THRONE

OF THE

ANCIENTS

Book Six
Stonehaven League

CARRIE SUMMERS

Chapter One

"OKAY, WAIT." DEVON leaned over and adjusted the padded canvas pants she wore over her regular armor, pulling the oversized waist up to the bottom edge of her rib cage. "Okay, now."

Even with the padding, she had to concentrate on avoiding tensing up as her opponent, all two and a half feet of him, advanced. Bravlon bared his teeth in what was meant to be a ferocious snarl. But the recent loss of the dwarf child's two front baby teeth and his disgustingly adorable green eyes totally hosed his attempt. Devon fought an impulse to grin like an idiot and blather in baby talk as his passive spell effect washed over her.

She swallowed, a faint clamminess slicking her palms.

> You resist *Adoration*. Barely. (Success chance +55% due to acquired resistance)

Devon edged back a step and tore her eyes from the kid's face. When she focused on his weapon hand and the movement of his feet, she had better luck resisting his spell. As long as he didn't make a cute little noise or something.

Bravlon sidestepped, knees bent like he'd been taught, and seemed to be looking for an opening. Devon kept her fists up, legs ready to spring as she adjusted her stance to match his movements.

Around them, the stone buildings of Ishildar hemmed a marble-paved square, the ancient stone smooth beneath their feet. Most of the buildings showed centuries of decay in their fallen archways and toppled pillars, but a few lifted intact facades over the square. The late morning sun pulled sharp shadows from what had once been intricate wall carvings but were now gentle, age-muted undulations in the stone.

Bravlon kept circling, which made her think the lessons about waiting for an opening were starting to take. Too late, she realized that his training was indeed working, but not in the way she'd figured. A final step to the left brought her square into the glare of the sun, forcing her to squint and snap a hand up to shade her eyes.

The moment she dropped her guard, Bravlon shouted and sprinted forward, stumpy legs pumping furiously. He swung his wool-wrapped warhammer in a wide arc, aiming for her hip.

Devon tried to jump aside, but the padded trousers—and her crappy *Dodge* skill—made her too slow. She watched while, as if in slow-motion, the heavy head of the warhammer slammed into the pointy part of her hip bone.

And she was still watching as a chunk of her midsection dissolved into shadow. A surge of nausea clenched her stomach as the angular head of the warhammer passed through her body, a cold and unwelcome invader. It didn't exactly hurt, and she didn't take any damage, but she honestly would have preferred the dull ache of an in-game injury to the sensation of having the blow sink through her flesh and out the other side.

> **You have gained mastery in a combat form:** Shadow Shifter - Tier 1 (+3% mastery)

You are now at 28% mastery of this tier.

Devon clenched her jaw to push back the wave of sick. The form's evasion was easier to handle if she didn't actually watch attacks pass through her body, but the physical sensation was still pretty horrid. According to Aijal, the Esh Shadow Master who had granted her the form, she would probably get used to it over time. It was important that she *could* sense the attacks that the form's ability prevented. Otherwise, she might not know she was in danger. At Tier 1, *Shadow Shifter* only prevented around 30% of melee attacks from damaging her. The rest would do full damage.

"That would have hit—" Devon said a split-second before something slammed into her kidney. She coughed and staggered, a sudden ache radiating from the impact point despite the padding on her body and the weapon. "Ouch."

She dashed forward a few steps to get out of range before turning, intent on complimenting Bravlon on the quick follow-through. A squeak of surprise left her throat when she spotted Greel standing behind the child. Devon sighed. Why did the lawyer have to show up right when Bravlon landed a big hit?

"Nice maneuver," the lawyer said as he clapped Bravlon on the shoulder. "Though the contest isn't particularly fair. Perhaps later I can instruct you in how an opponent with actual skills might have avoided that blow."

Bravlon giggled and raised his warhammer again.

Devon's health bar flashed and started to refill. She glared at Greel as she pressed a fist to her back where the hammer had struck. The blow had landed higher than she'd expected, near the top of the padding. Bravlon was growing fast. If she was going to continue playing targeting dummy for the kid, she was going to need padding for her chest and shoulders, too.

"What do you want, Greel?"

"You made such a big deal of your new combat form. I thought I should come see it in action. But now that I have, I'm not sure it was worth the journey from Stonehaven." The man gestured down one of the wide streets of Ishildar toward the outskirts and the savanna beyond.

Devon rolled her eyes. "Yes, I'm sure that's why you came."

The lawyer snorted. "And perhaps I wanted to check in on what sort of *lessons* you're giving Dorden and Heldi's young progeny. He does realize that most opponents will fight back, right?"

Devon took a deep breath and counted to five as she exhaled. "You know as well as I that I can't attack him."

"Oh?" Greel said, raising an eyebrow. "Afraid of a little retaliatory damage, huh?"

Shortly after Bravlon's "birth," which had actually been a protracted summoning spell, his mother had buffed him with an ability that made him invulnerable and struck back at anyone who attempted to damage him. The buff would last until the little guy was a teenager.

Rather than dignify Greel's question with a response, she just sighed and turned back to the young dwarf. "That was a good change of momentum. Keep that—"

Devon swallowed her words and threw out her arms for balance as the earth heaved, then jerked hard to the side. She stumbled, barely keeping her feet as the earthquake rocked Ishildar. At the edges of the square, the walls of ancient buildings shook and released puffs of dust. A square-cut stone tumbled from a decaying arch and smashed down on courtyard flagstones, sending rock chips flying. Pigeons erupted from building eaves, flapping and squawking.

After the initial surprise, she bent her knees and let the ground shimmy beneath her. Bravlon grinned, clearly enjoying the ride, and Greel stared at the ground, lip twitching as if in annoyance at the interruption. The whole shake lasted maybe twenty or thirty seconds, longer than most of the tremors that had rattled the area recently, but not enormously so. The quakes had been going on for days, ever since Devon and her friends had pushed the demon army south from Stonehaven and erected a shield to hold them there. The trembling meant Hezbek was even busier than usual supplying parties exploring Ishildar with healing potions—rockfall had caused more injuries than combat lately—but the quakes hadn't done much damage otherwise. The real concern was that the timing was too coincidental. The tremors were related to the demonic presence; Devon was sure of it. She just wasn't sure how.

When silence fell over the street, she turned back to Bravlon and dropped into a combat crouch.

"What was I saying?" she asked him, pointedly ignoring Greel.

"Momentum!" Bravlon chirped.

"Right. You did a good job changing direction so fast. But make sure you don't try the same trick twice in a row."

"Anyway..." Greel said, drawing his knife and examining his cuticles as if looking for hangnails to trim.

Devon raised her eyebrows in mock surprise. "Oh, you're still here? Sorry. I figured you'd have left after assuring yourself of my continued incompetence."

He smirked. "Now that I realize the depths of the disservice you're doing the lad, I figure I might as well deliver a message from Jarleck. Perhaps it will convince you to leave off these so-called lessons."

Devon sighed and straightened, raising a hand to Bravlon to ask for patience. "Jarleck knows I'll be back this evening."

Greel shrugged. "True, but I *did* tell him I planned to spend the afternoon in one of the city's libraries investigating historical legal documents detailing the trade arrangements between Ishildar and her vassal societies, and he asked if I knew whether you were in the city today."

"Sounds to me like he was just trying to change the subject. This might surprise you, but not everyone finds the legal arrangements of dead civilizations to be an interesting conversation topic."

He huffed and curled his lip in disgust. "And this might surprise you, but not everyone has the curiosity of a land whale."

"A what?"

"Dumbest creatures to slide their ponderous way across the Rengen Wastes, which you might know if you spared any energy for learning about this world and its fauna."

Devon clenched her jaw and exhaled. "Seriously, dude. Jarleck didn't send you with a message."

"No, but he did say he had some stuff to talk to you about this evening. Apparently some decisions need making...though why he persists in involving you in these things, I sincerely can't understand."

"Maybe because I'm the leader of Stonehaven?"

"A fact which still manages to astonish me."

"More fighting!" Bravlon chirped, pounding his warhammer against the stone floor.

Devon turned back to the child. "Yes, let's keep on. Greel was just heading off to the library."

The lawyer gave an exaggerated sigh. "I suppose it is kind of Bravlon to provide you sparring practice appropriate to your skill level. I'm sure Jarleck wouldn't want to drag you away from such a worthy opponent."

Bravlon puffed his little chest upon being called worthy. The child straightened his plate helm and made a sound like a puppy growling. Devon just barely avoided smiling and cooing at him as he raised his weapon. She'd learned the hard way that if she failed to resist the *Adoration* effect, it usually ended with a wool-wrapped warhammer to the teeth.

"All right," she said, raising her fists. "Take your best shot."

Bravlon took a deep breath. "Gwory is mine!" he shouted in a high-pitched voice. With lips pulled back in an adorable snarl, he charged. Devon stepped the wrong direction when the kid feinted, and her breath left her lungs as the warhammer pounded her belly.

"Ouch," Greel said, snorting. The man made more weird noises in his throat—laughter?—as he turned and stalked stiffly off, his twisted spine turning each step into a limp.

Jerk.

Chapter Two

DEVON SPOTTED JARLECK in one of his usual stations. Stalwart as ever, the man was standing on the palisade's wall-walk where he gazed out over the parapet. Her guildmate, Owen, was with him. Good. Devon had been hoping for an update on the *Illumin* barrier that was holding back the demons as well.

Climbing the final steps onto the wall-walk, she shaded her eyes against the red glare of the evening sun. As usual, the view from the wall made her breath catch; wide grasslands stretched far away to the west, the seed heads ruffled by gentle breezes. Yet scattered across the savanna, newly scorched patches marked the sites where demons had conjured flame. Areas of churned earth showed where her stone guardians had planted their heavy feet and stood firm against the ravaging horde. Quiet reigned over the area now, save for the clangs of hammers against anvils in Stonehaven and out in the player camp, a growing collection of canvas and hide structures connected to her settlement by a cobblestone road. But rather than feeling peaceful, that calm reminded her of the moment before a car crash, hurtling metal racing toward a collision with immovable stone.

Jarleck and Owen were deep in discussion, and Devon took the opportunity to turn and inspect the settlement from above. Stonehaven bustled as it always had, but the mood was different.

Devon's followers moved along footpaths with quick steps and hunched shoulders, often glancing toward the main gate as if to assure themselves that the walls still stood.

She glanced south toward Owen's barrier. Visible by day as only a faint line burned in the grass, the shield was evident at night as a faintly shimmering curtain sealing off Stonehaven and Ishildar from the demon army. It seemed such a flimsy thing to hide behind. That thought cured her impulse to dawdle, and she hurried across the wall-walk to speak to the men.

"Hi, Devon," Owen said before he turned to face her. Devon tried not to grimace. Owen's abilities, this extra-sensory awareness of the world—or of the pattern, as he described it—was kind of creepy sometimes. Especially when paired with his tendency to go all Yoda on her.

"I guess the pattern told you I wanted to talk to you?" she asked, trying to keep her voice light. It wasn't Owen's fault that the demonic AI, Zaa, had taken control of his mind and forced him to play for weeks as the demon general, Raazel. If not for Devon's efforts and those of Owen's girlfriend, Cynthia, Owen would still be trapped in the hell plane. Or maybe he would be leading Zaa's army in their march through the mortal realm. Either way, Owen's long period of deep connectedness with Zaa had granted his mind the capability to better understand the logic and—to use his words—the *patterns* of the game's creator AIs. He could even twist the rules of the world to some extent, a power which granted him this *Illumin* magic outside the constraints of ordinary class and skill-based advancement.

A faint smirk twisted Owen's lips, out of place with his otherwise haggard appearance. In the days since they'd gained a

11

respite from the demons' advance, Owen had been working non-stop, frequently needing to jog for miles across the savanna while refreshing the barrier.

"You give my abilities more credit than they're due," he said.

"So you grew eyes in the back of your skull?"

He smirked again. "Jarleck saw you coming, and I felt your footsteps." He stomped on the wall-walk, setting it shivering.

"Oh," Devon said. "So you can't guess which number I'm thinking of?"

"Probably thirteen, but I only think that because you like to pretend to be all edgy."

Devon snorted, glad to hear him sound a bit like his old self. "I have to act a little edgy to compensate for this monstrosity, right?" She jabbed a thumb over her shoulder to indicate her dragon-scale-sequined *Tiny Sparklebomb Backpack of Subpar Holding*. "Otherwise I might as well just give up and try to start a glitter-and-unicorns farm."

"It really is hideous," he agreed. "Anyway, as far as predicting the future, I might be able to guess what kind of quests your University building will cough up once it's finished, but..." A flash of concern darkened his features. "Actually, the pattern isn't looking too good for completing that before the demons find a way past the barrier."

Devon swallowed. "Wait. Are you saying we're going to lose?"

Her guildmate shook his head slowly. "Honestly, I can't really interpret what I see. Probably because the outcome depends too much on players, and they're not as woven into the pattern." He closed his eyes for a moment. "I feel the brightness of Ishildar and a dark flood lapping at her shores...not really new information, I know. Everything is just so uncertain."

Well, *uncertain* was a better status than *totally doomed.* Devon searched Owen's eyes as he reopened them. Despite the weariness on his face, the hollows of his sunken cheeks, his gaze still burned like he had a fever or something. "Seriously, how are you holding up, Owen? It's got to be hard to keep the shield refreshed." During the battle, some of her Stone Guardians had carried Owen across the savanna while he laid down the barrier, but soon after the fight, Devon had sensed deep weariness from her minions. A couple of them slowed nearly to a stop, just barely able to trudge back to Ishildar. The guardians, it seemed, could advance beyond the city's boundaries, but only for a short time. Unless another emergency arose, she needed to keep them within the borders they'd guarded for centuries.

Owen's jaw worked while he considered, his eyes growing distant as if in calculation. "I'm... I can hold. I've been sleeping in short shifts so that I can log in every few hours. At the very least, I've only needed to refresh the barrier due to natural decay in its strength. The demons seem to push lightly against it occasionally as if they're testing that it still stands. But I'd expected more of an assault by now."

Devon glanced to the south. "Maybe the barrier is stronger than you assume."

Owen shrugged. "Maybe. But I can't help worrying that they have another strategy."

Yeah, that was an issue, wasn't it? Between the earthquakes and the relative lack of activity from the horde, it would be naive to assume the demons were just biding their time. And anyway, even if

Zaa's forces had no other plan, Owen couldn't keep on like this indefinitely. The stalemate would break, and it would be far better if that happened on Devon's terms.

"How are things with Cynthia?" she asked. Owen had proposed to his girlfriend recently. His erratic schedule couldn't sit easily with the woman, especially after everything they'd been through in the last few months.

Owen sighed, once again looking troubled. "I can tell how much my playing worries her, but she does her best to understand that I'm doing what I feel I have to. Last night, she suggested we take a few days off. Grab a hyperloop out west or sail down to the Florida Keys. I explained why I can't, but you know, it's still hard for her to swallow."

Devon nodded. If she weren't already focusing all her resources on figuring out how to break the standoff in a positive way, Owen's situation would push her to it. Neither he nor Cynthia deserved to sacrifice another day to this game, but she couldn't tell him to quit, either, because the lives of everyone in Stonehaven depended on his barrier for now.

Sure, even if the demons took over the area, the players who'd set their bind points here could just log off, maybe find another game or leave gaming entirely. Life would go on for them. But this world was all that her sentient NPC friends had. And if Stonehaven and Ishildar fell, it seemed likely that no force could stand before the demons' advance. The mortal realm would be lost entirely.

She sighed and glanced up, spotted a pair of circling ravens. No doubt they were part of the awakened corvid society, the birds gifted with heightened intelligence by Ishildar's ancient magi. Every day, ravens and crows and magpies flew high over the demonic forces, reporting back on enemy movements. But their scouting missions had gained no more information than she'd just heard from Owen. Her total ignorance of the demons' plans sent a chill down her spine.

Lips pressed together, she turned her attention to Jarleck. "Greel said you wanted help with some decisions."

The fortifications master laid a hand on the parapet as he shook his head. "I told him it could wait."

Devon smirked. "I figured as much. He was just looking for an excuse to be a pest."

Jarleck raised an eyebrow. "He needs an excuse?"

Devon laughed, but her nagging worries made it sound hollow. "Anyway, how are things going?"

She pulled up the settlement interface and activated the fortifications tab as she spoke.

Fortifications:
Status: Castle - Basic
Completed:
1 x Main Wall - Stone
1 x Wall-walk
1 x Merlons
1 x Main Gate - Iron-reinforced Timber
5 x Watchtower
1 x Wicket Gate
1 x Outer Gate
1 x Dry Moat
1 x Drawbridge
1 x Dungeon
5 x Wall-mounted trebuchets

15 x Stocked barrels of pitch or tar

Bonuses: Castle - Basic
- Ranged Accuracy +17%
- Evasion + 39%
- Ranged Damage +25%
- Defensive Weaponry Damage +10%

Required for upgrade to Castle - Advanced
1 x Armory (complete)
1 x Inner Portcullis (70%)
1 x Large Ballista mounted on Inner Keep (complete)
1 x Water-filled Moat (90%)
5 x Wall-mounted Ballistae (complete)

She raised her eyebrows. "Looks like we're close to that advanced castle designation."

Jarleck couldn't help but look pleased with the progress. "The biggest step will be opening the headgate on the diversion ditch and finally filling the moat. It was something of a trick to bring the water under the walls without leaving exploitable weakness."

Devon nodded, thinking of the stream that ran through Stonehaven and disappeared, just as it had sprung, near the base of the semicircular cliff that guarded the settlement's back. The watercourse had been a mega bonus when it came to founding the settlement here. Abundant, readily available water that couldn't be poisoned upstream and that left the settlement in a way that wouldn't undermine the foundations or introduce secret entrances—pretty much a jackpot. When it came to filling the dry moat with water, they'd needed to construct a channel that *did* flow under the wall. Deld's stonemasons had painstakingly carved a series of grates that had been set into custom masonry at the base of both the palisade and the curtainwall. A determined infiltrator might chisel their way through, but they wouldn't do it unnoticed, and even then, the channels themselves were scarcely large enough for a child to wriggle through, much less an armed and armored fighter.

"Glad to hear it," she said. "Some people in your position might be too freaked out by the nearby army to keep building. It might seem kinda pointless. But we need every scrap of advantage we can muster. Are you worried about filling the moat?"

The man shook his head while absently pulling a pair of brass knuckles from his pocket and polishing them on his leather jerkin. Which reminded her, she ought to check in with Tamara to see how her training as a brawler was coming along. Devon hadn't known what to expect when inviting her friend into Relic Online, especially because Tamara had never really gamed before. But she was a natural, out-leveling pretty much every noob around. Between her and Emerson, equally inexperienced, but using that to his advantage—his tactics were unconventional to say the least—Devon had been forced to eat her annoyed words regarding the noob influx.

"The problem isn't with the fortifications, Mayor," Jarleck said.

Devon felt her shoulders slump a little when he used her title. She'd found that when her original followers fell back on formality, they were usually trying to figure out how best to deliver criticism.

"Just say what's on your mind. Seriously. You know way more than I do about a ton of things in this realm. If I didn't believe that, I wouldn't have made you our official quest giver and fortifications master."

"It's this policy about granting sanctuary to everyone even though we're out of space to make them citizens."

Devon nodded. The demon invasion had totally screwed up her settlement advancement track, and the local population was nearly at its cap while the construction and resource pipelines hadn't caught up. Until Stonehaven had enough buildings to fill the advancement requirements for Township, the settlement was stuck as a Hamlet. But seeing as there was a bloodthirsty demon horde rampaging to the south, and Stonehaven was the only defensible location around, she'd declared that everyone should be allowed free passage through the city gates. When an attack came, anyone who asked would be granted sanctuary inside the walls.

"They haven't been cutting into our stores, have they? We can teach them to hunt and forage for themselves, but our farms and the settlement's hunters just barely meet our food needs."

Jarleck shook his head. Leaning over the parapet, he pointed down into the so-called killing field, the area of empty ground between the inner and outer walls that was meant to leave would-be attackers vulnerable to archers on the palisade. Whereas the cliff at Stonehaven's back protected the settlement by being too sheer to scale on the outside face, the inner and outer walls made a semicircular corridor around twenty feet wide that defended the front half of the settlement. Devon had to lean far over the parapet, enough that her lower back tensed due to the sense that she might fall before she could see where Jarleck was pointing. At the far northern end of the corridor where it dead-ended against the base of the cliff, refugees from Eltera City seemed to have erected a temporary camp.

Devon grimaced. "Hard to get a clear shot at an attacking demon with a bunch of innocent civilians and their stuff in the way, I guess."

Jarleck let out a low grunt of assent. "There's another smaller camp at the other end. The thing is, there's no room to sleep inside the walls, but you can't blame them for being afraid to camp on the open savanna. Not after demons burned their original homes in Eltera City."

Devon straightened and crossed her arms over her chest, thinking. When she groped her way back to memories of tenth-grade world history, she seemed to remember similar descriptions of medieval fortresses and cities. The lucky citizens had homes inside the stronghold, and everyone else was forced to live outside. With good fortune, the town-dwellers made it through the gates and into the stronghold in the case of an attack, though sometimes they didn't. She also seemed to remember that the hovels and shanties outside the castle walls had sometimes brought about the fortress's defeat. Alleys hid attackers just as easily as they sheltered beggars, and by torching thatched roofs or canvas tents, an attacking force could both terrorize the population and provide smokescreens for the movement of troops. But usually, those ancient kings and lords had confronted the same problem Devon now faced. Building stone walls, not to mention defending them, was freaking hard work. When they'd laid out the line of the initial wooden palisade, the enclosed area had seemed huge. More than she'd ever be able to fill with NPCs and buildings. Now, the walls were overflowing.

She pulled up the settlement interface again.

Requirements for expansion to Township:

- Advanced NPC: 25/25
- Buildings (Tier 2): 15/27
- Buildings (Tier 3): 7/15
- Buildings (Tier 4): 0/2
- Population: 490/500

Filling out the final ten citizens to cap the population would scarcely dent the number of refugees camping around the settlement and screwing up the defenses. To house them all, she'd need to finish the construction requirements for advancement to *Township*.

She quickly flipped to the building lists, skipping over the Tier 1 structures because they were now unlimited in quantity and no longer part of the requirements.

Tier 2 Buildings - 15/27
1 x Medicine Woman's Cabin (upgraded)
2 x Crafting Workshop
1 x Basic Forge
2 x Kitchen
4 x Barracks
4 x Warehouse
1 x Smokehouse
1 x Tannery (in progress)
1 x Smokehouse (in progress)

Tier 3 Buildings - 7/15
1 x Shrine to Veia
1 x Chicken Coop
1 x Inner Keep

1 x Leatherworking Shop

1 x Woodworking Shop

1 x Tailoring Workshop

1 x Advanced Forge

1 x Stables (in progress)

1 x Barn (in progress)

1 x Weavers' Workshop (in progress)

Tier 4 Buildings - 0/2

1 x University (in progress)

No matter how many carpenters and masons she threw at construction, it would still be quite some time before the requirements were met.

"I can't just send the refugees away. The barrier could fail, and they'd be toast."

"What about Ishildar?" Owen asked.

Devon nodded. She'd considered that. The city had no walls, but the Veian Temple likely offered as much or more defense as the Shrine to Veia did for Stonehaven. But she didn't know that for sure, not enough to bet innocent NPC lives on. And besides, now that the jungle had been cleared, Ishildar was, in many ways, an urban desert. It was one thing to suggest that newcomers forage for themselves, but quite another to ask them to do that when there was no game or plant life.

She cast back again to her memories of those ancient real-world cities. Hadn't some of them had an inner stronghold as well as a wall surrounding the larger city? Even if she couldn't provide soldiers to guard another wall, hard stone could provide enough deterrent to allow residents to evacuate their homes and retreat to the greater safety of Stonehaven. But if an army were attacking, it wasn't like she'd be able to open the gates and let in innocent people. As she considered the dilemma, another detail about castles swam up from the depths of her memory. She glanced back toward the cliff that stood at Stonehaven's back.

"Isn't there something called, like, a poster gate or something?"

Understanding immediately flashed in Jarleck's eyes. "Postern gate. A secret exit that allows the keepers of a castle to evacuate if all is truly lost."

"But couldn't it also allow entrance?" Already, she imagined the layout, a wall built behind the defensive cliff, small cottages tucked up tight against the cliff's shielding bulk. And at the base, hidden behind the rearmost of houses, a secret entrance into Stonehaven. Of course, that would require tunneling through the cliff, but with war looming, she'd already recalled the dwarven miners from the Argenthal Mountains. Given the amount of ale brewing that was going on, she'd considered looking for a distraction anyway.

Nodding to herself, she opened the resources tab and checked the supply of stone and mortar. There likely wasn't enough for the wall in the current stocks, and access to the quarry had been sealed by Owen's barrier. But even if the vast sprawl of Ishildar made for terrible hunting, thousands of ruined buildings certainly provided materials.

Clapping her hand on the parapet, she started explaining her plan to Jarleck.

"I think it could work," the man said when she finished explaining. "I'll check with Deld tomorrow."

Good. It might not be progress toward ousting the demons, but it felt satisfying to solve at least one problem. And as a bonus, it likely skated around the restrictions on settlement advancement. She'd be willing to bet that once Stonehaven could officially upgrade to a Township, the additional area would automatically be incorporated into the town, giving her a head start on the next stage of progression.

She smirked. It wasn't at the level of a mechanics exploit Chen might come up with after forty-eight hours spent sifting through his spreadsheets, but it wasn't bad, either.

As for solving the demon problem, she was expecting reports about the additional troops she could expect from the surrounding territories as early as tomorrow morning—a couple of hours after sunrise, she would hurry over to Ishildar for her daily meeting with the leaders of the various groups she'd tasked with wartime preparations and Ishildar's exploration. It was tempting to ask for updates now, but nobody, not even NPCs, became more effective by being micromanaged.

Best to log out and get a little rest herself, because the following days would just get busier.

She touched Owen's shoulder before leaving, meeting his eyes. "Keep me up to date on how you're coping, okay?"

He nodded. "Thanks, Dev. I will."

Chapter Three

"YOUR MAINTENANCE REQUEST has been added to the queue. Please allow ten to twenty business days while we evaluate the costs and schedule a repair. Thank you for contacting Juniper Terrace. Apartments, and so much more. Is there anything else you need assistance with?"

Devon pulled her phone from her ear and stared at it in disgust. Ten to twenty *days?* Weren't these people under some kind of contract to provide livable accommodations?

She jabbed the button to put her phone on speaker. Her *phone.* What kind of place required you to make maintenance requests via voice anyway? Shouldn't there be some kind of messenger portal?

"I need this fixed sooner," she said.

"Okay, I understand that you wish to escalate the urgency of your maintenance request for..." The obnoxious robo-woman cut out with a click, and then a recording of Devon's voice was spliced in. "My stupid blind cord broke, and now it's stuck diagonally open. I can't close it, so anyone on the balcony can watch me eating my cereal."

Devon cringed. Maybe that hadn't been the best way to report the issue. "Yes, escalate please."

"Confirmation acknowledged. I can apply a higher priority to a request under one of a few conditions. Is this an issue of sanitation such as clogged plumbing or an infestation by disease-carrying rodents?"

"What? Have you guys had problems with rodent plagues lately?" Devon glanced at the grimy baseboard near the refrigerator.

"I'm sorry. I don't understand your response. Please answer 'yes' or 'no.'"

Seriously? The apartment complex's automated system had to be at least thirty years old with this level of stupidity. She could buy an espresso maker capable of better language processing than this.

"No. I don't have an overflowing toilet or rabid ground squirrels. But there's a dude who lives a couple of doors down and is always trying to stare through my window."

"Okay, I understand that there is no sanitation concern. I can also reprioritize your request if there is an extreme risk of injury or death due to this issue. Examples of such conditions are exposed wires, particularly those throwing sparks, or ceiling fans that appear to be at risk of detaching. Note that if there is a fire actively burning in your apartment, this automated system cannot notify emergency services. Please dial 911."

"Well, I might die of annoyance that you people are using a robo-answering service from 2015 to deal with requests from your paying tenants."

"Okay. Response acknowledged. I understand that you may die, and therefore, I am flagging this issue as potentially life-threatening. A manager will review the request during business hours. Thank you for contacting Juniper Terrace. Apartments, and so much more. This call has now reached the maximum allowable recording length. Goodbye."

Devon's phone screen went black, the connection cut. She stared at it for another few seconds, kind of dumbfounded. At least this so-called manager would be forced to listen to the recording in the morning. Er...wait. She focused on the clock in the corner of her vision, commanding her implants to pull up the calendar.

Ugh. Of course, there was the whole weekend thing complicating the business hours statement. Since it was Friday night, that meant she had two full days to deal with her stupid window being open to the world. Any nosy jerk could walk by and laugh at her attempts at cooking, or weirder, stare at her while she lay on the couch, unmoving while she spent hours immersed in Relic Online.

Uncool.

For about the thousandth time in the last week, she contemplated moving. She could afford it now—her bank branch had been hassling her over messenger about doing something more with her money than letting it collect in her checking account. But opening a savings account or a money market thing or whatever they were blabbing about would require her to physically go into the branch and talk to someone. Security reasons, they claimed. Which made her wonder if her bank got its technology from the same place as Juniper Terraces.

Anyway, moving sucked. After getting kicked out of her mom's house—which at the time had been a monthly rental of a single room in a decaying motel—she'd been forced for years to tumble from trailer to apartment to employee dormitory depending on where the rent was cheapest. So even if her current place was crappy and apparently prone to rat infestations, it was nice to be able to stay put.

Plus, moving would mean taking more time away from the game. Time she didn't have right now.

After staring at the broken blind for a few seconds, she shuffled into her bedroom and dug through the laundry basket. A bit of rooting netted her a threadbare robe and a smock-tunic thing she liked to wear when feeling bloated after eating too much bread. She toted them back to the kitchen, pulled a chair in front of the window, and managed to wedge the hems of the clothing items into the crack behind the blind housing, creating a makeshift curtain. As she hopped down to inspect her work, a message pinged her interface.

Her heart sped up a little when she saw it was from Emerson. Of course, she knew it was dumb to get excited. They hadn't even been on a date yet, unless you counted hanging out in their digital bodies watching drunken dwarves run through the edges of a bonfire. One of the Stoneshoulder fighters had accidentally caught a spark in his beard and was now in mourning over the lost volume where it had burned.

Anyway, it had been so long since her last date...when was it? Just after she'd passed the GED and found a job cleaning up fur at a pet groomer's? She remembered showing up for the blind internet date at an ice cream shop smelling like dog shampoo. But beyond that, she couldn't recall much about how the date had gone. Not well, she gathered. Like her other scattered attempts at romance, it hadn't worked out. There were plenty of reasons, usually involving Devon freaking out because the whole process required a bunch of small talk, which always baffled her. That and she couldn't help thinking of the train of asshole men who had passed through her mom's life.

Devon's in-person conversations with Emerson had been different. For starters, she hadn't had to come up with random stuff to talk about, hoping it sounded interesting, but knowing it was just filler. And the whole pro-gamer thing wasn't weird with him. Seemed that a lot of the time, people *said* they thought her job was cool, but when they realized she spent most of her time either in a VR pod or lying around unaware and probably drooling, they got a little weirded out. When she was feeling self-confident, she thought they might be concerned that a real-life relationship in the mundane world wouldn't compare to the excitement of virtual reality. When her self-esteem was in the gutter, she imagined that they viewed her like a slovenly couch potato.

Either way, her gaming wasn't a problem for Emerson. And if a relationship ever happened, they could hang out in both real life and Relic Online.

Great, except he was also her boss. Devon really didn't like the way the power dynamics stacked up there. He didn't seem like the kind of guy that would fire her if they got involved and it didn't work out. But the whole "not having to worry about affording food" thing had been pretty nice for the last few months. She didn't like the idea of risking that.

Hey, got time to talk? the message read.

"Yeah, sure. I was just going to microwave something to eat," she subvocalized to send the response.

So I've got these unspent attribute points...where should I put the points, you think?

She breathed a sigh of relief at the same time she felt a little twinge of disappointment. She'd been kind of hoping he would ask about meeting up in real life—no matter what happened, she wasn't going to have a relationship that only went on between their avatars. But she also wasn't sure how she'd answer the request. Geeking out about stats was a way easier conversation to have.

Spending points and making character decisions was Devon's bane when it came to her own avatar. She was too allergic to forums and chat channels to really get into the metagame and plan her progression ahead of time—not that other players could help much with her character since she had unique classes and abilities—and character choices just felt so *permanent*. Basically she was afraid of commitment and screwing up.

But when it came to someone else's character progression, she had no problem rendering an opinion. Shuffling to the fridge, she grabbed a beer, cracked it, and dropped into a seat at the kitchen table.

"Shoot me over your character details," she said. "Let's get your toon ready to kick ass."

Chapter Four

FREED FROM THE jungle, Ishildar could almost be a different city. Sure, many—okay, most—of the buildings were still in ruin, gap-toothed arches hanging over leaf-strewn paving stones, courtyard fountains filled with dust. Heaps of rubble covered floors that had once been tiled with beautiful mosaics. Yet despite the centuries of decay, the city still held a stately grandeur. Before, it had been choked, suffocating. Now Ishildar was proud and ready to rise again.

Devon leaned her ironwood bike against a pillar near the edge of the savanna and yawned as she took a deep breath of the crisp morning air. She could ride all the way to the council meeting, but she preferred taking her time and letting the city wrap around her. Awakened from the curse, the ancient metropolis seemed to shine with an energy she couldn't quite define. A flow of...something. She'd known all along that there was power and potential here—for better or for worse, the game had totally cast her as the hero protagonist, the leader in the fight against Zaa. She was meant to do more than simply hold back the demon horde for a time, and the city's vast sprawl somehow held the key to her chance at victory.

But she had yet to figure out how to use it.

In the days since Owen had established the barrier, she'd been attacking the problem on multiple fronts. It had been tempting to throw all her resources into exploring the city and searching for clues as to how they'd bring its power to bear. But since she didn't know what they were looking for—and the game hadn't forked over a quest or anything to help her—it seemed stupid to bet everything on finding some miracle weapon hidden in the ruins. So she'd been continuing to send scouts and messengers into the surrounding region, the historical territory that the city had ruled. Any potential allies were being called to send fighters and resources. Jarleck continued to upgrade Stonehaven's defenses, and she'd asked her head stonemason, Deld, to begin planning out restoration efforts in the part of the city surrounding the Veian Temple.

Still, it felt too much like she was just biding time. During this morning's meeting, she planned to discuss a more aggressive defense agenda with her followers. Actually, that was the wrong term. It was time to set an agenda focused on attacking.

As she marched toward the building they'd chosen as the council hall, Devon laid fingers over the *Greenscale Pendant* and activated *Ishildar's Call.* Moments later, the minds of the city's Stone Guardians connected with hers. She felt their ponderous thoughts, their ancient joy at greeting their liege. The nearest guardian, a golem she'd named Knobble Knees on account of some stone protrusions on its legs, raised a massive head over a nearby roof. She felt the question emanating from deep in its stone mind. Did she need a ride?

She smiled and shook her head. "Not going far."

As she probed the Guardians' minds, she received a faint sense of the conditions in the city. Sometimes it was hard to accept the added awareness as real since she had no similar perceptions outside the game. Maybe it was like being a psychic or something—if that were really possible and the people who claimed to have ESP weren't total liars. Regardless, she could perceive each golem as she might sense someone sitting back-to-back with her but not quite touching her body...if she could also tell something about the unseen person's mood and what they were looking at.

It was weird. But cool.

In any case, aside from a small group of NPC followers she'd sent to explore the northwestern quadrant of the city—far enough from Stonehaven that they'd brought supplies to spend the night—the city was largely quiet. Too quiet, really, for an ancient site that had supposedly just been reawakened after centuries of slumber.

There had to be something she was missing.

The building they'd taken to calling the council hall was fronted with a long row of towering pillars forming a grand colonnade. When standing between the columns, Devon often imagined the ancient residents of Ishildar walking before her in pairs and groups as they enjoyed warm evenings. Now, sunlight slanted into a deserted open-air corridor. Wide archways led into the hall itself. Devon hurried across and stepped through an opening.

Inside the echoing chamber, dozens of high windows admitted beams of light that fell on a polished stone floor. A forest of immense columns supported a soaring series of vaults in the ceiling. The air smelled faintly of dust and the birds' nests wedged between stone ribs high above. Despite the windows, the hall was dim compared to the glare in the streets outside, and Devon stood blinking while she waited for her eyes to adjust. One hundred meters long and fifty deep, the hall could host an army.

Right now, it hosted a heavy stone table, a few benches, and a motley crew of NPCs and players that were all that stood between a demon horde and the mortal realm.

Devon took a deep breath and glanced at her skills window, focusing on the section with the most advanced values.

Skills - Tier 3:

Combat Assessment: 20

Leadership: 25

Up until now, she'd focused on inspiring loyalty by listening to her followers and attempting to balance their individual needs with those of the Stonehaven community. She'd been kind while trying to appear confident. In peacetime, that had worked well—*Leadership* was her highest-rated skill.

But war had come to Stonehaven and Ishildar, and now it was time to do more than organize. It was time to command.

She ran her eyes over her NPC followers and player friends, calculating how best to use them as she approached the gathering. Rather than take the seat they'd left open at the head of the table, she stood, knuckles planted on the stone tabletop.

There were nearly two dozen humans and humanoids making up her council now, the number having grown from the small handful of leaders she'd chosen during Stonehaven's founding. Her former guildmates had joined her inner circle. More NPCs had been promoted to advanced status, allowing them to assume leadership roles not just in combat but also as heads of trade professions and construction crews. Two long-limbed and milky-skinned Esh represented the Mistwalker race, the remnants of one of Ishildar's ancient vassal societies. A sleek-feathered raven named Gustwing, representative of the coalition of awakened corvids, perched on the table beside Hazel, Stonehaven's petite scout and Tamer-class NPC.

The other awakened race that had recently arrived in the area, a herd of fleet-footed horses known as windsteeds, had no representative in the hall, but Hazel would represent their interests and carry Devon's commands to the alpha stallion.

After acknowledging everyone with a nod, she turned to the newest arrival at the table.

"I'd heard you arrived yesterday," she said to Perlda, leader of the felsen. "Thank you for making the journey."

Of the five societies that once paid fealty to Ishildar, only two remained—as far as she knew, anyway. The felsen—a blue-skinned, hardy, and diminutive race—hailed from the Argenthal Mountains to the east of Ishildar. Their leader was a stringy middle-aged woman with white tufts of hair sprouting at wild angles from her scalp. She carried a gnarled staff and frequently wore a scowl. It probably didn't help that some of Devon's other NPC followers had adopted Devon's nickname for the mountain folk, calling them smurfs as often as they used the proper term.

Rather than sit on the stone bench, which would put her nose around the level of the tabletop, Perlda knelt on a thick hide that had been folded a few times to make a cushion. Her staff lay on the table before her, but she kept fingers on it as if faintly suspicious that someone might try to snatch it away.

"The felsen"—the woman glanced pointedly around the table as if daring someone to call her a smurf—"owe you a debt that will take a generation to repay. Even if that weren't the case, we would honor the bonds our ancestors forged with Ishildar."

Devon tipped her head in gratitude. "I hope it won't strain that bond for me to ask you to bring every fighter to the field. We need each of your archers and...darters." Was that even the right term?

Many felsen were ambush fighters, using blowguns to fire darts drugged with compounds that slowed enemy movements.

"We are ready to defend our homeland."

Devon hesitated a moment. The next request was kind of a big ask given what she knew about the felsen's attitude toward their racial powers. "And I need you to speak with your ancestors. We need their help as much as we need your living fighters."

Perlda's face went stony. Long ago, the working of her people's ancestor-magic might have been a pleasant task. Requests had been made with respect. But when their civilization had fallen after the double gut-punch of Ishildar's loss and an advancing orc army, the shamans had forcibly bound their ancestors into service as poltergeists that had haunted the mountains for centuries. The ancestors weren't too happy with their descendants these days.

"The consequences could be unpredictable," the blue-skinned woman said.

"I prefer unpredictability to the certainty of a loss to Zaa's forces."

"Keeper, I understand your thinking but—"

Devon raised a hand to silence her. She ignored the impulse to buckle under Perlda's scowl. "This is not an indefinite binding and it's definitely not forced enslavement. This is a plea for help ensuring the continued survival of their descendants."

Perlda still looked skeptical as she ran her thick-knuckled fingers over the length of her walking staff. Some of Devon's other followers shifted awkwardly in the silence.

Devon stepped around the bench to get closer to the table, the stone edge pressing into her thighs. She wasn't quite tall enough to really loom over the gathering, but she imagined the angle made her look a bit more imposing. "As you already mentioned, many of your ancestors swore an oath to Ishildar."

"But the ones that did have drifted ever further from us, lost in time. Every year they become less substantial...less like their mortal kin and more like a collection of emotions. I don't think that a reminder of their bond to a vanished place will serve for anything but to recall to them the sadness of the city's fall."

"But it's no longer an oath to a lost place. Ishildar is restored, and I am its Keeper. Anyone oath-bound to the city in any age is now oath-bound to me. Your ancestors are my vassals—and I don't believe I need to remind you that the living felsen are sworn to me as well."

Perlda lowered her eyes at the hard edge in Devon's voice, her fingers now dancing back and forth across the staff.

Shavari, Veia's priestess and one of her chosen prophets, abruptly stood and planted her palms on the table. "Should oaths extend beyond death? Is it not enough to navigate trials of life? Death should bring rest and communion with Veia."

Devon shot her a hard glare. Shavari flinched as if struck; the woman clearly wasn't used to being questioned.

"Now is not the moment for a discussion of theology," Devon said. "And in case it wasn't clear, while I appreciate the wisdom and perspectives of everyone gathered here, the time for debate has passed. Bring me suggestions outside this hall if you feel the need."

Shavari's mouth worked, producing silent words, and after a moment she dropped to a seat.

You have lost reputation with Shavari: -10 Reputation.

Devon rolled with the blow, keeping her face even as she dispelled the popup. Game mechanics mirrored real life in many ways. A player had to make trade-offs, sacrificing certain possibilities to achieve other outcomes. Shavari had brought Devon the fourth relic of Ishildar, the *Ironweight Key*. Without it, Devon wouldn't have been able to take command of Ishildar. But the priestess was still just one woman. Despite her buffs and the occasional ability to see the future in visions sent from Veia, Devon couldn't sacrifice her authority to remain in the woman's high regard.

And anyway, Devon didn't need Shavari to understand the potential futures facing her settlement. Either they'd find a way to beat the demons, or Stonehaven, Ishildar, and the vast continent beyond would fall under demon control.

Shavari could sulk if that's what it took for Devon to save her city.

She turned back to Perlda. "How many felsen fighters can you bring? And how many of you can speak to your ancestors?"

Perlda spoke in a flat voice. "There are thirty of us of fighting age. As for who can commune, only three of us have the talent."

Only thirty? Devon was careful not to let her disappointment show. "Are you able to predict what aid we might receive from your ancestors? Providing they agree to help, I mean."

Perlda's knuckles were white where she squeezed her staff, and her voice trembled faintly when she spoke. "The last time we worked any appreciable magic was in the years of my great-grandmother three times over. I fear the attempt will do more harm than good."

Devon took a deep breath. The woman was naturally stubborn, and it had shown in her early objections. But now that she realized Devon wouldn't back down from the request, her fear made her honest. Tampering with the ancestor magic could be dangerous. Devon had personally been on the receiving end of malicious pranks by the felsen poltergeists, the spirits having turned spiteful after being forced into the role for so long.

But Devon had an advantage she'd been ignoring lately. She'd been playing the game extra carefully for fear she might let her followers down or get them killed. Her caution had kept her from taking advantage of an edge that the game had handed her the first few days of play.

Stalking around the table, she came to a halt beside Perlda. Devon opened her character sheet and glanced at the special attributes section.

Bravery: 10 (+3 Stonehaven Jerkin)
Cunning: 7

When she heard her awareness over the *Bravery* attribute, a tooltip popped up.

Grants an additional chance of success against foes or situations that would otherwise be too difficult for your level.

Way back when she'd started her journey through Relic Online, her *Bravery* score had given her the necessary edge to defeat an ogre she otherwise wouldn't have been able to scratch. Well, *Bravery* and *Cunning* put together with a bit of help from a special skill,

Improvisation. Few players had these special statistics, probably because they were too unbalanced. But not only had Devon received them as rewards for her unique play style, she had also received the ability to convey some of the benefits to her followers.

She laid a hand on Perlda's skinny shoulder and met the woman's eyes. "Your ancient kin will listen to you. They will follow your commands if you give them in my name."

Devon almost felt the courage surge through her hand and into Perlda's body.

> **Your follower has received a special attribute point:** +1 Bravery.

> *Seriously, it won't always be that easy. Typically, you transfer advantages to your followers by serving as an example, not by touching them and hoping for something to happen.*
> *But she was being an annoying wusscake, so you got a bonus this time.*

Dismissing the message, Devon wondered how she could have neglected the advantage for so long. But as resolve replaced the dismayed scowl on Perlda's face, she forced herself to stop regretting missed opportunities. All that mattered now was the future.

She turned back to face the group.

"Shavari," she said, prompting the woman to jerk in surprise.

"Yes...Keeper?" the woman said with obvious reluctance.

Devon ignored her hesitation and plowed on. "I need to know more about the Veian Temple here in the city. Every benefit it provides us. Will you please investigate?"

"I—much of what my order teaches may not apply to such an ancient structure."

"But you are still the most qualified. Please take the next few days to investigate and report back with a list of capabilities. I want to know about any spells we can activate, any passive defense beyond the *Ishildar's Blessing* effect." Devon glanced toward the upper corner of her interface where the buff granting added *Damage* and *Accuracy* vs. demons had been a permanent fixture since she'd taken command of the city and cleared the debris from the temple.

Shavari held Devon's gaze for a moment, long enough that Devon glanced through her interface to find her reputation score with the woman—145, just on the lower end of *Friendly*. Shavari hadn't sworn a formal oath, which would have probably boosted her score into the *Staunch Ally* range and eliminated this little power struggle. But now didn't seem the time to ask for that kind of promise.

"You'll have my report as soon as I believe I've made a thorough investigation," the woman said at last.

Devon nodded. That was about the best response she could hope for considering Shavari's mood. But the missed chance to secure the woman's absolute loyalty by swearing an oath reminded her of something she'd been procrastinating. She turned to her paladin friend, Torald, and another player she'd invited to join the council, a druid named Magda. "I've been putting off the ceremony you guys need to complete your quest for way too long." Apparently, the players were supposed to formally swear fealty to her as Keeper of Ishildar to receive the reward at the end of a long quest line. Devon was seriously dreading the process. A bunch of players kneeling before her, probably role-playing out the whole thing? It was like a nightmare for someone who typically avoided human interaction. But she was going to have to suck it up and take every advantage she could get.

Torald shrugged. "To be fair, you've had a horde of demons to contend with."

"Yeah, but it sucks to be stuck one step away from completing an epic quest. I'll make time this afternoon. Should I come to your camp?"

Torald averted his eyes when he answered. "Actually, some of us have drawn up a plan for the ceremony. We've worked with the town woodcarvers...we were planning to unveil your throne once Ishildar was restored, but the demons kinda put some kinks in the plan."

Oh hell. A throne? She sighed. "And where, exactly, were you planning to hold the ceremony then?"

"Your chambers in the inner keep. We have—"

Torald swallowed his words when a series of nails-on-chalkboard screeches pierced the echoing silence of the hall. He jumped to his feet, yanking out his sword as thumps followed the squeals and something blocked the light from one of the entrance archways.

Devon jumped back and summoned a *Glowing Orb,* throwing it at the wall before shoving mana into an insta-cast *Shadow Puppet.*

Footsteps clicked against the floor, a large shadow moving through the forest of pillars that supported the high vaults in the ceiling.

The benches emptied as combat-class players and NPCs prepared for a fight, and the representatives of Stonehaven's tradespeople hurried to huddle behind the fighters.

"Hail, Keeper," a deep voice called.

Devon hesitated, interrupting the casting process for the *Wall of Ice* she'd intended to slam down between the intruders and the council table. "Uh. Hail?"

The clicking footsteps pressed closer. Devon held her breath.

A piercing cry shook the hall as a griffon paced into view, the talons on its front legs tapping against the marble floor, leonine hind legs padding silently. The beast spread its wings wide in a space between pillars, the feathered limbs spanning at least twenty feet.

"What the...?" Hailey muttered.

Astride a saddle fastened to the griffon's back, a bare-chested man raised a hand in greeting. Long, flowing hair fell beyond his shoulders like a fricking mane, the tips bleached by the sun. Devon blushed when she saw he was wearing just a loincloth. And...had he rubbed himself down with oil or something? Why were his muscles so shiny?

"My liege lady. Heroine of Ishildar. Your light shines after centuries of darkness, and I have come to bask in it."

"Holy shit. It's Fabio," Jeremy, her troubadour friend, said in a false whisper.

Chen snorted, his little stick golem pressing the back of its hand to its forehead before collapsing in a swoon.

Devon stammered. Her face burned with embarrassment over having a nearly naked dude giving Torald a run for the most ridiculous praise possible.

"Uh. So I guess the Skevalli griffon keepers didn't vanish after all?"

The man leapt from his mount, landing on the marble floor in a cat-like crouch. He stood slowly, long muscles working in his thighs. He stared at her from beneath lowered brows.

When he opened his mouth and actually kind of...*growled* at her, Jeremy literally collapsed on the floor, hooting with laughter.

"I have come to place myself in your service. Any *need* you might have, I will satisfy it, my liege. This is my promise."

The griffon opened its beak and gave a keening screech as the man tilted his head to look at her from beneath lowered brows. His best attempt at a burning stare, she gathered.

Devon swallowed. Just...great.

Chapter Five

OKAY, WELL, SO much for laying out a comprehensive battle plan and setting her minions marching out to conquer the demon horde. After Fabio's arrival, Devon's composure had been totally shot. Like, babbling-idiot, why-the-hell-did-the-game-decide-to-create-that-kind-of-NPC shot. Even after she'd told the half-nude dude to take a seat at the table, hiding his way-too-skimpy loincloth from view, he'd continued to alternate between staring at her adoringly and growling low in his throat.

Totally, completely, not what she was looking for in a VR game. Her friends knew it, and Tarzan—his other new nickname—had created more entertainment than they'd enjoyed in months, judging by their reactions anyway. Even Owen had been forced to leave the table and step outside so that he didn't destroy his sensei/prophet/Yoda image by laughing.

Anyway, the guy's name wasn't Fabio. It was Prince Kenjan, and he was heir to the Skevalli Vassaldom. And yes, it did appear that he'd oiled his skin, because he'd also brought her a flask of the stuff, claiming it was a rare extract from a nut that grew only in crevices high up the walls of gorges in the Skargill Mountains. +2 Speed, apparently, but only if the user had greater than 60% exposed skin.

In other news, Veia was an asshole.

And Devon had already regifted the nut oil to Dorden. Not that she *wanted* to see a bunch of hairy dwarves streaking around wearing nothing but their beards, but the Stoneshoulders seemed most likely to appreciate the gift, if only because their short legs made their natural movement rate lower than the average human's.

Back in Stonehaven, having cut the meeting short, she was hiding in a back room in the lower level of the keep, collecting her wits and making notes so that the next meeting would stick to the agenda. Prince Kenjan had lifted off on his mount, claiming that he needed to feel the wind in his hair at least a few times a day, while everyone else had set about the business of fortifying and no doubt wondering what the hell they were going to do about the demon army.

Devon sighed and bent over the parchment she'd stolen from Greel's little office on the lower level of the keep. Her notes so far weren't all that useful.

-Felsen fighters: Only 30 smurfs...enough for a raid on Gargamel and Azrael maybe. Otherwise?? See if they can make more blowdart poison for Stonehaven's archers? Wait, does poison even work against demons?

-Felsen ancestors: 3 shamans. How many poltergeists can each spawn? Hoping one thousand million. Harass demon army from behind. Distract them with ghost lights and sounds. Steal their weapons and stuff. Also, haunt them so they get stuck in combat and can't regen health.

- Hazel: Apprentice more scouts. **We have to find out why Ishildar matters.** Won't happen if I keep wasting time sending random and unqualified search parties.

- Shavari = investigating Temple. What else? Figure out if it's worth improving Reputation with her.

- Greel: Ugh. Ask him to search through the libraries and records for anything we can use. Even if he gloats and acts self-important.

She dipped her quill into the ink and mentally ran through her list of allies. The corvids were great scouts. The awakening stones had also granted trickster-type powers to many of them. Some could read minds, while others could plant notions in people's heads. A few preferred to work their magic by imbuing shiny objects with the power to charm a person into performing a task for the bird. That kind of creeped Devon out, but it could also be useful if the demons were susceptible.

Windsteeds had an innate ability to sense the other members of their herd, which made for good coordination of mounted unit movements over distance, but it required the riders to blindly trust the horses unless they had a Tier 2 skill in *Animal Communication*. Right now, her only followers who had that were Hazel due to her Tamer-class proficiencies and Greel because he spent so much time talking to his chickens.

Leaving the awakened races for later, she bent over the paper and scratched down notes for the remaining groups of followers.

-Jarleck: Fill the moat. Supervise the wall extension for refugees. Investigate added fortifications for Ishildar.

-Mistwalkers: Figure out which Esh can train players in new skills and spells.

-Hailey: Can her *True Sight* ability help figure out the source of the earthquakes? Like, can it look underground for stuff or is it just good for inspecting mobs?

- Players: Form up into raid groups w/ Esh. Power level! (Can we bring other player groups in? Is there a route into Ishildar that doesn't go through the demons? Ask Hezbek.)

-Oh yeah...what about the NPC trainers? See if they can level past 20 (and train skills past that).

Devon stopped writing and stared at the last item. That was the real issue—aside from whichever mystery benefits Ishildar might still grant her. She needed a bigger army, and she needed them to be as high level as possible. ASAP. But now that Ishildar was restored, bringing peace to the immediate surroundings, where would they find the enemies they needed to grind out experience?

Raids against the demon force might do it, and they'd have the bonus of reducing the size of the horde, but they were also risky because attacks would require dropping the barrier long enough for a Stonehaven force to pass through.

There was really only one region near Ishildar that she hadn't explored—the maze of chasms and gorges that cut through sheer stone and made the Skargill Mountains nearly impassable. And someone who apparently knew that area quite well had just arrived to put himself at her disposal.

Devon sighed as she scratched a final line onto her notes.

-Ask Fabio for info on Skargill XP opportunities.

A chime and a flashing notification at the edge of her vision made her jerk before she remembered she'd set the alarm herself. Time for her daily training session with Aijal. She yawned and blinked the grit from her eyes, muscles aching as she stood. Just a few in-game hours into her play session, and already her Fatigue was at 60%. On the way to her beating at the hands of the Shadow Master, she'd have to pick up a *Savanna Energy Tonic* from Hezbek.

Leading the forces of good against the army of darkness was hard fricking work.

***

Devon just barely avoided Aijal's attack, the blunted lance passing a centimeter from her ribs. Landing awkwardly after her quick sidestep, she nonetheless tried to strike with a quick slice of her dagger, the weapon catching nothing but mist as the Esh turned insubstantial.

Overbalanced, Devon couldn't recover when her toe caught on an acacia tree root. She managed to get her shoulder tucked to convert the fall into a roll rather than a face plant, but the mistake still left her vulnerable. Aijal's lance stabbed down beside her ear, vibrating the soil beneath the back of Devon's head. The

Mistwalker's raised eyebrow made it clear that she hadn't missed by accident.

Devon lay there for a moment to catch her breath, and then pulled open her character sheet. She selected the option to show any values that had changed during the last day of playtime.

<u>Skills:</u>
Dodge: 5 (+2)
Riposte: 2 (+1)
One-Handed Slashing: 15 (+1)

<u>Combat Forms:</u>
Shadow Shifter - Tier 1: 30% Mastery (+5%)

<u>Abilities:</u>
Downdraft - Tier 1: 43% Mastery (+1%)
Backstab - Tier 1: 67% Mastery (+12%)

Aijal held out a hand to help her up. As Devon climbed to her feet, she kept her eyes off the Shadow Master's face. It was kind of embarrassing to get so thoroughly trounced every sparring session. In every other game she'd played, the best way to learn her class had been to go out and fight mobs, improving her play skill at the same time that her character statistics improved. But she had a settlement to run and an army to build, not to mention a couple of unique classes played by no one else in the game.

The other problem was the lack of mobs—the same problem that made it hard for her to order her army to power level.

Among the players in the camp, the practice of sparring to raise skills was common. Devon had even been talked into a match against Torald—a somewhat embarrassing memory she didn't like to relive. But the other players had pretty much maxed out the progress they could make play-fighting each other. For them, further advancement required real enemies.

Devon, on the other hand, had just gained a class specialization for which she had some major skill holes. A Shadowcaster extended the spell repertoire of a Sorcerer and the illusion and trickery of a Deceiver, but it brought its own flair, some of which was melee-based. Devon hadn't spent much time going toe-to-toe with enemies, and it showed.

And just Devon's luck, it usually showed most right when an audience arrived to witness her incompetence.

"Hey Hailey," she said as her friend stepped into the shade of the acacia tree where Devon and Aijal had been sparring.

"How's it going? Ready for your big moment on the throne?"

Devon groaned and checked her in-game clock. "I still have an hour of freedom before I have to deal with becoming the official leader of a rabid gang of do-gooders. If I teleport to the Stone Forest bindstone, I'll probably have enough of a head start that they'll never catch me."

"Especially when your griffon-riding slab of man meat swoops in and sweeps you into his oiled arms."

Devon grimaced. "Don't even start."

Hailey laughed, and if Devon wasn't mistaken, even Aijal looked faintly amused.

"Thanks for the lesson," Devon said, ducking a shallow bow to the Shadow Master.

"It's my pleasure to have a pupil who shows so many avenues for growth," Aijal said. "I take it you have preparations to make for your ceremony? If so, I have waiting tasks."

Devon blinked. Wait. Avenues for growth...was the Esh teasing her? The woman's big, liquidy eyes held no clue, and the expression on her milky face was as inscrutable as always.

"Yeah. But before you go, a quick request. Before our morning council tomorrow, can you work with Torald and Magda to gather a list of leaders from the Esh force and player camp? I want each of them to take command of a raid-sized group of fighters that will start training together. We need our communications and tactics working."

Aijal inclined her head as she turned to leave. "I'll set to that next."

"Want to help me pick out an outfit for this stupid thing?" Devon asked Hailey. "I guess if I really want them to think they're doing the right thing, I should probably try to look like a worthy leader."

Hailey snorted. "Shopping gives me hives. But man, I wish I could go back and tell me from a year ago where Relic Online would take us. Just thinking of you having to sit through this would have been enough entertainment to save me like half my subscriptions to premium streams."

The smile abruptly fell from Devon's face as Hailey's words struck. "You are *not* going to livestream this, okay?"

A strange look crossed Hailey's face, and she actually stammered before getting her next words out. "Yeah, no problem. But hey, Dev? You have time to chat soon?"

"Sure. Is this about whatever happened between you and Bob?" She whispered the wisp's name in hopes that she wouldn't accidentally summon him.

Hailey swallowed, and Devon noticed that she had double handfuls of her robes caught in clenched fists. "Yeah, kinda. Is tomorrow good? It might be a long convo."

Huh...Whatever this was about, Hailey seemed to be taking it really seriously.

"Sure. Let's explore the area around the council hall after the meeting. Talk while we walk."

"Sounds good." Hailey gave a little salute and turned. "See you in the throne room, princess."

Devon shot her friend a mock glare for the princess comment but waved as Hailey turned to leave. Just as the woman passed out of earshot, a minor earthquake rumbled deep in the earth. Shoot. Devon had meant to ask Hailey to try to look into that with her seeker abilities. She needed to remember that first thing tomorrow.

Chapter Six

JEREMY HAD SCROUNGED up a lute from somewhere and was sitting outside the main entrance to the inner keep, strumming it and humming stanzas. As Devon approached, decked out in a ridiculous velvet outfit that Emmaree, the tailor, claimed was the most queenly garb she sold, he cracked a wide, shit-eating grin.

"Nice threads, Elvis," he said.

"Shut up, dude." Devon clawed at the clasp for the short cape that was digging into her jugular. This sucked.

"I've been composing a song for the feast dinner. Want to hear the chorus?"

She felt her lower eyelid twitch. "Feast dinner?"

"Duh. How many coronations have you been to that haven't included horns of ale and roast piglets afterward? How else are you going to create leftovers for us poor serfs? Cast-offs from your high table and all that."

"I'm so glad this amuses you. I hope you can contain the urge to burst out in song while people are swearing their oaths. It's the end of their first epic quest line."

"Just the sort of occasion that should be heralded with glorious war ballads."

She glanced toward the darkened entrance to the keep. This was really, really going to suck. There was nothing Devon hated more than being the center of attention. She sighed. "Anyway, I don't remember putting you on the invite list."

Jeremy grinned and stood, the peacock feather in his floppy hat-thing bobbing flamboyantly. "But you see, I've been deputized by the planning committee. I have a *job*." He raised his eyebrows dramatically.

Oh brother. Clearly, someone didn't understand how much Jeremy loved to torment her. "Have I mentioned that I liked you better when you were out of phase with the physical plane?" In their previous game, he'd played a planar priest, which meant that he was often only in weak contact with the group.

He smirked and strummed a quick riff on the lute. Rolling her eyes, Devon stepped toward the keep entrance.

"Uh, nope. Sorry. You have to wait here." Jeremy trotted forward and got in her way, the stupid peacock feather dipping forward and tickling her face.

She knocked it away and stepped back. "Seriously, Jeremy. I'm ready to get this over with."

From within the entrance chamber to the keep came the sound of someone clearing their throat. Wood thumped against stone, and Hezbek stepped into the light falling through the doorway, her walking staff leading the way. "I asked him to delay you while I assured that the preparations were complete."

Hezbek glanced up over Devon's shoulder. Turning to follow her gaze, Devon spied a raven shuffling sideways along a shop's awning. If she wasn't mistaken, it was Gustwing. The bird bobbed his head as if giving a signal.

Hezbek sucked her teeth and nodded. "Good."

A moment later, a popup appeared in Devon's vision.

Hezbek has invited you to join her group.
Accept? Y/N

Devon's eyebrows drew together as she accepted the invite. "Why the group?" she asked as she stepped back a few paces and peered up toward the windows in the upper floor of the keep.

"Because, as you say, your teleport sucks."

Devon blinked, utterly confused, as Jeremy's health bar joined the group interface. "We're going somewhere?" she said stupidly as magic began to shimmer around her. Her body started to tingle as the bits and pieces disassociated from each other, and moments later, all went black as she vanished from Stonehaven.

The sounds of cheering swelled to fill her ears as she sensed hard stone taking shape beneath her feet. The afternoon sun warmed her shoulders, and her *Sparklebomb Backpack*, hidden beneath the velvet cape, pressed into her spine between her shoulder blades. She opened her eyes to Ishildar, and with a glance, determined that she was in the center of a crossroads near the council hall.

Half a dozen grinning faces stared at her.

"Surprise," Dorden said.

"Huh?" She glanced around again, lip twitching when she noticed a sort of chair-thing fastened to poles and shaded with a silk canopy. Plump scarlet cushions sported gold-thread tassels, and there was a drink holder near one of the arms already equipped with a full, gem-encrusted goblet. "No."

"Oh yes," Jeremy said. "You get to be in a *parade*. We've got people set up to line the streets from here to the player camp and from there to Stonehaven. It's going to be awesome."

Devon felt her shoulders sag. She searched the gathered faces for sympathy but found none. Even Hailey just shrugged and seemed to be on the verge of laughing.

She blinked again. "You really intend for me to sit in that thing?"

"And be carried, yes," Chen said. "I'm counting on at least five skill-ups in *Manual Labor*. And Torald sends his regrets about the little misdirection regarding the throne and the inner keep. We had a sneaking suspicion you might protest the pomp of this kind of procession."

"But you planned it anyway."

He shrugged and smirked. "Who doesn't love a parade?"

Groaning, Devon started toward the chair. "I sure hope there's alcohol in that—"

A rumble from deep in the earth cut off her words. Planting her feet and bending her knees, Devon threw her arms out for balance as the earthquake rolled beneath them. Smiles faded from the surrounding faces as the trembling grew violent. A swift heave of the earth sent her stumbling, and a sudden gap between paving stones caught Devon's toe. She went sprawling, and for once, she wasn't the only klutz knocked off her feet. At least half the people in the intersection lost their footing.

Devon rolled, worried for Hezbek, and breathed a sigh of relief when she saw the woman levitating over the shaking earth. Thinking to do the same, she gathered her weight and prepared to stand. But the sight of Aijal stopped her cold.

For the first time in Devon's memory, the Shadow Master's face showed stark emotion. Shock. Fear perhaps.

"What is it, Aijal?" Devon shouted.

"Devon," Owen shouted over the grating and cracking of stone. "The pattern says—"

"No!" Aijal hissed, cutting him off. "I'd stopped focusing on our racial bond, thinking the Rovan exterminated..."

"What? What is it?"

"The starborn camp. Would you say it's directly south of here?"

Devon yanked open her minimap. "Yeah. Almost exactly."

"Grab your swords. Now. They'll need our help."

Chapter Seven

DEVON'S CLOSEST NPC and player friends had been in the group planning to escort her throne thing through the parade, and now each of them threw off their celebratory mood and yanked out their weapons. Devon snapped open the clasp holding the cape to her neck and swung her backpack around to get at her inventory. There wouldn't be time to change back into her armor—damn...she should never have agreed to this stupid ceremony—but she jammed her hand into the pack to activate her inventory interface, focused on her *Frostwielder's Belt*, and felt it drop into her hand. *Night's Fang*, her dagger, was sheathed in a socket on the belt; as soon as she buckled it on, she drew the blade and started running.

Hazel raced ahead in the mad dash, shading her eyes and scanning the skies. A moment later, Gustwing flapped down from the heavens and landed on her forearm. The scout's steps slowed as she listened to the raven's quiet *gorboling*. Hazel's face went slack. A chill crept into Devon's guts. Hazel rarely showed anything but a smile.

Devon cursed under her breath as she forced more speed from her legs. After snapping off a few quick commands to the raven, Hazel tossed Gustwing into the air. With a few mighty flaps of his shining wings, the bird was gone. Most likely heading to Stonehaven to call the settlement's fighters to action.

Near the street leaving the intersection, Devon skidded to a halt and spun. She looked back to see Hezbek standing alone in the center of the slate pavements. The medicine woman stared off toward the south, the direction of the player camp, a sorrowful look on her face. After a moment, she shook her head and turned to Devon.

"You're not on a refresh timer for that teleport are you?" Devon said.

"No. I'll be fine, child. Just...something about today reminds me of my past. Of the times we celebrated our victories and respites too easily, knowing the threat was still there. But then...even in war, you have to find time for joy, right?"

Devon wasn't sure what to say. She shifted her weight between her feet, listening to the retreating footsteps as her other allies ran toward the southern edge of the city.

"Go," Hezbek said. "Your people need you. With good fortune, I'll see you back in Stonehaven on the other side of this."

As light sprang from the elderly woman's hands, Devon whirled to catch up with the others. Before turning onto a south-bound street, she glanced back to see Hezbek surrounded by a pearly nimbus as her teleport spell took hold. A breath later she'd vanished.

As Devon sprinted forward, chasing after her friends, the *Fatigue* bar in her interface steadily rose. She passed the stragglers, starting with Dorden, his stumpy legs pumping like pistons. But she didn't want to be wiped out before they even reached the savanna, so when she caught up with Hailey, she slowed to match the woman's pace.

"Hey," she panted, "how big is the range on *True Sight*? Can you get a picture of what's happening at the player camp?"

Hailey shook her head, her arms pumping lightly as her slipper-clad feet whispered over the flagstone pavement. "But I doubt we're going to like what we find."

"No—"

Another violent jerk of the ground stole her words as it threw Devon forward. Her foot landed hard, jarring her knee and hip. She tripped and fell forward, cracking a knee against the flagstones and scraping the palms of her *Gloves of Deceit,* one of the only armor pieces that had fit with her fancy outfit.

"Ow." Devon gathered herself, climbing to a crouch and rubbing her aching knee with her forearm. Hailey offered her a hand up.

You gain resistance: +1% versus earth-based damage.

Just trying to lighten the mood here. Klutz.

"I swear you could trip over a feather. What's your *Agility?*" the woman asked.

Devon peeked at the attributes section of her character sheet, shuffling sideways as the earth rocked.

"Twenty-one with gear," Devon said as she started trotting forward. "That's not *that* bad, right?"

"Well, it's not terrible for a caster. Maybe you're just extra clumsy."

"Thanks." Already the quake had stilled, and Devon sped up again.

"Hey...uh..."

Devon looked over her shoulder to see Hailey standing stock still, eyes wide as she stared at the southern sky. Belly *definitely* full of ice now, Devon turned.

Over the tops of the final buildings standing between her and the savanna, a column of oily black smoke rose steadily into the sky. "Shit," Devon muttered as she sprinted to the street that emptied onto the savanna. Glancing down it, she shook her head, aghast. Judging by the amount of smoke, nearly the entire player camp was on fire.

Flowing like silk, Aijal raced past. When she reached the end of the street, the Esh Shadow Master dissolved into a cloud of mist that hung in the air for a moment before streaking across the grassland toward the scene. Hazel dashed into the field and whistled. A shrill whinny answered the scout's call, and the drumming of hooves vibrated the ground. Before Devon reached the edge of the grassland, one of the windsteeds thundered into view, mane and tail streaming. Zoe, the war ostrich, followed close on the horse's heels, her neck stretched out nearly horizontally, her useless wings flapping. The horse slowed just enough for Hazel to grab a handful of its mane and vault onto its back, then the trio set off for the player camp at a gallop.

"Wait," Devon shouted as Dorden, clattering in his platemail, sprinted past and banged his warhammer against his breastplate to summon the mule he'd taken as a mount.

"If ye think I'll stay here while me starborn friends contend with merciless enemies, ye are sadly mistaken," the dwarf shouted. He seemed about to launch into a tirade about the Stoneshoulder Clan code of honor, but Devon raised a hand and tossed him a group invite. She grabbed Hailey's arm and did the same to the Seeker, then focused on Owen, Jeremy, and Chen and added them to the party.

Devon cast a glance at a few bikes leaning against a nearby wall—most players used them for commuting between the camp, Stonehaven, and Ishildar—then shook her head. The player camp was nearly equidistant from Ishildar and Stonehaven, so it wouldn't make much difference from which direction they approached. Given the smoke, though, she worried that her friends' small encampment was already lost. If that were the case, she needed to be at Stonehaven to save what she could.

Motioning her group members forward, Devon ran toward the dwarf so that everyone would be in spell range. When she went through the mental gymnastics to start casting *Journey*, her group teleport spell, scintillating magic filled the air around her. She felt herself growing lighter, her contact with the ground becoming insubstantial. She swallowed in preparation for the sensation of dissolution, and a moment later, Ishildar vanished.

Chapter Eight

DEVON'S STOMACH SLUICED into her lower abdomen like wet gravel as she rematerialized at the Shrine to Veia. Her senses returned in quick succession, the smell of green grass tinged with smoke, the sun on the crown of her head, the shouts from the forward areas of the settlement. She blinked away disorientation and reached for her dagger's hilt as she searched Stonehaven for enemies.

Ranged fighters stood shoulder-to-shoulder on the main palisade. They faced outward, the tension in their bodies obvious even from the shrine's position at the rear of the settlement. At least the walls were still secure. Nonetheless, Devon's heart hammered in her chest as she made eye contact with Hailey, then started for the front of the settlement at a run.

"Devon," Owen called from behind. Devon slowed enough to look over her shoulder. The faint outline of a figure was steadily consolidating as someone began to respawn beside the shrine. Feet planted near the condensing figure, Dorden tugged his beard while adjusting his grip on his warhammer—he'd never been all that comfortable with the respawning process. A couple of seconds later, a bright glow surrounded the incoming person, ending with a flash and a pop.

Devon hurried back to the shrine as the new arrival, Torald, dropped to a knee in the grass. His usually gleaming armor was black with soot, reflecting the sunlight only where deep gouges marred the plates. He knocked the helm from his head and ran a hand through his hair. Hollow eyes met Devon's gaze, and he shook his head.

"What happened?" she asked.

With a groan, Torald clambered to his feet, then stooped and grabbed his helm. He stuffed the armor piece into his *Manpurse of Holding*, and his eyes went distant for a moment. Devon guessed he was making a quick check through his inventory to see which item the game's death penalty had randomly stripped from his possession and left at the site of his demise.

"Torald?" she prompted.

Torald shook his head and blinked. He pressed the tips of his armored fingers to his forehead. "We didn't have any warning. I was polishing my armor and waiting for the parade when the first pillar of hellfire erupted so close. Maybe thirty feet away."

"Hellfire?" Hailey asked.

Torald blinked again. "It was surreal. Like it wasn't happening. At least that's what I thought before the heatwave knocked me flat. Have you ever smelled molten earth? The ground turned to liquid, white-hot glass."

Devon glanced from Hailey to Owen and back. Both her guildmates shrugged. Devon stepped forward and grabbed the big paladin by his soot-stained shoulder plates. "You're in shock, Torald. But we need answers. Who was it? Demons?" She glanced again at Owen, whose barrier had been holding back the horde for the past few days.

The man closed his eyes. "The *Illumin* curtain is undisturbed."

"Did it extend underground?" Hailey asked, putting a voice to Devon's internal frustration that she hadn't taken more action to figure out the source of the earthquakes. Given the intensity of the tremors that had hit just before the smoke appeared, Devon was now sure they were related.

Owen shrugged, a troubled expression crossing his face. "I guess I don't know."

"I couldn't get a proper *con* on him," Torald said, referring to the *Combat Assessment* skill in old-school gamer vernacular. *Con* was short for *Consider*, which had once been the common name for a similar skill. Coming from anyone but Torald, the usage wouldn't even snag Devon's attention. Because the paladin so rarely broke character, the word sounded almost foreign.

"A *con* on who?" she said.

"It said Archdemon Gaviroth. No other information. Not even a level or a skull and crossbones."

"Great," Hailey said.

"Do you recognize that name, Owen?" Devon asked, hoping the man's experience in the demonic plane would be some help here. But even as Owen slowly shook his head, the ghost of a memory scratched at the back of Devon's mind. Owen wasn't the only one who'd spent time with his mind trapped in the hell plane. In the early months of Relic Online, the demonic AI, Zaa, had used Devon's unconscious mind while she slept, co-opting her mental processing to control and develop a demon war priestess, Ezraxis.

Devon might not recognize the name, but she sensed that Ezraxis did. The emotion the name conjured was something like fearful reverence.

She shivered.

"There were maybe half a dozen lower-level mobs with the archdemon."

Torald's eyes turned to the shrine as more figures began to materialize. He shook his head in dismay.

"So to sum up," Hailey said, "you guys got hit by a hellfire-wielding archdemon and maybe six of his lackeys."

Torald nodded somewhat dumbly. Devon had never seen him like this. Maybe he'd taken his role-playing a step too far and now couldn't handle a confrontation with his creator goddess's nemesis.

Or maybe he'd already grasped something that Devon's mind was working around towards. With a spell that could melt stone and a challenge rating too high for whatever scale *Combat Assessment* used, what the hell good were Stonehaven's defenses? It sounded like the only saving grace they might have was the repelling effect from the Shrine to Veia. At the very least, this archdemon would need to hammer at Veia's protections for a little while before smashing Stonehaven flat.

"Infernal Tyrants and Demonic Ravagers they were called," Torald said. "The lackeys, I mean."

Devon shook her head. Details didn't matter. Dragging the paladin by the elbow and motioning for the others to follow, she dashed toward the front of the settlement.

The movement seemed to jar some sense back into Torald's skull, and by the time the small group had reached the stairs leading up to the palisade's wall-walk, his eyes seemed brighter. He shook his head and muttered something under his breath. Devon caught the words *divine light* and *benevolent creator* and felt mild relief that her friend was at least back to his old self. The stairs shuddered under their feet as the group sprinted up the steps to join Jarleck at his post.

For a moment, Devon couldn't speak. She was glad that the player camp was a couple of miles away, too far to make out details, because the truth had to be horrific. Burned-out husks of structures were just barely visible on the edge of the pool of what looked like slowly cooling lava. Heat shimmered the air, and flames ate at the grass surrounding the former camp. Each puff of wind tore scraps of cinders from the blazes, tossing them deeper into the savanna.

At the forward edge of the camp, between the molten earth and Stonehaven, a massive figure cut a dark and wavering silhouette from the glow of the fire. Before it, rising no more than thigh-height on the monster, figures cavorted. But the archdemon wasn't advancing. Not yet.

For at least thirty seconds, no one spoke. There wasn't much to say.

"Maybe our defenses are better than we think," Dorden finally said. "Maybe the shrine can keep them back now that Ishildar is awake."

Devon wanted to believe that, but she couldn't quite have faith.

"You with us enough now to answer some questions?" Hailey asked Torald.

Torald shrugged, then nodded. "I serve Veia and Devon for as long as I walk this realm. Any answers I can produce are yours."

Hailey hesitated a moment, seeming unsure how to respond to flagrant role-playing in this situation. "You said they surprised you. Didn't the camp set a watch?"

A faint line formed between Torald's eyebrows as he considered the question. "Now that you mention it, yes. I don't see how that beast could have approached without being seen."

"You didn't even hear anything? Nothing seemed out of the ordinary?"

He shook his head, but then seem to reconsider the answer. "During the last couple of quakes, I thought I heard howls rising from the earth. I was sure it was my imagination."

Owen cursed under his breath. "The creases in the pattern make sense now. The opposing Esh faction. I thought some might have escaped, but I assumed they could do no harm." His eyes went distant, and a parade of expressions crossed his face. "And now I wonder..."

Devon didn't have a chance to ask what he wondered because as the man trailed off, a mighty earthquake shook the settlement. The wall shuddered, foundation stones grating against one another. She flung her hands out to grab the railing and still struggled to keep her balance.

With a roar, a massive pit opened in the savanna ahead, pulling down a wide section of cobblestone road that connected Stonehaven and the player camp. Shrieking and howling, demons began to pour from the crater.

Her breath locked in her chest, Devon watched in horror as similar pits opened all across the savanna. Between them, sunken trenches formed as subterranean tunnels collapsed. Within two or three minutes, the area writhed with demon flesh.

Chapter Nine

HAILEY AND OWEN were talking in clipped tones, Hailey asking why he couldn't just cast an *Illumin* barrier around Stonehaven, Owen answering that it couldn't hold against this, not for long, and speculating that the demons had left his other barrier alone because they wanted the element of surprise.

Devon listened, but only intently enough to catch the gist. The roar in her head consumed the rest of her attention, the despairing thoughts tumbling one over the other.

There had to be hundreds...no, thousands of demons out there. Stonehaven and everyone in it were totally and completely hosed. There just wasn't a freaking chance. The situation was so bad that she wasn't sure whether to cry or laugh or throw herself off the wall. So instead, she grabbed the *Starlight Rod* from her *Sparklebomb Backpack*. Focusing on a random demon, some new variety with mottled, skin-colored wings, she held the rod up and activated its special ability. A bolt of pure-white light lanced from the heavens and speared the demon through the chest, leaving a smoking hole. The monster toppled.

You receive 5500 experience.

As she let her arm fall to her side—the rod had a cooldown of ten minutes and was useless until that was over—Devon stared despondently over the field. Her eyes unfocused as self-pity washed over her in full force. When a glow appeared before her, she assumed it was Hailey or Owen performing some equally futile casting.

The glow booped her nose.

"I abandoned my game of Lord of the Rings Risk for this? Really? You're now officially the Keeper of Ishildar, and you're standing here like a brainless toddler while Zaa's army prepares to obliterate all life in this part of the mortal plane? I am seriously disappointed in you. Actually, that doesn't begin to express the depth of emotion I'm working with here. I'm tragically frustrated. Inconsolably demoralized. Righteously—"

"Did you have something useful to say, Bob?" Devon said, batting at the wisp as it danced in front of her eyes. "Or did you just come to gloat about how I wasn't worthy of restoring Ishildar? Because if so, let me help you out. Yup. You called it. We lost. Now if you wouldn't mind shutting your trap, I'm guessing I have about five more minutes to enjoying the settlement I've built from nothing. Five minutes and ten seconds if we try to fight back."

"For once, I don't disagree," the wisp said.

"Good. Then why don't you get back to defending Middle-earth and leave me to wallow in my misery."

"Uh...because I'm apparently a glutton for punishment? You do remember that Ishildar was going to be critical in this war, right?"

Devon balled her fists and pressed them against the top of the waist-high parapet. "And I wasn't quick enough or smart enough to figure out how to use its resources. I get it."

"Hey Dev," Hailey said. The woman was still standing beside Devon. Out of the corner of her eye, Devon saw her friend make an absent motion with her fingers. Just beyond the cleared area outside Stonehaven's curtain wall, an imp fell under Hailey's *Charm* spell and shrieked while it tore into one of its comrades. Two more down. Just a few thousand to go.

An imp fluttered over what seemed to be the boundary where the Shrine to Veia's ability to weaken the demons cut a line in front of the settlement. It screeched as its wing beats slowed, gravity dragging it toward the earth.

Settlement has come under attack by an invading force.
Stonehaven's ownership is now: Contested 0.5%.

This couldn't be happening, but it was. Devon growled and pummeled the falling imp with a *Flamestrike*, ending its pathetic life. But another demon, a low-level thrall, edged a toe over the boundary, shrieking in fury at the debuff but still advancing.

"Yeah?" Devon said, turning a shoulder toward Bob in what a sane being would recognize as a dismissal.

"Never mind," Hailey said. "I was noticing that none of the tunnels passed under Stonehaven. At least, none of the tunnels that collapsed did—there aren't any trenches within twenty feet of the walls. I was going to say that they weren't advancing out of the grass."

"Owen, can you reinforce the shrine's barrier?" Devon asked. "Use your *Illumin* to create a secondary wall? Maybe we can hold them off."

"And what?" Hailey asked. "Wait for them to starve us out?"

An arrow streaked from the battlements and impaled the advancing thrall through the eye. It fell, half in and half out of what seemed to be Stonehaven's region of control. A status bar had popped up in Devon's interface indicating the contested status. Across the line, low-level demons kept shoving at the barrier. Crossing it, dying, but slowly pushing back the line of control.

"Whoa now," Bob said. "Getting from 'five minutes' to 'long enough to starve' is kind of a leap, don't you think?"

Devon turned a glare on the wisp. "Seriously, I know you're some freaky fragment of a self-creating AI hive mind, but you really could be a little more sensitive here."

"I'm just *saying*, if you stand around waiting for Stonehaven to burn, two things will happen. One, Stonehaven will burn. But on the bright side, two, you'll be dead so you won't have to witness it."

"Technically, we'll probably be caught in a death-respawn loop back at the shrine once they get control."

Devon spun to see Chen, a few steps down the stairs. She glared at him for stating the obvious.

"I don't know whether it's better to be stuck in a spawn loop or just plain dead," she said, thinking of all the basic NPCs who depended on her for their lives. She turned again to the battlefield, arrows now peppering the advancing demons non-stop. For every hellhound or imp or thrall that fell, another just climbed over the corpse and advanced on the walls. And behind the ranks and ranks of cannon fodder, the darkness-cloaked form of Archdemon Gaviroth advanced, his lackeys forming a crescent before him.

Near the center of the fortifications, the barrier appeared to buckle as squealing demons pushed forward in a slavering crowd. Spells from half a dozen casters slammed down on the group, momentarily popping the line back into place, but within a few seconds, it had buckled all over again. Devon dropped a *Wall of Ice* in the path of the advance, the frozen barrier spanning the cobblestone road that led up to Stonehaven's drawbridge.

A tongue of flame licked out from a *Demon Conjurer's* raised hand, reducing the ice to a puddle.

The advance pressed onwards until an imp was shoved forward by its companions to die, arrow-quilled, on the drawbridge.

> *Stonehaven's fortifications have come under attack.*
> **Structure is contested:** Drawbridge - 10%
> **Stonehaven's ownership is now:** Contested 2%

Devon shook her head as heavy lances from the ballistae speared the horde, some flying straight through one demon and into another. Ichor sprayed, but still, the demons came.

Her makeshift army didn't stand a chance against this.

"We've already lost," she said, voice flat but certain. Penned into a settlement with no escape, an unbeatable force bearing down. Unless...

"You have the spyglass?" she asked, whirling on Jarleck. The man stood looking over the parapet with the same despondent expression that had likely been on her face just a couple minutes ago.

He slowly turned his attention to her, face slack with shock and despair, as he pulled the device from a holster on his belt. It was one of Stonehaven's most prized communal items, purchased from a sailor refugee who had come from a village near an inland sea north of Eltera City. The brass of the lens housing was cool against her palm.

Devon raised the glass to her eye and peered toward Ishildar. Over the heads of the horde and through the cloud of imps fluttering above it, she spotted untouched grassland, a strip maybe fifty or a hundred yards wide. One of her early quests, which she had only recently finished, had been to restore Ishildar's Veian Temple. When she'd completed the quest, everyone in the area had received the buff that increased their combat stats versus demons. There'd been no mention of a shielding effect, and Shavari hadn't yet reported on her assigned investigations. But due to that empty strip, Devon had to assume it existed. More, she assumed the shielding was much stronger than that offered by the small Shrine to Veia. Strong enough to provide sanctuary for a time.

She dropped the spyglass from her eye and stared at the road that joined Stonehaven to the ancient city. Part earthen wagon track and part cobblestone pavement, it was now entirely thronged with demons. She shook her head slowly. Even with bikes or windsteeds and with every fighter riding out as a shield to try to defend the non-combatants, there was no way she could get the population across the miles of the savanna. Most likely, even the best fighters would fail to run that gauntlet with no one to defend but themselves. But provided the defenses could hold for a little while longer, there was still a chance to get her followers to safety.

Bob hung expectantly at the edge of her vision, vibrating with what appeared to be a tremendous effort to keep quiet.

Devon glanced back toward the shrine, taking an indulgent moment or two to let her gaze linger on the streets and buildings and *life* that filled Stonehaven. She'd built this place plank by plank, stone by stone, decision by decision.

Behind her, out on the savanna, a howl went up from the demon horde. Thousands of voices shrieked and wailed, and above it all, she heard a rasping, two-toned voice that some deep part of her recognized as Archdemon Gaviroth.

"Forward, worms!"

Clenching her fist around the *Starlight Rod*, Devon sprang for the stairs. She whirled to face the defenders, focusing on Owen. "Lay whatever barriers you can. Make them fight for every inch of ground." When her guildmate nodded, she turned to Jarleck. "Shoot anything that comes within range, but as soon as you see my signal, I want you to pull everyone off the wall. Fall back to the rear of the settlement, and herd any stray citizens who are lingering too long. We'll gather at the shrine."

Bob executed a loop the loop but made no other comment. Hailey followed its glow with her eyes before turning back to Devon. "I'm guessing you have a plan?"

Devon nodded. "Fetch Hezbek, and help her bring every mana potion in our stock." To Torald, she said, "Tell the respawning players to spread the word through the settlement. Villagers should grab whatever they can: food, clothing, weapons. But only what they can carry. We have to be quick."

***

A structure's ownership is now neutral: Drawbridge - Time remaining: **1 day, 4 hours**

If the original owner does not restore the contested state, ownership will transfer to the captor when the timer expires. Captors may lower the delay by making improvements to the structure.

Structure is contested: Moat - 30%

Structure is contested: Outer gate - 5%

Stonehaven's ownership is now: Contested - 3%

The citizens of Stonehaven streamed toward the shrine carrying their belongings in their arms. Despite the sunny day, it felt as if a storm hung over the region. The roars and howls of the demons were wind lashing the town, and the attacks against the walls—rocks thrown by cackling imps, gushing hellfire that washed against the *Illumin* barrier and rippled the air with unimaginable heat—were thunder and lighting. Smoke filled the sky over the savanna, black and choking.

A storm of destruction. A demon apocalypse.

Devon was barely holding herself together.

Standing alongside one of the wider village paths, she waved the villagers on, urging them with words that came out too curt and clipped. Jaw aching from clenching down hard on her panic, she swallowed and kept glancing toward the palisade. Stonehaven's soldiers still lined the battlements, but now there were a few holes in their ranks. The demons couldn't physically pass the shrine's and Owen's defenses, not yet. But a few clever imps had discovered that *Illumin* did nothing to stop their hurled rocks or thrown lances.

Few of the settlement's fighters were advanced NPCs—she had only been able to promote twenty-five of her followers. If any of the advanced citizens died, she'd be able to resurrect them at a Veian shrine. But for the basic NPCs now missing from the soldiers' ranks, death was final.

She closed her eyes for a moment, scarcely able to handle the thought.

Clenching her fists and straightening her shoulders, she peered again through the streets. Aside from a few stragglers trying to drag along too many possessions, the evacuation of the forward areas of the settlement was nearly complete.

Laying her hand against the back of a woman she recognized as a shopkeeper, a seller of enchanting reagents, she pressed gently, urging the woman to hurry. Raising her other hand high, Devon cast *Glowing Orb*. When the blue-white light appeared in her palm, she tossed it up high then targeted it with her wind spell, *Downdraft*. The gust sent the orb flying over the rooftops, and when it reached the height of the wall-walk, she targeted it with *Flamestrike*. A column of fire appeared in the air over the city, harmless due to the precise targeting, but bright enough to capture the attention of the men and women on the wall. If not for the circumstances, she might have taken a congratulatory moment or two to pride herself on the improvised flare.

Using *Ventriloquism*, Devon projected her voice to the area beside Jarleck. "Now. Retreat, and quickly. Carry the stragglers if you have to."

Smoke had begun to drift and billow over the wall, and it was growing harder to make out crisp details, but Devon thought she saw the man nod. Moments later, fighters began to file toward the staircases, firing arrows and bolts and ranged magic only when the procession slowed or stopped as those near the front of the line negotiated the stairs.

From out on the fields beyond the walls came shrieks of triumph, the demon horde rejoicing in the defenders' retreat.

Devon told herself that the stinging in her eyes was from the smoke, and maybe that was partially true. Either way, she wiped away the water that threatened to spill over her lower eyelids and turned for the shrine, spine straight.

Stonehaven was lost, but the demons wouldn't have any more of its citizens. Not while Devon could still do something to save them.

She dashed through the grass at the edge of the footpath, tossing words of encouragement as she sped past the procession of villagers. At the Shrine to Veia, Chen, Hailey, and Owen stood together. Hezbek sat on a low, rounded boulder rubbing her walking stick between her palms. The twirling motion of the staff had drilled a shallow hole in the earth before the stone.

"Where's Torald?" she asked. She hoped the paladin hadn't snuck off to do something stupid.

Structure is contested: Moat - 45%
Structure is contested: Outer gate - 15%
Structure is contested: Curtain wall - 2%
Stonehaven's ownership is now: Contested - 3.5%

Chen pointed toward the farm plots and the warehouse that had recently been constructed near them. Torald and Bayle, one of Devon's original NPC followers who was both a fighter-class citizen and one of the town's farmers, stood in the wide double door that led to the darkened interior of the storage building. The woman appeared to be pouring the contents of some grain sacks into

Torald's *Manpurse of Holding*. Devon's eyes widened. The idea was genius. She might have to stop making fun of his manpurse.

When she spotted Tom, Bayle's husband and the town's most senior cook, standing nearby, she shrugged out of her *Tiny Sparklebomb Backpack of Sub-par Holding* and pressed the straps into his hand. The cook stared at her, a startled look on his perpetually sunburned face.

She nodded toward the warehouse. "My bag can't fit nearly as much as Torald's, but you have five minutes to grab as many ingredients as you can stuff inside. Choose whatever supplies will stretch the furthest, not what will taste the best."

The man blinked and ran a hand over his balding skull. He appeared to have forgotten his sunhat in his hasty dash to the shrine—if this escape plan worked, she'd have to make sure to get one of the crafters to improvise another for him. The man seemed to turn into a lobster if exposed to moonlight. She didn't want to know what would happen to him after an afternoon under the actual sun.

She nodded encouragement. "That's all. Get to it."

Jerking straight, he gave a little salute and ran off, bound for the storage shed near one of the town kitchens.

Devon turned to Owen. "We'll need time. Can you cast concentric shields around the shrine area? I want them to have to break through one at a time. And I'm hoping the shrine's power strengthens the closer we get to it."

"Hey, Devon?" Hailey said. "We'd be more help if we knew what was going on."

Devon hesitated a moment. Had she not told them? As if in answer to her unspoken question, Greel snorted. She peered over Hailey's shoulder and spotted the man herding a flock of chickens forward with a stick. The birds were his pride and joy, the only creatures that experienced the pleasant side of his personality. Well, them and the windsteed he'd persuaded to carry him around sometimes, a fact that irked her a little because no amount of sweet talking had convinced any of the horses to give her a chance.

"Have you ever known our illustrious leader to be clear in her communications? Or even more uncommon, do you recall her asking for advice about a situation?" the lawyer snapped.

"Dude, it's really not the time," Hailey said.

The man raised an eyebrow. "I think it's precisely the time. The decisions made in the next few minutes will likely determine the fate of everyone here. If I were ever to decide to hold my tongue out of fear of being called abrasive, now would certainly not be the most opportune moment."

Devon sighed and then blinked as she realized something. The last time she'd seen Greel, he'd been racing from the council hall in Ishildar to the edge of the city. Despite his twisted spine, the man was fast when he wanted to be. She assumed he'd been not far ahead of Hazel, and that the two of them must have reconsidered the suicide mission once they got a better look at the remains of the player camp. A retreat to Ishildar would have been the safest ploy, especially for a man who had repeatedly claimed that he only remained in Stonehaven out of self-interest.

Or so he said. Devon had seen him put himself at risk for her and her followers enough times to know the truth.

"Where's Hazel? And if you have something to say, be quick. We don't have time to listen to one of your lectures."

He curled his lip, then circled his hand in the air. "I believe you were going to elucidate regarding your plan. And I haven't seen Hazel since the council hall."

"Ill-loosa-what?" Hailey asked.

Bob abruptly popped into view from somewhere in the vicinity of Devon's feet. The wisp shimmered as if in pleasure. "Tell me you play Scrabble," it said, swirling around Greel's head. "My sibling-selves are sorely lacking in skill."

Devon glared at the wisp. "Elucidate is a snobby word for explain. And the plan is simple." She nodded toward Hezbek. "We're leaving."

Her friends' eyes turned to the medicine woman. "I don't get it," Hailey said.

"The word's origin is sometime in the mid-16th century of the starborn realm, deriving from the Latin—"

"Bob! Shut up!" Hailey and Devon said together.

Hezbek planted her walking stick and pressed up off the boulder. Setting her feet, she then used the butt end of the stick to drag forward a sack of clinking potions. "I believe Devon plans to use me as what you starborn sometimes call a taxi."

Comprehension dawned on Hailey's and Owen's faces, but Greel looked completely mystified.

"How many points is the X worth in Scrabble?" Chen asked. "Because I'm guessing by the look on the lawyer's face that he's never heard the word *taxi* before."

Bob rose about three inches in the air and seemed to notice Chen for the first time. The wisp slowly drifted closer to the teenager, whispering to itself.

Devon batted at it, hoping the annoying ball would just dematerialize or something. "It's starborn slang for someone who has a class ability that allows them to teleport other people. Hezbek can evacuate groups then come back alone to gather more passengers. I'll help too, once I'm sure everyone is behind Owen's barrier."

"All right. I'll admit it seems like a reasonable plan given the circumstances." Greel ran his eyes over the settlement as if abruptly coming to terms with its loss. He blinked a few times—was he banishing tears? Devon glanced away to give him privacy. "But where to?"

With her group teleport, Hezbek would be able to take the citizens of Stonehaven anywhere in the world that she'd previously traveled, limited in range only by the scaling mana cost that increased with distance.

But Devon wasn't ready to give up entirely. Stonehaven was lost, but Ishildar wasn't. And since Hezbek could only transport one group at a time, mana was a concern.

"The Veian Temple," Devon said. "It's our best hope, the strongest protection we have. I can only teleport between bindstones, so I'll lead my groups south from the edge of the Stone Forest."

"And the livestock?" Greel asked, nudging his chickens into a tighter circle with his stick. "Where do they fit in your little plan?"

Devon stared down at the birds. It wasn't that she didn't care, but if it came to it, humans would take precedence over poultry. Fortunately, she didn't have to tell that to the lawyer because Tom's arrival with her obnoxious glittering backpack gave her an idea.

Taking it from the cook's hand, she bent down and started scooping chickens into the bag.

Greel opened his mouth as if to protest, then clapped it shut.

"Are we ready, then?" the medicine woman asked.

"The sooner, the better."

Hezbek grunted as she hefted the bag of mana potions. Fishing through it, she pulled out a small pot, tossed it to Devon, then retrieved another and tossed that as well. Shuffling toward the shrine, she started tapping people on the shoulders and motioning them to follow. Once a small party had congregated within spell range, Hezbek closed her eyes while light flowed from her hands. Moments later, the group vanished in a flash.

Stonehaven's exodus had begun, and not a moment too soon, because as citizens shouted in surprise to see some of their number vanish so abruptly, shrill screams rose from the edges of the crowd.

A young man in the apron of a leatherworker's apprentice climbed on a stump and pointed, his eyes wide with fright.

A demon had reached the top of the palisade.

Chapter Ten

Warning: *Attacking this creature will cause your alignment to shift toward evil. Many residents of Aventalia's settlements and cities can recognize evildoers by their auras. You may be refused entrance to these hubs, and in some cases, you may be killed on sight.*

Ashley snorted as she dispelled the pop-up. What was it with this game and its attempts to be her conscience? If the designers or the content-creating AI or whatever didn't want her grinding XP on a bunch of giggling Glacial Fairies, why make them so easy to kill? And anyway, it didn't matter if she was flagged kill-on-sight by the major city factions. Either she'd wait to visit those places until she was high enough level to fight off the guards, or she simply wouldn't bother. Yeah, maybe it meant missing out on vendor access—if she cared about collecting and selling loot in an economy that was designed as a constant cash sink to keep players on the grinding treadmill. But for someone smart enough to see through this artificial alignment crap, it was way easier to steal whatever gear and consumables she needed from the NPC villages she cleared. Like, for instance, the glittering set of miniature ice palaces she'd glimpsed on the surface of the glacier ahead. There was probably some pretty unique loot inside. Ashley just had to get rid of a few fairies to get it.

Starting with the so-called Glacial Fairy Guard sitting dead ahead.

Placing her feet carefully, Ashley advanced the final few steps to get in range of the fairy's back. The gossamer-winged woman hummed to herself while she wove what looked like ice-worm silk into some sort of blanket. Nearby, the fairy's Neve Moth companion dozed in the arctic light, its wings flapping languidly.

If these were the guards, clearing the icy village ahead was going to be even easier than the camp of fairy scouts she'd wiped out at the toe of the glacier. She probably didn't even need her *Stealth* skill here.

Honestly, Ashley had never really liked grinding out experience on easy mobs. This was a game after all—the whole reason she played was to have fun and challenge herself. But just like in every other game she'd played, the biggest challenge of all was player-versus-player combat. And the leader of Ashley's PvP-focused guild had big plans for the coming weeks. Phase one of which was getting everyone leveled up ASAP.

Adjusting her grips on her dual-wielded daggers, she raised her arms high and aimed for twin points just behind the fairy's collarbones. The NPC wore some kind of tunic that most likely had inherent armor and resistances despite the insubstantial appearance. But against a level 23 player with a brand-new Assassin specialization and a *Backstab* skill in the tier 4 range, it wouldn't matter.

"Hello," Ashley said in the split-second before her daggers bit into porcelain-white flesh. Her lips pulled back from her teeth as she felt the blades make contact, first the faint resistance of the armor, then the grating of a knife against bone.

And then the resistance suddenly vanished.

Ashley fell forward, her blades screeching as they skittered across the hard ice where the fairy had been sitting. She recovered, ducking her shoulder and turning her head to the side to roll out of the missed attack. She came up quick, her *Agility* and *Focus* scores granting reflexes far beyond what her real-life body could manage, even after a decade of martial arts training.

She whirled to face the spot where the fairy had been, squinting against the blue-white glare of the sun reflecting off the glacier's surface. Her target and the moth had both vanished. Some sort of teleportation? A phase effect?

Ashley smiled. Okay, so maybe this wouldn't be as boring as she'd imagined.

Tinkling laughter filled the air, seeming to echo off the jagged peaks that hemmed the river of ice. A cloud of ice crystals abruptly coalesced from the polar air, hazing the scene and tickling Ashley's skin where they melted and beaded up in droplets that ran down her face.

"You can come out now," she called, blades raised.

A gust of wind stirred Ashley's hair as a shadow passed overhead. The moth? She crouched, tense, and activated her *Heightened Perception* ability. No way was the fairy going to beat a stealth-heavy class at her own game.

"Hey. Ash. Status report?" The voice seemed to roll over the landscape, booming from the high mountain ridges.

Most obnoxious voice-chat setting ever. Only the moderators of the guild channels could use it, a configuration called *god-voice* or something. Seriously, Nil could be such an asshole. But he was also her guild leader and the only person that could sign off on her promotion to the lieutenant level.

"Kind of in the middle of something here," she muttered, mentally thumbing the toggle to send her voice through the chat.

"And you can't handle multitasking? I thought women were supposed to be pros at it. Seeing as you have to nurse babies and cook dinner at the same time."

Ashley gritted her teeth. Yeah, Nil might pretend to be joking, but he said that kind of shit often enough that she had to think he partially believed it.

A spray of ice jetted through the crystalline fog, too quick for Ashley to dodge. It plastered the side of her face, filled her ear, and cracked her neck as it whacked her head to the side. A dull ache filled her skull as a few hitpoints fell away from her health bar, but the real problem was the debuff that sprang up in the upper corner of her interface.

Ability: Deadened Senses
An icy cold has sunk into your body, chilling your awareness.
-35% Perception | -20% Dodge

Ashley shivered as the crust started to slide off her cheek, the ice inside her ear trickling down deeper into her ear canal. She rose onto her toes as she spun at the waist, searching the glittering haze for movement. The fog only seemed to thicken, muting sounds and obscuring the scenery. Directly above, a faint hint of blue sky showed through, but everywhere else was white, white, white.

A snowball flew from the shining fog, landing at her feet. Too late, Ashley realized it was just a distraction. As her eyes followed the missile, she lost focus on her surroundings.

The fairy laughed as she materialized and sliced through the tendons in the back of Ashley's knee. Growling, Ashley spun and slashed with her primary hand, her blade catching on *something*. But before she could focus on her target long enough to get a *Combat Assessment*, the fairy flitted back into the fog. Another debuff appeared.

Ability: Hamstrung
-7 Agility

Another puff of wind stirred the air, the only warning before a barrage of dagger-like ice crystals streaked down from above. If Ashley had been prepared, she might have been able to dodge. Still reeling from the strike to her knee, she took the brunt of the attack, a dozen icicles piercing her flesh.

Ashley's health fell to half.

"Damn it," she cursed as she started to run into the haze, hoping to get clear of the fog before the fairy struck again.

"Sounds like someone can't handle a little teasing," Nil's voice boomed. "Toughen up, Ash."

"Can you just shut up for a minute?" she said, pissed at herself for forgetting she had her voice chat toggled. "I'm trying not to die."

"Ah. In over your head again. Got it."

Ashley's boot slipped on a patch of blue ice, and with her knee rendered unstable by the fairy's slicing of the tendons, she couldn't recover. She went down hard, her face scraping across a section of the sun-pitted glacier. Another barrage of icy needles flew down from above. She felt one sink through her neck, the frigid dart just missing her spine.

Another 15% of her health disappeared.

Unwilling to give up, she scrambled awkwardly to her feet and started running again.

She didn't see the crevasse until it was too late, the void opening below her foot. She pitched forward, cracking her knee on the far rim of the yawning crevice. Still quick, even with the debuffs, she stabbed down with her daggers on the glacier on the far side. The points of her blades bit into the ice for a moment, catching in a small fissure. Yelling through gritted teeth, she pressed harder on the hilts, willing the metal to grip as her body slammed into the wall of the crevasse.

Arms trembling, she paddled her feet against the glass-smooth ice. One of her daggers squealed as the point slipped, and then caught again.

A tinkling laugh filled the air.

Ashley looked up as the fairy once again appeared from the fog, small wings stirring the suspended ice crystals as they slowly fluttered. The fairy's fine features twisted into a grimace, baring a row of perfect white teeth. She kicked, hard, knocking Ashley's blades from the ice.

She fell, at first slowly, then sliding faster and faster. Bouncing off one and then the other side of the crevasse, she winced as her skull cracked against ice.

The crevasse faded from icy white to velvet blue then black. And then the walls disappeared altogether as they drew back into a wide, subterranean chamber.

Ashley's shout echoed before she slammed down on the bedrock beneath the glacier.

You have been slain by the ground.

Respawning...

"Oh, shit," Nil's voice filled her ears moments later. Not the booming god-voice of the chat program, but his character's semi-annoying nasal whine. He laughed. "Guess you *were* busy, huh?"

She opened her eyes to the guild longhouse and the bindstone near the blazing hearthfire.

She sighed. "Yes, and now I'm not. So what did you want?"

"Good news," he said. "You remember Stonehaven."

"Yeah...?" The man had an unhealthy obsession with that stupid player city. That and an irrational hatred for the woman, Devon and her friend Hailey, both of whom had been key in defeating the guild when they'd tried to take the settlement. As far as Ashley was concerned, it was a waste of time to keep going after that crew, especially since the game seemed to be handing them unfair advantages.

"Well, seems their fortunes have changed. I've just learned that Stonehaven is exceedingly vulnerable at the moment. We strike at Devon and her friends now, and they won't stand a chance. Sweet revenge, my friend."

Okay so, Ashley was *not* Nil's friend. But as for the vulnerability...now that sounded interesting.

"Do we have a plan?"

"It's...coming together. You'll get details on your part as soon as they're ready."

Well, that was unsurprising. Nil believed the best way to control a guild was to control the flow of information. As long as he made it seem like he was the only person who could run things, he didn't have to contend with threats to his position. For about the hundredth time in the last week, Ashley considered pulling up the guild interface and clicking the 'Leave' button. But seeing as the next-best PvP guild was basically a group of incompetent noobs, she didn't have anywhere else to go.

Yet.

Every day, she put out little feelers with her guildmates, looking for would-be defectors. If she could just splinter off something like thirty percent of the membership, they could get out from under Nil's thumb. But so far, she wasn't getting much traction. The other members basically considered her a peer, not a leader. Which was why she needed to stay on Nil's good side and get that lieutenant promotion. And staying on his good side meant walking a fine line between kissing ass and acting tough.

"Care to clue me in on *when* we plan to move? Because if I'm going to *do my part*"—she made air quotes as she said the last words—"it would be easier if I weren't frantically trying to repair my gear because my guild leader distracted me in the middle of a hard fight and got me killed."

He sneered at her, curling his lip and adjusting his ugly-ass evil-druid tunic. "Don't blame your failures on me. And we'll leave as soon as my inside guy gets me the information I need on the vulnerabilities in Devon's current status. We aren't going in until we know exactly where and when to strike. Because this time, we aren't going to stop attacking until we've killed every one of her NPC followers and we have every one of her player friends spawn camped."

An inside person, huh? Nil had been busier than Ashley thought. Of course, he'd had the guild harassing the streamer chick, Hailey, for weeks. But ever since the woman closed comments on her stream and stopped going active on messenger, she'd assumed there hadn't been much action against the Stonehaven people. Which honestly had been a relief. Ashley had never been cool with the out-of-game harassment. Nil claimed it was an intimidation tactic that made the targets less effective in PvP combat. But that was bullshit. Nil was just an asshole.

An asshole she still needed.

She forced herself to nod appreciatively. "Sounds like I should stick close then."

He grinned, oblivious to the forced enthusiasm in her tone. "I'm hoping we'll be dancing on their corpses by this time next week."

Chapter Eleven

Hi Emerson,

While processing payroll, our system came back with an error when attempting an electronic deposit to a contractor, Hailey Landers. The bank rejected the deposit, saying the account had been transferred to a charitable trust, and that deposits are blocked until the new administrator takes possession as-is or consolidates the balance into one of their existing accounts.

Sorry to bother you with this, but the contact information for Ms. Landers seems to be out of date. The message we sent to her bounced. You're listed as her direct supervisor. Any idea on how to get in touch?

Thanks!
Shauna Johnson, Payroll Specialist
E-Squared Finance & Accounting
Message: sjohnson@e_squared
Voice: x2910

Emerson yawned and brushed the message out of his vision. He could deal with it during the work week. Maybe by then, Shauna Johnson would have figured out the problem on her own. It wasn't like Hailey was incommunicado—work had kept him busy lately, so he hadn't logged in much, but he definitely remembered spotting her recently. Once, she'd been coming out of Stonehaven's Tailoring Workshop, and another time she'd been bent over an old scroll in one of Ishildar's courtyards.

So she hadn't been abducted by aliens or anything. Even if accounting couldn't figure out how to navigate their own records, Hailey would surely notice if her paycheck went missing. Neither Shauna Johnson nor his player employees needed him to act as a secretary.

He yawned again, absently scratching at the stubble on his cheek while he stirred his Cheerios. The weak January sun fell through the glass doors that led to his modest patio where dust collected at the base of the white stucco walls and a potted cactus stood forlornly on the brick-red ceramic tile. When he'd bought the condo, there used to be a little breakfast table out there, but the chair had attracted birds, and he'd gotten tired of cleaning up their droppings.

He'd never been much of a breakfast eater, but today was the start of a three-day weekend with no looming work obligations. The demon threat had temporarily been dealt with, which meant he could find some baddies to slaughter—NPCs he could actually defeat for experience rather than attacking as a human sacrifice to gain his higher-level friends the advantage of distracted enemies.

Imagining the battles to come, he finished fueling for the challenge, then dropped his bowl and spoon in the dishwasher. Dusting off his hands and grinning with anticipation, he shuffled to his recliner. The faux-leather upholstery squeaked as cushions rubbed together when accepting his weight. Sighing, he tugged the handle to extend the footstool, closed his eyes, and activated Relic Online.

His condo faded to black, and then Emerson was *burning*.

Flames covered his body, his skin blackening and bubbling. He gasped, and furnace-hot air seared the inside of his lungs. He tried to scream, but his vocal cords were already incinerated.

You have been slain by hellfire.

Respawning...

"Ow," he said as he fell to his knees in the grass. He curled his knees to his chest and clenched his eyes shut.

"Got another here," someone shouted. "Okay, dude, let's get you up."

Emerson felt hands snaking around his body, trying to get a grip. He forced his eyes open and saw white light shimmering in a curtain a few yards away. Beyond that, demons howled and raked claws against what had to be a magical barrier. Blinking, Emerson looked up at the person who was trying to help him. He didn't recognize the face, but it was human, at least. Nodding, he climbed shakily to his feet.

Standing beside the Shrine to Veia, Owen had his eyes closed and his hands outstretched. Emerson glanced from him to the barrier and back, then noticed the Veian prophetess NPC standing nearby. A radiant halo surrounded her, and streams of light flowed off it, traveling across the ground to bolster Owen's shield.

"Uh?" he asked the man who had helped him stand. "Er?"

"Someone can explain on the other end. For now, we need to get you on the taxi out of here."

A message appeared in his vision.

> Hezbek is inviting you to join her group.
> **Accept?** Y/N

"Okay, I guess?" he said. So much for leveling up today.

Chapter Twelve

"SO IT'S REALLY gone? I mean, not gone, but lost, I guess?" Emerson asked.

Devon had spotted his character wandering around Ishildar's Temple Square with a bewildered look on his face. Throughout the afternoon, players had been logging in, dying in a pool of hellfire-melted glass, and respawning in the tiny safe area around the Shrine to Veia. But now that the flow of incoming players had slowed, Devon had left the teleportation duties to Hezbek. She had work to do here: a secure camp to establish, followers to reassure, and after that, she needed to craft a plan for the future.

"Well, it's technically contested. They still need to finish capturing a few buildings. Not sure what criteria the game uses to determine that. Maybe they have to perform some sort of demonic ritual to finalize it or something. Anyway, we still hold the area around the shrine thanks to Owen's newest barriers and its natural defenses. But that won't last forever."

"Then what happens?"

"It seems like whenever they capture a structure, the status goes to neutral, and a countdown timer starts. If we attack and, you know, shift the line of control to include any of the structures before the timeout, we can flip them back to contested. Anyway, the longest timer I've seen so far is on the main palisade. They have to keep it out of the contested state for two days or something. Then it becomes theirs. I guess the whole settlement becomes neutral once all the structures have been captured."

He reached out and touched her hand. "I can see all that info in my interface. What I mean is, do you think there's no hope of taking it back?"

She felt the blood rush to her face. Duh. Of course he could see that. She would have realized that if she weren't so frazzled. Devon sighed. "I don't know. I have no clue how we fight that archdemon. He's too high level for us to get a *Combat Assessment.*"

Emerson gazed around the square. She guessed he was taking in the chaos of the refugees as the situation sunk in. "I'm sorry. I wish...I just wish I could do more."

She blinked away the sting of frustration from her eyes and started walking again. "Maybe we can rebuild once we figure out how to take the settlement back. I just wish I had a clue how to do that. I guess the only good thing right now is that we saved most of the people. My teleport spell sucks, but I'm glad I have it."

Still, though she tried to be positive about the lives they'd saved, Devon couldn't help thinking back to those gaps in the line of defenders on Stonehaven's palisade. Basic NPCs who had been killed in the attack were never coming back. Many had left spouses behind, and at least one had had children. Most people would laugh at her for even worrying about the losses. They were just NPCs, after all. Devon knew Emerson understood, though. His beliefs about the NPCs' level of sentience were the same as hers. For a moment, Devon considered opening up to him and telling him about the ache in her lungs when she thought of the fallen fighters, but she was afraid she'd break down. Maybe they could talk about it after she'd finished the mountain of tasks before her.

"But you think we're safer here? I mean, I'm not questioning you. I'm sure we are. It was just...well, I've never been killed by hellfire before. It wasn't very pleasant."

Devon smirked. "And you are the settlement's expert on death."

Emerson scratched the back of his neck, the gesture he used when he was slightly embarrassed. She nudged him with her elbow. "Hey, so, I never got to formally thank you for the kamikaze runs. You know they made a big difference, right?"

Under the tutelage of Greel, who had never been particularly concerned with the psychological effects of his actions upon others, Emerson had been granted a unique class, Frenzy. He wasn't *required* to die over and over, but his ability set made him rather effective at charging into unwinnable situations and scoring more blows than an average fighter would. Emerson really had helped in the final stages of her quest to restore Ishildar and push back the demons, so as long as he wasn't too traumatized by his repeated deaths, she had to admit that Greel had trained him well.

"A noob has to find some way to help out, right?" he said with a shrug. Emerson nodded toward a quiet alcove opening off the temple square where Hailey sat on a stone bench. Bob bounced in the air before her face. "Looks like your wisp has found someone else to pester. Speaking of...do you ever contact Hailey out of game? Someone at corporate was trying to reach her, but apparently the messenger contact the company has is invalid."

"Not often. I thought you had her contact in your personal list?"

Emerson shrugged. "When I originally got in touch to hire her, she gave me a temporary handle. Said that her livestream sometimes attracted weirdos, so she preferred to stay semi-anonymous. I'd assumed HR got actual information out of her, but I figured it wasn't my business to ask for personal info. The handle I had expired a while back."

Devon shrugged. "Well, lately it seems like she's on all the time. If somebody really needs to get in touch, they should send a GM to talk to her avatar."

Emerson nodded. "I'll pass that along."

They'd nearly reached the far side of the square, and Devon slowed, chewing her lip. "I'm trying to be strong, you know. But it's kind of hard. I keep thinking about how this is all Bradley Williams' fault. He could have shut down Zaa's server cluster, but he let this happen. Makes me want to head down to HQ and punch him in the teeth or something."

Emerson stopped, planting his feet. His avatar, all six-and-a-half feet of solid game flesh seemed to vibrate with contained frustration. "I know. I can't stop feeling like I should have been able to do more. I mean, this is ridiculous—a full-on, brutal invasion. Do players really like this kind of thing?"

"I don't know. I mean, yeah, challenge is cool. I get that Bradley thinks this good-versus-evil war is like the best content ever, but if we can't stop the demon army, I don't know who will. Seems like a great way to permanently break the game."

Devon ran her eyes over the activity in the square. Across the open space, people were erecting makeshift tents and organizing the meager provisions they'd brought along. She shook her head—such a ragged group. But at the same time, her followers didn't show the despair Devon felt. Despite being forced to abandon their homes, they seemed to believe that she would somehow save them.

But how? Unless Ishildar offered up a miracle in the next few days, Devon had no clue what they would do. They might be able to pull the same sorts of teleport evacuations, her followers fleeing the leading edge of the army as it spilled across the continent. But what about when they reached a far shore?

And as for the players, they'd either flee with Devon's followers or have their experience reduced to death loops around their individual bind locations. Once the demons took possession of the spawn points, they only needed to camp out and slay each player as they respawned. Even for someone as obsessed with Relic Online as Hailey, there would be no reason to play anymore. The woman would probably log out, and Devon would never hear from her again.

But that was the worst case. It wouldn't come to pass if she could just figure out what she was supposed to do here.

"I guess I better get back to Mayor-ing."

"Keeper-ing, right? You're more than a mayor now."

Devon smiled. Emerson did have a knack for helping her feel better. She hesitated for a second, then gave him a quick hug. "Thanks for listening. If you've got some free time, I'm sure Torald and Bayle could use help tallying our food supplies."

Emerson tossed her a quick salute. "On it, Mayor keeper Devon."

Chapter Thirteen

"WHAT HAPPENS IF I get found out?" Hailey asked.

Until Bob had abruptly materialized and asked to speak to her, she'd been helping with the regrouping efforts, healing the scraped knees of Stonehaven citizens who had fallen while rushing to the shrine and casting her *Calm* spell when it looked like someone was about to panic. Now she felt on the verge of panic herself. Apparently, the denizens of the arcane realm had intercepted E-Squared communications regarding failed deposits to her dead body's bank account. She had *no* idea they were still trying to pay her; Hailey had assumed that someone—the care facility most likely—would send word of her death to the company. She'd hoped that would have been the end of it. Seeing as she now lived as a pattern within the game, there wouldn't be any logins or network activity to track. It wasn't like her guildmates were going to email the company to ask if she was dead when she saw them in-game all the time—and anyway, she'd also planned to tell them what had happened. Well, Devon anyway.

Of course, she hadn't planned on the noob, Valious, revealing himself as Emerson. Major wrinkle in her "no one is going to notice that I've gone on living inside the videogame" plan. She could trust her guildmates—probably, anyway. But an E-Squared employee who also happened to be her boss? That was a lot more complicated. If she'd known he was going to be rolling a character and playing around Stonehaven, she would have said her goodbyes and started a journey to some other area of the world. In fact, it might still be a good idea. But given the situation with the demons, leaving might not even be an option. Devon knew more about the surrounding region and whether there were routes out of the area that didn't cut through demon territory, but asking her would require getting some alone time with the other woman. Seeing as she hadn't even been able to get enough time to confess her situation to Devon, it might still be a while before she could ask questions.

Bob glided side to side through the air as if contemplating. "My relationship with the mortal realm is somewhat passive. I'm more of a leech than, say, a hammer."

"Um. What does that even mean? For someone so good with words, your metaphors suck."

"It means that I and my arcane brethren-selves get a ton of input. Data I mean. But we don't have any output. We can't make changes to the real world. As in, I can't just slip into the records of the finance department at E-Squared and reverse those payments."

Hailey's brows drew together. "So a hammer can change financial records? I still don't get it."

"Okay, forget the hammer. I'm just saying that I'm not sure what to do."

Hailey planted her hands beside her thighs on the bench. "Back to my question then. What happens if I get discovered? They delete me or something?"

"I have no idea. I mean, I've been through Bradley Williams' email quite a few times, and the only thing I've really been able to determine is that he would be difficult to model as an entity. There doesn't seem to be much of a robust pattern in his decision-making. I suspect he takes advantage of dice-rolling or alcohol to assist his processing algorithm."

The wisp slid side to side as if contemplating. "Though I will say this: that your information pattern would be difficult to selectively delete due to the company's lack of visibility into the servers. I suspect they'd mess up several other things in the attempt. So if it's any consolation, you probably wouldn't be erased alone."

Hailey sighed. Some help Bob was. It seemed her guesses were as good as the wisp's. So what did she think Bradley Williams would do? If it were her company, and she'd just learned that corporate software had created a digital representation of a human mind, then allowed that person to "upload," she would probably try her damnedest to forget she'd ever discovered that fact. The implications were way too morally complicated, as far as she was concerned.

Even now, living fully in the game, she didn't like to think about the implications. It was far easier to tell no one than bear responsibility for unleashing immortality on the world.

Somehow, she doubted Bradley would have the same qualms.

Regardless, the failed payments were a pretty huge problem. Even the little stuff, like having left her livestream channel hanging, could cause problems. She needed help from someone with a real-life body, an ally who could help with investigations at the very least. Devon obviously had a lot going on right now, but maybe she could find some time to lay out her situation to her friend.

Tomorrow.

For now, Hailey sighed and stood and went looking for people who could use a little healing.

Chapter Fourteen

I'M ON YOUR balcony with cookies.

Devon jerked in surprise when Tamara's message flashed across her vision.

"Sec," she subvocalized as she planted her fork in her microwaved macaroni, stood, and started for the door.

And what's going on with your curtains?

Devon twisted the deadbolt and tugged on the door handle, admitting a gust of January air as the door swung aside. Tamara's slight form was wrapped in a puffy blue coat that doubled her size. Her ever-present oxygen tube ran over her shoulder to her backpack. She smiled and lifted a plate covered in a tea towel.

Devon quickly stepped aside to let her pass, then shoved the door shut. "Since when are you awake at 2 AM?"

Tamara turned to face the makeshift curtain arrangement and cocked her head in confusion. "I got up to pee and thought I should check the forums real quick—bad habit I know. I saw players talking about what happened to Stonehaven. Figured you could use a friend."

"And cookies, apparently." Devon plucked the plate from her friend's hands and set it down on the table. She pulled out a chair for Tamara then retook her seat in front of her congealing macaroni.

"The blind is broken, and the complex won't even look at my maintenance request until Tuesday."

"I don't see why you stay here," Tamara said. "I mean, now that you have a real salary and stuff. I get not spending everything you make. Way better to have some savings than go back to wrangling tourists at Fort Kolob if you lose your job. But still."

Devon shrugged. "Laziness, I guess. And yeah. I'd rather live here for the rest of my life than go back to the Fort."

Tamara smirked as she gestured toward the cookies. "Eat some before they get cold. They just came out of the oven fifteen minutes ago."

"Wait. You baked these?"

"From a mix. It's not like I whipped them up from scratch."

Devon plucked a cookie from the plate. Yep. Still warm. The chocolate chips were half-melted, oozing over the top. She shook her head, wondering where her friend got all these crazy skills. As she bit down, a slightly crunchy exterior gave way to a gooey and delicious middle, and she rolled her eyes with pleasure.

"Better than that sloth steak you used to eat?"

Devon laughed. Now that brought back memories. She hadn't tasted sloth meat since the jungle had retreated from Stonehaven.

"Seriously, Dev, I'm so sorry about the attack. It sounds like you guys managed to retreat to Ishildar, though?"

"Most of us. I lost a few NPCs." Devon's voice cracked a little when she said it out loud.

Tamara laid a hand on her forearm. "So, what now? People on the forums said it's something called a base battle?"

"I guess you could call it that. Seemed more like a rout than a battle."

"But the ownership is still contested, right?"

"Yeah, I guess that's true. We still have full control of the Shrine to Veia. Hezbek has been binding people at the temple in Ishildar and then teleporting them into Stonehaven at our little pocket of control. We're making suicidal attack runs out from the shrine in hopes we can keep structures contested for longer."

"Then it's not over."

"No, not yet. We aren't making a dent in their forces, but I think we're slowing them down. At least, that's how it looked last I was in there. My head was swimming, so I had to log out."

Tamara broke a cookie in half, leaving part on the plate and nibbling at the other. She seemed to be lost in thought, but the distance in her gaze made Devon think she might be checking the forums for updates. Devon was tempted to do the same, but she knew that would just lead to her logging back in. She would do more good for Stonehaven if she got some sleep before playing again.

"Even if we slow the change of control, though, we hardly have any supplies. I kinda think we're safe in Ishildar until they fully establish ownership over Stonehaven. They're stronger than us by a lot, especially that fricking archdemon. But attacking on two fronts would spread them too thin."

"What do you need for supplies?

"Food, mostly. But if we solve that, we'll need crafting supplies for armor and weapon repairs. Plus components for potions and stuff. Still, the basic issue is we're only safe enough to slowly starve."

"Sucks," Tamara said, summing things up pretty concisely.

"Yeah. I'm sorry this has been your first introduction to gaming. Joining up on the losing side of a war and all."

Tamara snorted. "Don't even say that. War or not, the game has been awesome. Next-best thing to my first bike. Seriously, though, what happens if the demons really do take over? Wouldn't that ruin the game?"

Devon dropped her palms to the table in exasperation. "Pretty much. It's seriously infuriating what an idiot Bradley Williams is. I think he honestly has no clue how strong the demons are. At least, I hope it's cluelessness because otherwise, he's just a psychopath."

"But it's not totally hopeless, right?"

Devon shrugged. "I was always crap at base battles when the odds were even."

"Somehow I doubt you're actually as terrible as you think. Maybe you just need to, I dunno, look at the problem a different way."

Okay, so Tamara had a point. Devon hadn't even known about the contested structure mechanic until the demons attacked. There was probably even more going on than Devon realized. For all she knew, the demons might have established a base or control point between Stonehaven and the coast. That was a potential vulnerability.

Not only that, but she'd also been thinking of Ishildar as a temporary sanctuary and retreat. If there were more to the base mechanics than she'd seen so far, maybe she could get some advantage by formally establishing the city as a friendly base.

She didn't want to get too excited, not after how badly they'd been beaten today, but she couldn't help feeling a flicker of optimism. For now, though, she really needed to get to sleep. Especially with the new information giving her something to go on, she wanted to be totally fresh when she logged in tomorrow.

"You want to crash out here?" she asked, not sure what the etiquette was for gently kicking someone out so she could go to bed.

Tamara smirked and glanced at the couch. "I think it's time I head home and leave you to your cookies."

"You're going to take some, aren't you?"

Tamara glanced at the plate with mock horror. "And wind up as big as I look in this coat?"

"Wait, so you want to sacrifice me to the gods of chocolate and butter, but you won't face them down with me?"

Tamara laughed. "Just pace yourself. I imagine you'll survive if you take the battle slowly. Besides, you already know I think you should eat more than you do because of the gaming."

Devon glanced at her now-cold macaroni and pushed it aside before grabbing another cookie. Good point on needing to fuel for a potential marathon session ahead. "By the way, fair warning: when you log in, you'll probably be instantly incinerated by hellfire. Drop me a message when you respawn at the shrine, and I'll come and teleport you out."

Tamara's brow furrowed. "Hellfire sounds...unpleasant."

"Yup, so I hear. But at least it's a quick death, right?"

"If you say so."

***

Settlement: Stonehaven
Size: Hamlet
Ownership: Contested - 65%

Devon grimaced and quickly switched tabs to a settlement interface page she'd almost always ignored entitled *Regional*. For most of her time in the game, it had shown a high-level map of the area with pins for the named areas she'd discovered or heard about. The Argenthal Mountains hemmed Ishildar to the east with the Felsen Spire marked in their heart. To the south of Ishildar stood Stonehaven, and beyond that, the Fortress of Shadows and Noble Coast—demon territory now. West and southwest, the Drowned Burrow stood near the Mudpots of Ven, an impassable area of boiling mud that lined Ishildar's western boundary. North of the ancient city, the Stone Forest was a narrow strip of petrified trees standing between Ishildar and the cracked landscape of the Skargill Mountains.

Also marked were the bindstones that Devon could teleport between. Together with the Shrine to Veia, she could travel to the edge of the Stone Forest and a bindstone in the foothills of the Argenthals. Not much in the way of a transportation network, but she hadn't had much time to explore in search of more stones.

She shifted her weight on a stone bench tucked into one of Ishildar's secluded courtyards, a place she'd come to assure she could have a little time to search through her interface in peace. Somewhere in the empty buildings behind her, a bird or small animal rustled, but otherwise, the area was silent.

Okay, hopefully this would work.

When she focused her mental attention on the map pin for the ancient city, an options button appeared, which she clicked.

    -History
    -Population

-Resources

-Ownership

Note: *Information on settlement population and resources is limited for settlements which you are neither the manager nor a citizen.*

She smirked as she focused on the *Ownership* button and clicked. Duh. Maybe it should have occurred to her to look for something like this *before* Stonehaven was overrun. But she tried to console herself with the notion that the whole "you are now the Keeper and supreme ruler of the city" thing had led her to think she might just be done.

Settlement: Ishildar

Size: City (ruined 94% - at 100%, settlement will be considered 'vanished' and will not be able to be rebuilt)

Ownership: Unowned

Special: Ishildar may only be managed as a settlement by an individual who has met the qualifications to be named as its Keeper. Currently, the Keeper of Ishildar is Devon. Non-Keepers may reduce the ownership status to 'contested' or 'unowned' by attacking and occupying the city, but control cannot be transferred.

You meet the requirements to assume ownership and management of Ishildar.

Accept? Y/N

When Devon clicked 'yes,' a chime rang through the city, sounding similar to the *ding* that heralded a level-up notification. Devon curled her toes as she felt the little thrill of accomplishment that the sound created. It was totally Pavlovian, of course, a conditioned response after so many years of gaming.

Still. If someone could invent a device to give her dings for real-life accomplishments, things like, say, figuring out how to hard boil eggs so that the shell wasn't all stuck to the white part when she went to peel it, Devon would totally be a more functional adult.

Congratulations! **You are now the official owner of Ishildar (Uncontested).** You remain the owner of Stonehaven (Contested - 66%)

Additional settlements pay fealty to you based on your region of control. You may now access information and requisition resources from the following settlements (available supply depends on vassal settlement morale and your reputation with factions within the settlement).

Settlements sworn to Ishildar

Felsen Spire

New Galvan

Chasm View

Vulture's Rift

Settlements sworn to Stonehaven

Player Camp (ruined 100%, defunct. Any remaining materials will vanish in 2 days, 3 hours)

Devon grimaced at the reminder of the player camp's fate, and her brow knit when she looked at the names of the other settlements. Felsen Spire she recognized, but what the heck were those other three? When she focused on the names, little information windows popped up.

> **New Galvan - Population 75:** Built upon the site of an ancient felsen holdfast that was known as Galvan, this village was founded by the residents of Felsen Spire after the orc infestation was cleared from the Cavern of Spirits.

> **Chasm View - Population 45:** Clinging to a high cliff face in the Skargill Mountains, this village is the residence of the royal family of Skevalli griffon riders. Other residents include the Skevalli royal court, councilors, and their families.

> **Vulture's Rift - Population 523:** Wedged tight into a deep chasm in the Skargills, this township is the main population center for the remnants of the Skevalli people.

Whoa. Nice. Devon hadn't had a chance to talk to Fabio—er, Prince Kenjan rather—about his people and the help they might be able to offer. Actually, she'd been actively avoiding him due to the whole loincloth and growling issues. But a settlement large enough to qualify as a Township meant they already had more infrastructure than she'd managed to create in Stonehaven. Like it or not, she was going to have to meet with the guy.

Before closing out the settlement interface, she glanced back to the main page and saw both Stonehaven and Ishildar listed. Ishildar's status caught her eye again. Ruined 94%. Okay, so she knew that already, but the fate of the player camp made her think. It was listed at 100% ruined with a note that it was now defunct and would soon vanish.

If the same fate could befall Ishildar, then unlike Stonehaven, the demons wouldn't even need to capture and occupy the city's structures. Destroy 6% more of the already-ruined city, and her new base would be toast.

"You look as if responsibilities are pressing heavily on you today."

Devon jumped and brushed away the settlement interface at the sound of Hezbek's voice. Despite the *thump-shuffle* the woman made as she crossed slate paving stones with the help of her walking stick, Devon hadn't heard the woman approach.

"I guess it's pretty hard to feel good about our chances right now."

Hezbek patted Devon's shoulder before planting her walking stick and grabbing it with both hands to help her settle onto the bench. Her breath came out in a puff when she touched down.

"I must admit, I've seen many battles in my time. Wars that raged back and forth like angry waves on a shore. I don't recall a time when the odds were so uneven. But we're still alive, aren't we? As long as that's true, we haven't lost."

Easing her legs straight, the medicine woman crossed them at the ankles. A faint grimace crinkled the area around her eyes when one of her knees cracked.

"Have you slept, Hezbek?" Devon asked as she swiveled to give the woman her full attention.

Hezbek had tipped her head back against the wall of the building which formed a backrest for the bench. Sun fell on her wrinkled face, etching the lines even deeper. She looked at Devon through the corner of her half-closed eyes. "I'm debating whether I should lie to you."

"I asked Emmaree to make sure there is enough bedding set aside to make you comfortable."

"And extra padding for those who were injured in the evacuation, too. Emmaree told me. There are more scrapes and bruises than I expected, to be honest. For those who aren't losing health over time due to a severe wound, I'm apparently supposed to let their natural regeneration provide the healing. Only so many bandages to go around."

"I'm glad she's properly conveying my orders," Devon said.

"Delivered as if they were commands from Veia herself, and Emmaree the chosen prophet."

Devon laughed as she thought of the little halfling woman browbeating people into following her directions. Emmaree had already fled the demons once, making a desperate voyage across the Noble Sea with a ragged group of survivors—the last remaining population of her home continent. They'd arrived with fewer supplies than Stonehaven's evacuees had brought to Ishildar, and somehow they'd managed to carve out a new home in the swamp surrounding the Fortress of Shadows. The woman's survival expertise could be critical in the days ahead.

Loosely clasping the walking stick, Hezbek's hands were pale beneath the scattering of age spots. Her mouth lay slack rather than curling into the faint smile she so often wore.

"I don't suppose I could just order you to go rest," Devon said.

"You're smarter than you look."

Devon sighed. "Well then, maybe I can get your advice on what you think our next steps should be."

"Maybe you could. Though I don't know whether I have any insights you haven't already explored. The plan to keep Stonehaven's status contested by making attack runs seems to be working. Or at least, delaying the change in control. There is an issue that concerns me. Two, actually."

"Oh?"

"If we find ourselves in a position to fight for real, more than these quick attacks by your starborn friends that we expect to end in death anyway...Well, I hate to say it, but we're critically low on potions. While evacuating Stonehaven, I used all but two of the *Savanna Mana Potions*, and I didn't have bag space to bring any of the other varieties. Perhaps my contributions aren't as dramatic as when I was a working sorceress, but I like to think my elixirs provide some edge to our combatants."

"Are you kidding? They're indispensable. Marmie told me recently that they're the main reason her adventuring supplies shop stayed in business. And I heard some other starborn talking about them. Complaining, actually, because even though some of the starborn have the *Alchemy - Potions* skill, they can't produce anything to compete with your concoctions."

Hezbek's lips twitched in a faint smile before she managed to contain it. "Well, I'm pleased to hear that I can still offer something to the cause. Except now, I have nothing but the empty jars and vials from the potions I used in the evacuation. If there were any way to gather more ingredients, though…"

> **Hezbek is offering you a quest:** Component gathering, now with DANGER. (repeatable)
>
> *The ingredients for Hezbek's potions are out there, in the savanna, under the hooves of hundreds of demons. Make your way out from the city to get her the good stuff.*
>
> **Objective:** Obtain 5 x Termite Mound Chunk, 3 x Acacia Sap, 5 x Pollinated Wild Rye Stalks, 1 x Wild Yam Tuber
>
> **Reward:** Choose 2 x Savanna Health Potion - Major or 1 x Savanna Mana Potion - Mid
>
> **Accept?** Y/N

Devon nodded and accepted the quest. Back in Stonehaven when she'd made notes about the defense of the area, one of her action items had been to get her army leveled up. Ingredient hunting might not be the most effective XP, especially since groups would probably wipe as often as they found quest components, but she'd still get the benefit of the two birds, one stone thing by sending parties out.

"You don't mind if I share the quest with others, do you?"

Crow's feet deepened in the corners of Hezbek's eyes when she smiled. "Of course not, child."

"So what was the other thing? You said two issues were bothering you."

The woman's smile immediately fell away. "I'll be honest. You weren't the first person I thought of when I considered asking for help getting the ingredients."

Devon blinked, unsure how to take that comment. "Okay..."

"And not just because you've got a whole settlement's worth of people to look after. I happen to know that your *Stealth* isn't as high as one might hope for someone of your experience."

"I did finally get it almost to Tier 2..."

Hezbek chuckled, but the laugh lacked joy. "I know you've tried. I've seen your...training. It's somewhat reminiscent of a strange dance they perform in Rimeshore when the winds carry mind-altering spores from lichen growing on the northern glaciers."

"Okay, maybe we can just move on. Who did you think would do a better job?"

"You know I've used Hazel to gather components quite often. She usually picks them up on her scouting ventures. It would certainly be easier to obtain this stuff if someone could move undetected among the demons rather than cutting their way across the savanna."

"And?"

Hezbek's brow furrowed. "And, well, the problem is I can't find her."

Devon sat straighter, eyes shooting toward the exit to the courtyard and the street leading to the Temple Square where her followers had set up their makeshift camp. "Nowhere?"

"I've asked around. Now, it's entirely possible that she's out in the city somewhere, maybe continuing the search for advantages. But I thought you should know."

Devon thought back to the last time she'd seen the little scout. When Aijal had raised the alarm about the player camp, Hazel had dashed off, swung up astride her windsteed mount, and set off at a gallop across the savanna. In the chaos that followed, Devon didn't think she'd glimpsed the woman anywhere.

She yanked open her settlement interface and paged over to the section listing Stonehaven's Advanced NPCs. Her spine relaxed when she saw Hazel's name still listed. If the woman had died in the demon attack, there would be some sort of status update near her name, right? Advanced NPCs could be resurrected, but it was kind of hard for the manager of a settlement to accomplish that if they didn't know the NPC was dead.

Still, her experience losing followers was pretty limited. She'd never actually checked whether her assumption was true.

Hezbek's hands dropped from her walking staff when she saw Devon's reaction. Clearly, the woman had been hoping Devon had a ready answer about Hazel's whereabouts.

"Well, I suppose we ought to formalize her absence as a problem as well," the medicine woman said.

> **Hezbek is offering you a quest:** Hazel's Fate
>
> *Find out what has happened to Hazel. If she's alive, bring her back. If not...well, better hope that the Shrine to Veia remains under your control or that the Veian Temple provides NPC resurrection.*
>
> **Objective:** Determine Hazel's location.
>
> **Reward:** 25000 Experience
>
> **Accept?** Y/N

Devon accepted as soon as the quest text flashed onto her interface.

Chapter Fifteen

"HERE," DEVON SAID as she thrust out a package. A leather cord neatly tied the stacked items together.

Fabio looked up from beneath lowered brows, holding her eyes in what she assumed was supposed to be a smoldering stare. Rolling one muscular shoulder and then the other, he pushed up from his totally-prostrate-on-the-ground bow, planting his tanned hands on the flagstones. Keeping his eyes locked with hers, he slid a foot forward so that he was crouched kind of like a runner on the starting blocks. Then he slowly rose until he towered over her, way, way, way too close.

She shoved the package forward again, jamming it into his actively flexing abs as she took a step back. Thank goodness she'd requested to meet him in the relative privacy of the courtyard where Hezbek had found her exploring her new settlement options. She'd never be able to have this conversation with Jeremy and Chen clowning in the background or just rolling on the floor laughing at her situation.

Of course, she hoped Prince Kenjan—he had a third nickname now, Prince Ken Doll—hadn't gotten the wrong idea about the private location. She felt a horrified expression creeping onto her face and pushed it away.

With one of those low throat growls, the man accepted the package and tugged at the tie, the corded muscles rippling across his forearm as his fingers worked. Midway through untying the string, he paused and tossed his mane, the motion ending in another obnoxiously long stare.

As he shook out the items, a loose-fitting tunic and a pair of drawstring cloth pants, he stared in confusion, then turned a faintly hurt gaze on her.

Devon coughed up her prepared lines. "After assuming the position of Keeper, I consulted with my lawyer and historian on how I might best resurrect the ancient customs between Ishildar and her vassal societies. Greel was able to uncover information about ceremonial garb that was gifted by the Keeper to the Ishildar's most esteemed vassals, something to mark them as favored whenever they visited the city."

She forced herself to keep eye contact. It wasn't even a complete lie; Greel had assured her he could find—or forge—a document with similar meaning. As long as—in his words—he didn't have to have his vision burned out by the sight of so much oiled man-flesh whenever the ridiculous man brought his griffon in for a landing.

She flashed Prince Kenjan a hopeful smile.

The man seemed to be turning her words over in his head. Or maybe he was trying to figure out how one dealt with the concept of "clothing."

"My queen," he said at last. "You honor me beyond measure." He started to fall prostrate again, but Devon snapped out a hand and caught his elbow. Kenjan froze, flexed his abs again, and stared at her hand as if it were some long-sought-after treasure. Devon covered her recoil by pretending to, just then, notice a thread on the tunic that she quickly plucked.

"So listen, I was hoping to talk to you about the resources your people can offer us." She gestured in the direction of Temple Square. "We weren't able to bring many supplies when we evacuated. Ishildar would be forever in your debt for any food you can spare. And I'd like to know more about the region where you live. Our forces need somewhere to train if we're to gain the experience we need to stand against our enemies."

He gave more throat rumbles as he considered, but he seemed distracted by the garments in his hands, a quizzical expression on his face.

"Do you need—I can help you get those on if you need."

With apparent relief, he shoved the clothes toward her. "Thank you, my queen. I admit...I've never... Well, this is my first time."

Devon stared at him for a moment.

"You've seriously never worn clothes? I mean... Seriously?"

He blinked as if it were a strange question. "Well, I should say it's my first time as an adult—at least when it comes to real garb, not the royal bindings and togas the servants wrap us in for formal audiences. I wore swaddling garments as a baby, and all Skevalli youth wear rompers while at play. But it's customary for fighting-age members of the royal family to leave our flesh exposed. As you might have noticed, our sacred nut oils increase in potency with every percentage point of skin left bare. Even when we aren't actively defending our homes, royal fighters must constantly train, guiding our steeds through breakneck races in the chasms, crossing swords with the fearsome basilisks that threaten our commoners."

When he mentioned the basilisks, his eyes narrowed, and his cheek twitched in apparent anger.

So not a joke, then. Weird.

Devon shook the wrinkles from the trousers, shoved her hands inside the waistband, and held the pants open. The prince seemed momentarily perplexed, but then nodded and stepped a foot through the first leg hole. He planted a hand on her shoulder for balance as he switched feet, and Devon squeaked, cranking her head to the side to avoid getting a face full of loincloth. The moment he released his grip on her shoulder, she dropped the pants and scuttled back out of range of his...loins.

The man stood blinking with the pants around his knees, and with a nod of encouragement, she pantomimed pulling them up. Once his trousers were fastened, there was just the problem of the tunic. Devon looked up at his towering physique and then raised the shirt in her arms as if judging whether she could even slip it over his head. The math didn't seem like it would work, so she decided to talk him through it instead.

"So this hole is for your head, and these are for your arms, and you sort of just stick all three through then scooch the shirt over your body. Got it?"

"I confess I'm just concerned that I'll look like a fool in front of you, my liege." Fabio took the garment and cocked his head. "It doesn't matter which side ends up in the front?"

"Well, actually it usually does, but these particular ceremonial items are intended to fit either way." Devon didn't add that she had an unfortunate amount of experience in wearing her clothing backward, inside out, and once in the case of a hoody sweatshirt, upside down. Like an idiot, she'd managed to shrug it on too quickly, only to find out that later that the hood had been dangling over her butt for the whole commuter bus ride out to Fort Kolob.

Prince Kenjan did as she said, accomplishing the task with more ease than she would expect given his confessed lack of practice. Maybe he was just nervous. Of course, despite getting the shirt over his head with relative competence, he took an inordinately long time to pull the cloth down over his abs. Which were still flexed, of course. Didn't his muscles get tired?

Once he was safely covered, Devon gestured toward the bench where she'd sat with Hezbek.

"Care if we sit? I don't want to gain extra *Fatigue*. I'm putting together a search party after this."

He followed her to the bench without hesitation. Once seated, he turned to her with an expression of genuine concern. "A search party?"

She sighed and nodded. "Stonehaven's scout is missing. I last saw her at the start of the demon attack."

He raised his hand and seemed to be planning to lay it on her knee in a gesture of sympathy, but he reconsidered and clapped it against his own knee instead. "I'm so sorry to hear that. If it's any help, I can take Proudheart up and search from above."

Proudheart, huh? That wasn't cliche at all...

"Thank you. That would be great, actually. All I know is that she took off into the savanna when we first saw the smoke from the demons' hellfire. She was riding a windsteed mount, and if she's still out there somewhere, she'll have a war ostrich by her side."

"Pardon? Did you say she was astride a windsteed?"

Devon's eyes widened as she spun to face him. "What? Have you seen her?"

He shook his head quickly. "Sorry. I haven't. But you are aware of the windsteeds' special powers, right?"

Of course. Devon pressed the heel of her hand to her forehead. "The herd can sense one another. As long as Hazel and her mount are still together, another windsteed should be able to guide us right to her. I can't believe I didn't think of it."

Prince Kenjan smiled, and it seemed more genuine than his smoldering looks. Needless to say, she preferred the newest expression.

"You were asking about supplies?" he said.

"Before getting to resource stuff, mind telling me a little bit about where you come from? I know your people used to live in the Stone Forest, but it sounds like your settlements are in the Skargill Mountains, now?"

He nodded. "Our histories from the migration have been passed by mouth through the generations. I gather there is as much myth as fact. Regardless, we retreated into the chasms shortly after Ishildar's fall and the great petrification."

"When the forest turned to stone, you mean?"

He nodded. "I assume you can imagine the difficulty in finding food where nothing living grows."

"Yeah. Got a decent handle on that."

He smirked, another departure from the previous smoldering stare. "Anyway, we've been in the Skargills since. My family lives in the royal aerie, a cliffside roost we call Chasm View. Those we protect have a home in the bottom of one of the chasms. A few generations back, we tried building another settlement on the walls of one of the canyons. But the site just wasn't defensible...too prone to attacks by rocs and harpies. Chasm View's location seems unique in the area, with a set of deep cracks that provide shelter. Anyway, given the choice of enemies, I prefer defending people from basilisks, king scorpions, and sidewinders. The harpies are horrid."

Devon was trying to pay attention to the history, but all she could think about were these new mob types he was mentioning. Even with the war and Hazel's disappearance and her people's status as evacuees, her gamer self immediately itched to head into the Skargills and get some XP.

She took a breath. Later. Hopefully.

Or maybe she could actually justify it as some sort of power-leveling and combat-training exercise.

Anyway... Later. Hopefully.

"You keep calling yourself the protector of your people. So the royal family helps destroy threats. Do you have other fighters?" She'd been hoping for good news on the build-a-worthwhile-army front, but it was starting to sound suspiciously like the Skevalli were a bunch of noob-like civilians.

"A fair question. And the answer is somewhat complicated." He smoothed his trousers, then plucked at the fabric, rubbing it between his thumb and forefinger. Given how slathered he'd been in oil, Devon wondered whether the cloth was getting all gooey and stuck to his skin. It didn't sound pleasant, but she wasn't going to back down now that she'd managed to get him dressed.

"Common Skevalli aren't helpless. They have a standing militia that fights off many of the attacks—"

"Actually, another question. You make it sound like the attacks are constant."

He shrugged, finally letting go of his trousers, but then starting to fuss with the sleeve of his tunic. A toss of his head sent a puff of some sort of scented oil fragrance from his mane. How much time did he spend oiling his body and working scent into his hair every day? Way longer than it took her to pull on yoga pants and run a brush through her hair, that was for sure.

"My father, the king, would be sorely disappointed to hear that I've been so lax with my tongue. I wasn't supposed to mention our difficulties."

Oh. Great. She'd heard this sort of game storyline before. Player meets a new character, representative of a settlement she hasn't visited before. The settlement is in trouble and in need of a hero.

Normally, she wouldn't be bothered by the cliche plot. It was always nice to have an objective, a good reason to head out and kill monsters for fat loot and glorious XP. But she'd kinda hoped that the Skevalli would be helping *her*, not the other way around.

Or maybe she was just being cynical, reading too much into what he'd said.

"But since you mentioned them, might as well finish the job then, eh?"

He sighed and twirled a strand of hair around his finger. "It's always a struggle, scratching out a home in the Skargills. I've mentioned how my people's stories may be as much myth as truth. In any case, when the stone sickness began to creep through our forest, freezing the trees and sending their leaves cutting down through the air as stone blades, the royal seer retreated to the reflecting pool and fasted for fourteen days. When she returned, she declared that our people would be isolated in the Skargill's maze of rifts for centuries. We would be in constant danger from the fearsome beasts that inhabit the gorges. The attacks would worsen up until the very end, and the royal family must devote everything to protecting the innocents, especially those with no griffons to call their own. And we must preserve the First Son's Duty. Someday, a hero would come, the seer said. And the eldest prince of every generation must stand ready to bind our people to her in the most enduring manner possible."

"Uh...?"

He nodded. "All my life, I've been groomed to become your consort and...to offer myself in marriage to the Keeper of Ishildar so that our fates might be—"

"Hold on a second. Sorry, but I'm not hunting for a husband." Especially not an NPC. What the hell was Veia thinking?

"Then I've failed. I was trained in the arts of wooing. Every morning, the royal servants have exfoliated my skin, rubbed tonics into my scalp to encourage my mane."

"Okay, lemme just stop you there. Can't I help you guys without this whole marriage thing? If it's just a problem with basilisks, I have a hundred or more starborn who need something to hunt. And if you guys have food and supplies and stuff, it benefits all of us to get rid of your problems."

"Every day at noon, I have retreated to my chamber to execute one thousand crunches." He lifted his shirt to expose his flexing abs.

Devon grabbed his wrist and pulled the hem of his tunic from his fingers. The cloth fell back to cover his stomach. "Isn't there some Skevalli maiden you want to marry? Maybe someone that rides around in a leather bikini?"

"I suppose I've never thought of it. My parents would have cast me out had I shown the slightest inattention to my duty and birthright." He sighed and dropped his head. "They may cast me out still when they hear that I've failed to charm you."

"Dude, listen. We're going to help your people anyway."

He cast her a look filled with hope. "And you'll explain to my father?"

> **Prince Kenjan is offering you a quest:** Nobody's Boy Toy
> *Convince the Skevalli king and queen that their son hasn't failed them when his attempts to woo you were unsuccessful. Ishildar and the Skevalli people can stand together without the rite of marriage to formalize the alliance.*
> **First Objective:** Eradicate the basilisk nest nearest Vulture's Rift
> **Reward:** An audience with King Jildan and Queen Kiela
> **Accept?** Y/N

With a sigh of relief, Devon accepted the quest.

"I'll make plans with my fighters tonight. We'll show the basilisks what happens when they mess with Ishildar's vassals, okay?"

He growled and gave her a smoldering look.

"Uh, hey...not necessary, okay?"

"Right." He pressed his fingers to his temples. "Habit. I may require help in re-learning my mannerisms."

She clapped him on the shoulder. "Maybe you should spend a little time with Greel."

Chapter Sixteen

"HEY, SO SORRY about Stonehaven. Sucks," Jeremy said as he trotted up to her. "What are your plans, boss lady?"

Something about his ever-present, shit-eating grin was just too much for Devon today. She shook her head as she tried to step around him. Jeremy sidestepped to keep her attention.

Devon gritted her teeth. Greel, Hailey, Torald, and his druid friend Magda were waiting for her at the edge of the city. Between Greel, aka "the chicken whisperer" and the druid, someone in the party ought to be able to speak to the windsteed herd and figure out Hazel's whereabouts. Devon already regretted the time she'd lost in finding out answers about the little scout's fate—she shouldn't have needed Prince Kenjan to remind her about the windsteeds' special capabilities. And she most definitely didn't need to waste time satisfying Jeremy's idle curiosity.

"Now we solidify defenses here and ready our forces to strike back at the demons," she said. "Honestly, Jeremy, it's not a good time." As she spoke, she pulled up the settlement interface to check on Jarleck's progress. Before meeting with Prince Kenjan, she'd spoken with her fortifications master about constructing defenses around Temple Square and its immediate surrounds. They couldn't count on the repelling effects of the Veian Temple to hold back the demons indefinitely.

Settlement: Ishildar

Fortifications
Status: Unfortified

Completed:
7 x Stone Guardian

Required for advancement to Fortified Camp:
1 x Bulwark (in progress - 10%)
3 x Watch Towers (in progress - 20%)
4 x Archer Platforms with Screens

Dispelling the interface, she managed to sidestep and squeeze by Jeremy, but unfortunately, he turned and fell in beside her. "So that's it? That's your strategy?"

"Right now, yes."

"I...see."

"Listen, I've got a lot going on. A follower to find. A society of griffon riders to protect. And I'm stressed because I always do crappy at base battles. I never know when to play offense or defense, and this case is way worse than a typical battle for control of a base. Obviously."

"If by obviously, you mean that the other guys outnumber us like ten to one and have an undefeatable archdemon, yeah. Obviously."

"Do you have anything useful to say, Jeremy?"

"You mean my sparkling wit and great fashion sense aren't enough anymore?"

Devon didn't answer, but rather hung a sharp right onto a cross street, her sudden movement cutting him off. Never one to get the hint, Jeremy hurried around to her other side and drew even with her again. His ridiculous feather hat plume bounced as he walked, occasionally kissing the top of her head.

She batted it away. "I'm serious when I say I don't like base battles, actually. If you have any suggestions on defenses, I'm all ears."

"And actually, I didn't chase you down just to be annoying. It turns out I do have a few ideas."

Just a few more blocks separated them from the edge of the savanna and her designated meeting spot. She slowed her steps. "Okay, spit it out then, I guess."

"Okay first of all, you're not off to a terrible start. Abandoning Stonehaven wasn't the best opening to a protracted control battle, but if you hadn't kept the pressure on by teleporting people in and striking out from the Shrine to Veia, you wouldn't even have a toehold. The problem is, you're still losing ground."

"I got that much, genius."

He smirked. "So now you have to change things up. The thing with this kind of control mechanic is the demons can't actually move Stonehaven from contested to neutral and start their possession timer as long as you keep just one structure contested. One-percent contested even. So I think from here you should do the bare minimum to hold control or partial control of the Shrine to Veia. It's the hardest structure for them to take because of its natural defense against demons, and you have at least two people who can teleport in there, straight into the heart of Stonehaven."

"And then I redirect my strike teams elsewhere?"

He nodded. "Exactly. The problem with attacking inside Stonehaven is the demons are way too strong there. It's a suicide mission every time. But they have the same problem you were running into with a hamlet-sized settlement, only it's worse for them. They don't have room inside the walls for their full army. If I were you, I'd start sending parties of players to make guerrilla strikes at the edges of their force. There might be ten times more of them than us, but as far as I know, the demons can't respawn. They can't even rez the higher-level NPCs like you can."

"A war of attrition."

He shrugged. "For now I think it's your best bet. Plus, your guys will gain XP."

"Okay, I guess that makes a little sense."

"I'm more than a pretty face and a songbird's voice, you know." He patted his cheek and made a little kissy face.

"Ew." She pushed him back. "So do me a favor, then."

He took off his hat and bowed. "Yes, boss lady?"

Devon rolled her eyes. "Let Hezbek know she can slow the teleportations into Stonehaven. Then can you please work with Aijal and Chen and get a couple of parties together to start attacking from the fringes. Advanced NPCs and players only, got it? Aijal was supposed to be organizing raid groups before all this happened anyway."

"As you wish, Highness."

***

"Man, talk about addicted. You're worse than me—sleeping in-game. That's dedication." The druid, Magda, laughed as she nudged Hailey with her elbow. None of the waiting party members had noticed Devon's approach, and they stood in a loose semi-circle at the end of Ishildar's street, their gazes turned to the savanna and the dark patches where demon groups gathered.

Hailey shrugged and laughed, but it seemed a little forced. "I guess I wasn't paying attention to my *Fatigue* bar. That and the sunbeam felt pretty good."

"What's this?" Devon asked as she stepped into the circle.

"When you sent me to round these guys up, I found Hailey totally conked out on a bench. Her inspect window even had a sleeping status."

Devon couldn't help noticing the little wrinkle that formed between her friend's eyebrows as she listened to Magda's explanation. Even if she wouldn't admit it, Hailey was sensitive. Given Devon's theory that something in Hailey's real-life situation was forcing her friend to escape into the game, she wouldn't blame Hailey for feeling defensive when teased about her play hours.

The best way to help her friend out here was to change the subject, so Devon quickly turned to Greel. "So. Think you can get anything out of the windsteeds? Or do you only speak chicken?"

She noticed that Torald had a hard time keeping a straight face after that comment, so she avoided eye contact. She didn't want him to bust out laughing; Greel was hard enough to deal with without being the subject of ridicule.

"I suppose your ignorance is understandable," Greel said, "seeing as you have been unable to acquire the *Animal Tongues* skill despite a moderate amount of effort applied in that direction."

Devon clenched her jaw. How did Greel know she'd been trying to pick up the skill after the awakened races arrived?

"Oh yes," he said, eyebrow raised as he straightened his shoulders self-importantly. "It's no secret that you've been trying. It's the staring contests with the livestock that give it away. And for your information, as mundane creatures lacking the awakening of the windsteeds and corvids, the chickens don't exactly speak. Our communication is more of a sharing of emotional states."

Torald snorted, but quickly covered it by pretending to cough. Devon blinked, clamping her lips into a line. But she finally couldn't help it, and the laugh came bursting out.

"And how do the chickens react when you share your angst over flaws in the settlement's legal documentation? Do they transmit sympathy when you rage about imprecise language?"

Greel narrowed his eyes. "I'll pretend that's a serious question. For your information, Sugarcakes and I often commiserate over the difficulties in our young lives. She was just a chick when the goblins attacked Emmaree's settlement near the Fortress of Shadows. Her mother was killed in the attack, and there was no regurgitated mash for her or her siblings. All but one of the other chicks died before we rescued her."

"Sugarcakes?" Hailey asked. "I'm guessing you named her?"

Greel turned an icy glare on the Seeker. "Her feathers reminded me of confectioner's sugar when she was young."

"Ohh...kay..."

"Anyway," Devon said, gesturing toward the savanna where the windsteeds grazed in a loose cluster. "Let's see what we can find out about Hazel."

As the group started toward the herd, motion at the edge of Devon's vision caught her attention. She whirled to see another windsteed approaching from the east—parallel to the city and within the demon-free strip of grass—at a thundering gallop. Froth dripped from the corners of the mare's mouth, and sweat pasted her coat to her flanks. Strangely, it appeared that the horse was carrying something in her teeth.

All at once, Devon's stomach dropped toward her feet. She recognized that horse. Hazel had been riding her the last time Devon had seen the little scout.

Chapter Seventeen

DEVON HUNG IN the air twenty feet above the edge of the savanna, her *Levitation* spell maintaining a soft cushion under her feet. Behind her, the rest of the party waited expectantly for her report. With Jarleck's spyglass clutched in one hand, she ran her eyes over the grassland to the south.

Before, there'd been a wide stretch of rolling, grass-covered hills broken only by scattered acacia trees, crumbling ruins of the Khevshir vassaldom, and the occasional rock outcrop where lions and hippogryphs lounged. Now, craters pitted the landscape and black scars smeared across the scene, long streaks where the grass had burned. Farther from the site of the former player camp, the burned areas were widely scattered and smaller, little patches where stray embers had landed and caught. But nearer the camp, the char grew denser and denser until scorched earth replaced all traces of grass. As for the player camp, nothing remained except for a glassy black bowl where the earth had been melted by Archdemon Gaviroth's hellfire.

Devon pressed the spyglass to her eye and examined the bowl. Baking under the midday sun, the wavy surface threw back glints of light. The glass itself was dark, almost black, with just a hint of translucence in the higher ripples. In the center, the smooth crater seemed to glow from within, a deep red that made her think the core of the crater was still molten.

At the edge of the bowl, angular lines caught her attention. It looked as if blocks of glass had been cut from the rim and removed, but with the distance and angle from which she viewed the scene, she couldn't say anything for certain. She pulled the spyglass from her eye and took a few seconds to compose herself before continuing her survey.

Turning to examine Stonehaven, Devon felt her throat clamp down. It wasn't just the destruction, though it was like a fist to the gut to see the holes where hellfire had melted through the curtain wall and palisade that had taken months to build. The worst part was seeing how the demons were changing her settlement. Atop the remaining parts of the main palisade where wood and stone merlons had provided cover for Stonehaven's archers, a row of wicked iron spikes now speared upward, their barbs like thorns. The stone itself was darker in color than it had been, though she couldn't say whether the change had been worked by magic or soot from some other means. Oily smoke rose from points along the wall, and when Devon gathered her courage and peered through the spyglass, she saw that yellow-green fire blazed in some kind of dark-iron braziers. Because the settlement was still contested, the crest that Devon had never gotten around to customizing still adorned a set of banners hanging over the battlements, but the cloth was now tattered and charred. She shook her head. It would almost be better if the banners were gone.

As a patrolling defender, a demon thrall, marched into the circular view of the spyglass, a barbed spear gripped in its claw, Devon tore her eyes away from her town. Staring would do no good, especially while Hazel needed her.

Once again, Devon turned her attention to the landscape beyond the player camp. A few miles farther to the south, a gray line of cypress and mangrove-like trees marked the ragged edge where the savanna met the swamp surrounding the Fortress of Shadows, the subterranean temple at the heart of the former Grukluk Vassaldom. Devon mentally ran through the windsteed's account that Greel had translated for the group. Hazel, Zoe, and the windsteed had been racing toward the scene of the player camp when the pits had opened in the earth, disgorging the demon army. Hazel had first tried to turn for the safety of Stonehaven, but the archdemon and his lackeys had blocked her path. She'd stood no chance of making it through, so she'd turned her mount in the opposite direction, figuring she might be able to circle around and eventually approach Stonehaven from the south. Or at the very least, she'd hoped she might find shelter in the swamp. The demon army had already come through that area and would be far more interested in advancing on Ishildar than flushing out strays from the braided channels of fetid water and boggy land.

Turned out that wasn't precisely the case—the horde might be focusing on a march north, conquering settlements along the way, but that didn't mean they were ignoring their rear flanks. When talking to Tamara, Devon had considered the possibility of a rear base between Stonehaven and the Noble Coast. She'd even wondered if she might be able to leapfrog the demon army, attack this other base, and force them to divide their forces if they wished to defend it. It turned out, she was right about the presence of another base, but to call it that might be something of an understatement.

According to Hazel, who usually judged these things well, Devon needed to see what was going on in the swamp's heart. Hazel had happened upon a raised causeway that struck through the swamp from north to south and had followed it, thinking that her duties as a scout demanded that she investigate. But just as she caught a glimpse of an installation, the construction anchored not far from the entrance to the Fortress of Shadows, she'd been spotted by a demon patrol. To escape, Hazel had been forced to flee onto an isolated peninsula of dry land surrounded by water too deep to wade. Turned out, not only was Zoe unable to fly, she couldn't swim either. Hazel and her war ostrich were pinned down deep in the demons' territory. Meanwhile, the windsteed's ability to swim combined with extraordinary speed had allowed her to return to Ishildar bearing Hazel's message and a hastily scrawled map.

Devon shook her head as she lowered the spyglass. It hadn't escaped her that spending resources on an expedition through enemy territory to rescue a single follower could be seen as an emotional rather than a rational decision. But there were a couple of counterarguments. First, Hazel had claimed that Devon needed to see the installation for herself. And second, as Greel had translated the windsteed's communication, Devon had received a quest update. To double-check that she hadn't missed anything, she pulled up the log.

> **Quest:** Hazel's Fate
>
> *You have discovered Hazel's whereabouts. And it seems the woman has discovered critical information about the demon army.*
>
> **Objective:** Rescue Hazel from the Grukluk Swamp
>
> **Objective:** Investigate the demon installation near the Fortress of Shadows
>
> **Bonus Objective:** Might as well rescue the ostrich, too. Hazel is fond of her.
>
> **Reward:** 250000 Experience

The thing was, Veia probably wouldn't nudge the NPCs into giving her quests that weren't important to the overall goal of saving the world. So even if it seemed a questionable choice to head south with a party of her best fighters, she could have faith in the almighty quest log.

As for a location to target with their expedition, the object that had come straight from the horse's mouth—quite literally and covered with frothy slobber—had been a hastily scrawled map. Despite what had surely been terrible conditions for mapping, Hazel's *Cartography* skill had won out, and the additions to Devon's in-game map marked this so-called installation with a pin. Another blip showed Hazel's location. So, altogether, it seemed that venturing into the swamp was the best way forward.

At least, that's what she hoped.

With a deep breath, she canceled her *Levitation* effect and sank to the ground. Landing lightly on her *Longstrider Boots*, she turned to face the group.

"I think we stand a chance if we use the terrain for cover and swing wide around the player camp. We'll need to take out some scattered groups of demons, though, and if the main demon force spots us, we're toast. Does anyone want to back out? I'll need to find a replacement quickly."

Silence reigned while her friends shook their heads.

"All right then," she said. "Buff up. We've got a woman to save. And an ostrich, I guess."

Chapter Eighteen

OKAY, THIS WAS dumb. Right? Or maybe it wasn't. Emerson really had no clue about this stuff.

He paced up and down the grocery store aisle, blinking in the godawful glare from the light bars overhead. What was it with store chains and migraine-inducing wavelengths? Some kind of partnership with the drug company? He stopped at the end of the aisle and glanced toward the shuttered pharmacy and the racks of over-the-counter medication that paid fealty to it. Was it his imagination, or was the light friendlier there? Like a promise of relief as you laid your trembling hand on a box of pain relievers.

Anyway—he blinked again—back to the task at hand. Why did there have to be so many kinds of chocolate? Cacao contents from 35% to 87%. Chocolate with coconut cream. Organic truffles. Raspberry infused with orange zest. Sea-salt sprinkled. Some kind of super-food variety with Himalayan berries that was supposed to make you look ten years younger without spending fifty thousand dollars a month on anti-aging therapy. Hell, they probably made chocolate that was supposed to raise your IQ to, like, Einstein-level. Stephen-Hawkins-level. So you could no longer think about anything but solving the universe's greatest mysteries.

Anyway...

Closing his eyes, he made a step forward and ran his finger back and forth over the shelf while he counted down from ten. At zero, he snatched the package under his hand.

Swiss-made milk chocolate with single-origin cacao from Bolivia. Probably fertilized only by the poo of a rare, cloud-forest-dwelling spider monkey. Probably picked by trained spider monkeys. Maybe the Swiss chocolatier was able to afford the carbon tax for shipping from South America to Europe and back to North America by paying the monkeys in bananas grown on the next plot over.

Speaking of price—he turned the package over and held it to the scanner mounted on the shelf.

Emerson grimaced when the price flashed on the readout. "Ouch," he muttered. It wasn't that he couldn't afford ridiculously overpriced candy. He still had a salary from E-Squared, and they probably wouldn't fire him for ignoring Bradley Williams' latest demand for a detailed report on why Veia's servers were working so hard lately. Was there something wrong with the AI's content generation?

No. The problem was that Bradley hadn't shut Zaa down, and now the evil AI's minions had crossed the realm boundary into the mortal plane. It was taking everything Veia had to get her NPCs coordinating a defense on the current front while preparing for assaults from new angles.

Actually, that was kind of wishful thinking on Emerson's part. Turned out, he'd run a query on the network traffic and the models he'd constructed of Veia's world view. Granted, it was just a model— the state of the world was spread across a neural network and through a set of quantum cores. In other words, totally opaque to someone looking in from the outside. Like a neurosurgeon looking at an exposed brain and trying to determine what her patient was dreaming about.

Okay, the exposed brain was kind of a gross metaphor. It was exactly the sort of analogy that turned conversations awkward at company parties, the biggest social events of his existence. Actually, the only social events he attended. But anyway.

Emerson waved his wrist in front of the scanner to authorize payment for the chocolate bar, then dropped it in his messenger bag and glanced down the aisle again. A single chocolate bar wasn't really enough for the situation, was it? Outside, the moon had risen, and the power-saving algorithm in Saint George's streetlights had flipped off all but a few of the bulbs. Movement detection would reactivate them, but for now, the autocab pull-through was painted in a pleasant silver. It was the kind of night when he would typically step out into his patio back in Tucson, careful to tiptoe around the bird droppings that marked the outline where his dilapidated patio furniture used to stand. He liked to look up at the moon and enjoy the sound of night birds, the stray chirps of crickets in the storm drains.

But he wasn't in Tucson, and the windows in his Saint George hotel room didn't even open.

Anyway, kind of stupid to be thinking of standing outside when it was actually the middle of winter. Saint George might be in a desert, but January wasn't exactly balmy.

Also, if he didn't want to make a complete idiot of himself tomorrow, turning up at Devon's doorstep and hoping he wasn't about to ruin everything, he ought to get some sleep.

After he figured out what the hell else to get her as a sympathy gift for having her home taken over by demons. With a sigh, he headed for the next aisle. Maybe the store had a floral section or something.

Chapter Nineteen

"WHAT IF THEY have, like, infrared vision?" Magda asked as the party filed across the savanna through the darkening gloom. It had been early evening when the party set off from Ishildar. First, they'd traveled east through the strip of demon-free terrain until they'd reached a point that would—barring detours to follow the most concealing terrain—grant them a relatively straight shot through to the swamp. Then they'd cut away from the city and out of the shelter of the Veian Temple's repelling effects. Between the falling darkness and the sense of exposure, Devon didn't blame the woman for worrying.

"I dunno. I guess we deal with it," Hailey said.

"I mean, maybe we're safer traveling in daylight. Maybe we can sort of blend with the grass. We could camp until dawn."

"Says the woman who has a whole quiver full of nature camouflage spells," Torald called over his shoulder.

They'd set the marching order to put Greel in front, his martial artist's reflexes complementing his ability to move stealthily despite his twisted spine. The paladin followed behind, leaving enough space that the clanging and squeaking of his platemail wouldn't blow Greel's cover, but sticking close enough that he could run forward and grab aggro if Greel was jumped. Hailey followed, ready to drop a heal over time on the tank at the first sign of danger, and

Magda came next. Devon brought up the rear with her *Shadow Shifter* combat form activated. If an attack came from behind, at least that granted her a 30% chance of avoiding damage.

Not very reassuring, but Devon couldn't think of a better alternative to the ordering.

"Anyway, infrared doesn't really fit the world, right?" Hailey said. "Wouldn't they just have a *Darkvision* skill like the rest of us?"

"Well, I wasn't thinking infrared exactly. More like 'ability to see the lifeblood pumping through mortal veins.'"

"Then if that's the case, it doesn't matter whether it's night or day," Hailey countered. "Maybe the darkness will let us spot the glow of their baleful eyes or something."

Torald seemed to shudder at the thought and adjusted his grip on his greatsword. He walked with the blade exposed, heavy steel held before his body. Just watching him hike that way made Devon's arm ache.

The party was trekking along a dry wash. The idea was that the grassy slopes on either side of the stream bed would conceal them from any creatures roving the grassland nearby. But the wash also prevented them from noticing approaching enemies. In truth, Devon would be glad when the gray light of dusk gave way to full night. Infrared vision notwithstanding, the darkness would provide as much concealment as the gully. Never a fan of moving through low-lying terrain where she'd have a disadvantage in combat, Devon would be glad to climb out of the wash and resume a straighter-line march for the swamp.

"I don't think we should camp, but what do you guys think about finding a spot to rest until full dark?" she asked. Though not in any danger of maxing out any time soon, her *Fatigue* bar had been steadily climbing since they'd set out from the city. Even if they crossed the savanna without incident, they still had at least a couple of hours of wading through the swamp to reach Hazel's position.

Ahead, the wash bent to the right. Greel stopped at the turn and whirled to face the group, fists balled.

"Have none of you people ever heard the term *stealth*? I don't know which is louder, your stamping feet or your annoyingly shrill yammering."

"That's why we put you in front," Magda said. "The point is for you to flush out anyone who might otherwise hear our melodious voices."

"The *point* is—"

Greel's statement ended in a strangled yelp when a dark shape burst from a waist-high stand of cattails and tackled the man. Or rather, the demon attempted to tackle the lawyer. Quick-stepping backward, Greel evaded the attacker as if he'd expected the appearance all along. The lawyer leapt into the air as the demon charged past, and he somehow kicked his legs in opposite directions. Devon winced, imagining the tearing sound her groin would make with that kind of maneuver, as one of Greel's heels slammed the demon between the shoulder blades. She actually jerked in surprise as the lawyer's other foot connected with the jaw of a second demon that seemed to have appeared out of thin air. A satisfied grin flashed on the lawyer's face as he landed, but he quickly turned a glare on the group.

"Little help here? Or do I have to do this on my own too?"

"Veia, bright goddess, guide my weapon in your work!" Torald shouted as he broke into a run. "Give me the strength to defend your creation against evil, and may my heart never falter."

"Seriously?" Devon heard Hailey mutter. "Wouldn't 'Veia grant me strength' work just as well?" Despite her commentary, the woman's cast bar was already active. A moment later, her *Guide Vitality* spell surrounded Torald with a glowing heal-over-time halo.

Just before the paladin reached Greel, another demon sprang from low brush beside the dry stream. Torald first elbowed the attacker aside, then hesitated. He whirled and raised a mail-armored fist. "Look upon me, foul beast. Look upon me and quail!" As he spoke, he pointed at the staggering demon.

Was that his...taunt? Devon guessed it must be because the paladin's shout seemed to have grabbed the demon's full focus, assuring that it wouldn't recover from its daze and turn on a different member of the group.

Ridiculous battle cries or not, Torald was a good tank.

"Wait, isn't a quail some kind of extinct bird?" Magda asked.

Hailey shrugged as she started casting *Self-Actualization*, a group buff that increased damage and effectiveness with class abilities. "I thought so. But I don't think they're extinct. Don't they have that weird head feather or something?"

Devon glanced at the sky—no moon, which meant no moonlight-based shadow puppets—before funneling mana into casting a *Glowing Orb*. When the cast finished, two balls of light appeared, one on her hand and one in the air nearby. She blinked, wondering for a split second if Veia had improved the ability, but then the floating ball executed a loop the loop.

"Oh. Hi Bob," she said. "Hey, mind floating up and watching for more—"

She stopped talking as the wisp streaked forward...*and booped Hailey's nose.* What the heck? Wasn't that their thing? As in hers and Bob's. Not that she liked having her nose booped. But still. First, there'd been that weird moment between her friend and the wisp just after Devon had exited the Vault of the Magi. Hailey had claimed that she'd explain the situation to Devon later, but it never seemed to be the right time, which made Devon wonder if she just didn't want to share. And lately, the wisp had been spending a whole lot of time with Devon's friend. Way more than Bob had been spending with her.

Devon wouldn't go so far to say that she *missed* the obnoxious ball of light, but...Okay, actually, she kind of missed it.

And now Bob was booping someone else's nose? After everything she and the wisp had been through together?

She shook her head and muttered something about traitors before casting *Levitate* to get a better vantage on the fight. His armor shimmering each time his heal over time pulsed, Torald now had four demons focused on him. Greel worked the enemies from their flanks, landing jabs to their kidneys and kicking the beasts in the backs of their knees. Eyes glowing green, Magda chanted as she sent a gust of leaves, no doubt razor-sharp, flying up the slope to tear through another trio of demons that had just appeared. Insta-casting a *Shadow Puppet*, Devon sent her minion arrowing up the hill and into the newcomers' midst. Lightning arced over the demons as the lightning-based shadow discharged its power. Smoke rose from the group.

"Incoming, other side," Hailey called.

Crap. Devon spun in the air to see another five attackers sprinting to the opposite edge of the wash. She threw down a *Wall of Ice* to slow their progress, then targeted the cluster with a tier 3 *Freeze*. The spell caught two of the demons, encasing them in ice.

Hailey's cast bar lit up as she attempted to charm one of the remaining mobs from the newest group, but the bar turned gray instead of flashing when the cast timer finished.

"Damn. Resist," she muttered.

Torald staggered as one of his attackers landed a lucky critical strike. He seemed momentarily dazed, and as if, only then, noticing the trio of women behind him, two of the demons that he'd been fighting spun and started running down the creek bed toward Hailey.

"Shit. Watch it, Hailey." Devon felt vaguely sick she realized they were losing control of the battle.

Bob spun a quick circle around Hailey's head. "I just thought you might like to know that, in the sense that Torald was using the word *quail*, it is an intransitive verb meaning 'to feel frightened or show that you feel frightened.'"

"Do you seriously have no sense of situational awareness?" Hailey snapped, batting at the wisp as she backpedaled and started casting *Crippling Self-Doubt* on the closest charging demon.

"On the contrary, I know quite well that your group is facing some tactical disadvantages here. Might I suggest—"

"Shut up, Bob!" Devon said.

The orb shrank and backed away as Devon hammered the advancing demons with a *Downdraft*. The gust of wind knocked them onto their backs and gave Hailey time to retreat a few paces as she tried another *Charm* on the demon she'd already debuffed. This time, the spell landed. As the charmed mob sprang to its feet, then tackled its friend, Devon turned her attention to the trio of mobs she'd hit with her *Shadow Puppet*.

Magda had landed her creepy *Heartwood* spell on one of the three, and it was now shrieking in terror as roots burst from its feet and branches sprang from its torso. While Devon watched, the druid raised a swarm of insects from the ground and sent them crawling toward the trapped demon. Death by one thousand little mandibles—she didn't blame the other two demons from that trio for having turned and started toward Torald and Greel. At least a blow from a greatsword or a well-aimed backstab would be a clean death.

She shuddered, looking toward the other side of the wash. The five demons on the gully rim had spread out into a line, likely to avoid getting caught in the area of effect of her *Freeze* and *Shadow Puppet* attacks and were quickly descending the slope. She used a quick *Combat Assessment*—all five were basic Demon Thralls between level 27 and level 29. A bit higher than her, Hailey, and Magda. Five against three wasn't great odds, especially since most of Devon's offensive spells caused fire-based damage, which the demons would just resist.

"Either of you have a snare spell?" Devon asked as she paddled the air with her feet to get some distance from the advancing line. It might not be efficient, but if she and Magda could kite the mobs, slowing their run speed and running away while wearing away at their health, they might be able to win this.

Shaking her head, Hailey cast her *Crippling Self-Doubt* debuff on one of the new attackers. "I was supposed to get one at level 20, but you know, no Seeker trainers out here in the wilderness."

"Nothing," Magda called, her tone suggesting faint confusion that Devon needed to ask. Most gamers would know the abilities of the other classes by now, but Devon had been too occupied with building and defending Stonehaven to comb through the forums—

not that she'd ever been very interested in reading about the meta-game anyway. And she definitely hadn't had many chances to group with other players.

"Aww, crap," Hailey said, pointing to the rim of the gully where yet another demon had appeared. Where the others had little useless wings, claws, and generally mottled skin, this one had a purplish skin tone. Stubby spikes stood from the flesh of its arms and thighs, the skin puckered and raw around the jutting bone. Lips pulling back from glinting yellow teeth, the demon raised its arms. Red light began to glow in the gaps between its claw-like fingers.

"Caster!" Devon shouted. Fumbling a little with the mental motions for her new spell, she eventually managed to start casting *Night Shackles.* Just as the light of the demon's spellcasting flared to a brilliant scarlet, Devon's counterspell fired, darkness surrounding the demon's hands and freezing its claws. With its casting ability temporarily silenced, the monster roared and charged down the hill behind its brethren.

"Damn it!" Torald shouted, a rare slip of character to curse in actual English. "I'm out of command points. Can't pick up the adds."

"My kingdom for an off-tank," Hailey muttered. "We're toast."

"Actually," Devon said. "That's a good point."

Flicking her fingers to dispel the Levitation effect, she dropped to the floor of the wash and turned to face the oncoming demons. Being a tank wasn't so much about armor—well, in most cases, yeah, it was. But it didn't have to be. The most important thing was damage mitigation or damage avoidance along with the ability to hold mob aggro. She couldn't taunt mobs to keep their attention, but maybe if she nailed them with enough spells, it would keep them pissed off at her.

She double checked that her *Shadow Shifter* form was still active, winced at the pain she knew was incoming, and yanked out her dagger. "*Barkskin* and heals, please. And whatever else you think might help."

The demons fell on her like rabid dogs.

Yep. It hurt.

Chapter Twenty

"WORST SPOT EVER to set camp," Magda muttered as they limped into the ruins of some ancient Khevshir structure. The building stood at the edge of the swamp, its toes in the water. In a few places, stone blocks rose above the damp, but most of the floor of the building was a muddy mess. Moss coated the walls, and in the light from Devon's *Glowing Orb*, a latticework of skeletal branches seemed to collect the mist that swirled in from the swamp, converting it into water droplets that splattered on their heads and shoulders.

Yes, it might be the worst spot ever—except that the walls and overhanging trees provided good concealment from roving demon patrols, and there was no way that Devon could walk another hundred yards without collapsing.

Stumbling to a corner where two decaying walls met, she went down on her knees, then fell over on her side as her *Fatigue* bar flashed to indicate it was 95% full. In her experience, she was just 3% away from seeing black spots and passing out. Her brain hurt from focusing on weaving melee combat with spellcasting, and her body ached from exhaustion and injury.

The best tactic she'd found during the six battles she'd recently off-tanked was to start the fight with a *Simulacrum* of herself active. The illusion confused some of the dumber demons, especially since around 30% of their attacks also passed right through Devon's flesh. But it was murder on her concentration to try to command her copy while fending off attacks, trying to dodge, and striking out with her sub-par weapon skills. At this point, the inside of her skull felt like pulp. Oh, and her gear was wrecked; the pieces that could take damage were all down to below 30% durability.

"Hey Torald?" she said. "Want to do your thing?" She made a vague hand gesture.

"My...thing?" he responded, copying her gesture.

"Yeah. That thing where you're just as tired as everyone else, but somehow you manage to build our campfire and get out food for everyone and, I don't know, tuck us in for the night?"

He gave a tired-sounding laugh. "Right. That thing."

The last time Devon had felt this tired, she and her group had just carried their custom-made ironwood bicycles through a couple of miles of jungle so thick you could hardly breathe without cutting out some free space with a machete first. But despite being as fatigued as the rest of the group, Torald and Tamara had leaned on their real-world camping experience and weird exercise hobbies, and they'd set up the camp while everyone else played dead. Thinking back, Devon couldn't help but smile at the memory of how disgustingly happy Tamara had been to have pushed herself to the brink of total systems failure. The woman was a fricking masochist.

Judging by the faint smile on Torald's face, he had fond memories of the experience, too. Or maybe it was just fond memories of his time with Tamara. As far as Devon knew, he hadn't worked up the courage to suggest meeting up with Tamara in real life, but those two had been pretty inseparable in-game lately. Well, until the demons had forced Stonehaven's evacuation, anyway.

Devon wasn't sure if Tamara had even logged in since then. Maybe the warning about spawning into a pillar of hellfire had made her consider a short break from gaming.

After stomping around from raised block to raised block, likely testing to see which parts of the floor were solid, Torald nodded to himself and reached into his *Manpurse of Holding*. Devon almost laughed when he actually pulled out a bundle of firewood tied neatly with a few pieces of twine. He was seriously such a Boy Scout. Exhaustion was making her slaphappy, and she started wondering whether there was a merit badge in LARPing, his main out-of-game hobby. As a teenager, Torald would've been all over that.

Devon's *Fatigue* had ticked back down to 90% by the time the paladin finished laying the fire, and as he pulled out a flint and steel, she spared him the work by sitting up and casting *Phoenix Fire* on the pile of wood. After the syrupy fire had enveloped the sticks and real flames had begun to crackle, she canceled the effect and then focused on the surrounding ruin. Despite the years of decay, the encircling walls provided a decent screen to keep the firelight from attracting attention, but it wasn't complete. Focusing on the few small gaps that would allow the glow past, she cast a couple of *Illusion* spells, creating patches that mimicked stonework and prevented light from passing through.

The effort of spellcasting stole more energy than she expected, and she flopped back down on the ground when her *Fatigue* hit 95% again. Turning just her head, she checked on the rest of the group. Everyone looked about as worked as she felt. If they hadn't found the ruin just in time, she suspected that they'd have ended up face-down in the grass, at the mercy of fate to decide whether a demon patrol would trip over them.

Dull-eyed, Hailey was digging through her small backpack. After a moment, she produced a leather-wrapped packet and opened it to reveal what looked like strips of dried mango. Saliva flooded Devon's mouth as her friend offered out a couple of pieces.

"Have I ever told you that you're the best Seeker I've ever grouped with?"

Hailey tried to laugh, but it came out as a tired little gust of air. "Thank Tom. He said we can pay him back by foraging for mushrooms in the swamp. Just as long as we don't sample them unless we've got enough *Foraging* skill for proper identification."

Devon almost asked whether the settlement's head cook had also given Hailey an update on the remaining food stores; now that she was away from Ishildar, she couldn't get detailed information on resource availability through the settlement interface, and she'd forgotten to check before they left. But she knew the news wouldn't be great, and it would just distract from the task at hand.

"That's a good point, actually. When we set out tomorrow—er today..." she said as she glanced upward. The moon had risen shortly after nightfall and had already traversed halfway across the sky. "Everyone keep watch for forage and especially for wild game. Well, actually, what kind of animals live in the swamp anyway?"

All of a sudden, Hailey burst out laughing.

"What?" Devon said. "I figure if we bring back some meat, it will buy us time to get another supply chain set up."

"Sorry," Hailey said as she wiped a tear from her eyes. "I'm goofy-tired, and when you asked what we could hunt in the swamp, I got this sudden image of Torald stuffing a manatee carcass into his manpurse."

Torald grimaced. "The owner of said manpurse gives that plan a preemptive veto."

Devon laughed. "Anyway, I guess we should set a watch order and rotate who gets to log out for food or nap or whatever. I'm thinking you should go first, Hailey, seeing as Magda found you sleeping in-game. Why don't you grab some real-life rest?"

All at once, Hailey looked stricken, and Devon wanted to smack herself on the forehead for having forgotten her theory that the woman was escaping some unpleasant real-life issues. Her friend stared at her feet for a while, and then finally met Devon's eyes. "Actually, I need to stay logged in for a while—got some character maintenance to do. I'll grab first watch."

From the following silence, Devon got the idea that the other group members were as skeptical as she was about Hailey's choice to stay logged in for so long. But like Devon, no one seemed to feel it was their place to comment.

"All right. Hailey has first watch. Any objections to just using our marching order to determine the rest of the rotation?"

When no one raised an argument, she nodded, then scooted over to rest her back against the wall. As she focused on the logout button, Hailey touched her forearm. Devon blinked to dispel the game interface and glanced at her friend. For just a moment, she felt a jealous frown on her face when she saw that Bob had appeared and taken up a perch on Hailey's shoulder.

"Have you got a second, Dev? I was hoping we could step outside for a couple of minutes. I want to..." She paused, seeming to fish for words. "I read in one of Ishildar's libraries about some kind of *Far Sight* ability. It could be pretty clutch for finding Hazel. I thought maybe you could give me a boost with *Levitate* so I could try looking over the treetops."

The woman was a terrible liar, and Devon got the feeling that everyone recognized the fabrication for what it was. But she didn't hesitate before grabbing hold of a chink in the wall and pulling with her arms as she shakily climbed to her feet. She swayed a little and nodded. "As long as you don't expect me to catch you if you fall off the *Levitation* spell or anything. I don't think I could lift a kitten at this point."

Chapter Twenty-One

HAILEY FELT LIKE her rib cage was shrinking over her lungs, making it harder and harder to breathe while she waited for Devon's reaction. Even though she'd told herself that she'd explain her situation to Devon gently, the moment she'd started talking, it had all come out in a rush. She'd started by explaining the auto-immune disease that had first struck around her twentieth birthday. First, the aching joints and circulation problems, then a rapid progression as her body started attacking her organs.

She'd already been on her own by then, her mom having passed away a few years before, and her dad living out his last couple years in a nursing home. They'd conceived her in their late fifties, an accidental consequence of hormone therapy and cheap—as in, poorly controlled—anti-aging programs. So when Hailey was forced to enter a care facility at twenty-three, her condition advancing so quickly that the doctors said she needed inpatient monitoring and care, no one had even been available to help her move in.

She'd lasted longer than the doctors had predicted. Almost ten more years, during which time she'd paid her bills by livestreaming her gaming exploits, hawking products as a minor digital influencer, and generally finding her place among a virtual community of gamers.

But the doctor had given her the final, grim prognosis around the time that Devon had returned from the hell plane having rescued Owen. He'd said Hailey had very little time to live and should put her affairs in order.

Enter Bob who, as a representative of Relic Online's arcane hive mind, a collectivist AI that had bootstrapped itself from spare processing and a steady stream of data, had approached her with a proposal. Apparently, the arcane realm's pursuit of knowledge and order included building simulations of human players. At the time, the construct that simulated Hailey had been nearly complete. She'd simply needed to transfer her awareness into the new digital substrate and, voila, her consciousness would live on indefinitely inside the game world.

Provided, of course, that the game world continued to exist.

"You're...you're dead," Devon finally said.

"My body is dead. I'm not."

"Like in science fiction and all those old LitRPG books."

"I guess so. I mean, it wasn't like the movies where there's some kind of brain scan that can automatically decide how to reconstruct a person. From what Bob tells me, the modeling process combines patterns recorded from the implants with observations of people's network traffic and in-game actions." She shrugged. "And so forth."

Devon shook her head, blinking. "Does anyone know? Besides Bob I mean."

"No one. I mean, it was pretty sudden. I could feel that my body was dying outside the game, and I had to make the choice. I'd tried to consider all the implications, but...it's kind of a big issue, you know?"

"Dude. Understatement."

Hailey felt a faint smile tug at her lips. Trust Devon to state things so concisely.

"So you can see why I haven't really known how to talk about it."

"And I also see why it's a bit awkward when someone suggests that you log out. Hailey, what happens if they find out? I mean, it's pretty much a game-changer for humanity."

"They meaning E-Squared?"

Devon shrugged. "I guess I mean...anyone. The company. The government. Religious leaders all over the world."

Hailey exhaled through loose lips. "I don't know. It was hard enough for me to decide for myself. I'm still not sure it was the right one...Catholic upbringing and all. I definitely don't want the responsibility for deciding whether or not to unleash this kind of thing on the world."

"Ugh. Yeah. Sounds great, real digital immortality. But there's that whole Law of Unforeseen Consequences thing."

"Right. And how good has humanity ever been at considering things ahead of time?"

"Heavy stuff, Hailey. It's like you've been doing that whole 'carrying the weight of the world on your shoulders' thing." Devon's mouth quirked in an ironic smile. "Even divided in two, that's still enough to crush someone."

Hailey hesitated, chest tightening around a knot of guilt. "I know. I—I hate laying this all on you. It's just—"

Devon cut her off by snatching her hand and squeezing. "I'm teasing you with the whole crushing thing. Sorry. But seriously, Hail. I need a little time to process this. It's pretty out there."

"Yeah, I get that. Anyway, I wanted to tell you earlier, but it's kind of a hard thing to bring up."

"Not exactly a small talk conversation." Devon's eyebrows drew together. "And I think it's more complicated than a simple choice of whether you want to reveal your situation to the world. Because regardless of your choice, you don't control the technology."

"Exactly. Like, on one hand I think about all the people I could help. People in my situation—the situation my body was in, I mean. But is E-Squared going to freely offer it to everyone? Doubtful. I can't help thinking about what they did to Owen, how their biggest concern about his coma was how it would affect their cash flow if the story got out. Part of the reason I ended up in a basic care facility just waiting for my organs to fail was that I wasn't rich or famous enough to be chosen for high-end therapies. If the executives in charge of Relic Online hear about what happened to me, I bet you anything their first thought will be how much they can charge people."

Bob, who had been perched quietly on Hailey's shoulder, its substance tickling her neck, shimmered in indignation. "As if the arcane realm would agree to provide patterning for characters at the behest of some money-grubbing CEO."

"You might change your mind if they threatened to power down the processor cores running your simulation," Hailey said. She sighed as she glanced up through the misty air to the hazy face of the moon. Unlike Earth's satellite, Aventalia's moon had a bluish cast, and the darker areas—the *seas* as they were called on Earth's moon—were more pronounced, their color a deep navy blue. For just a moment, she felt a touch of homesickness for the real world she'd never see again. But considering that her views of the night sky from her real body had been through a clean-room window for the last few years, the nostalgia didn't last.

"To be quite honest, I calculate around a 50% chance that the company would either attempt to delete your pattern or move it to an isolated testbed while they try to figure out how you were put together," Bob said. "Not that I expect they'd succeed without disfiguring the data. But as I've mentioned before, there is a high degree of uncertainty in my predictions due to Bradley Williams' status as a—to borrow your term—loose cannon."

Devon's brows drew together. "Can we back up a second? Aren't you concerned that they will just look up your avatar and see that you never log out?"

Hailey was still a little fuzzy on the details of that answer, though Bob had reassured her it wouldn't be a problem. She shrugged as Bob rose from her shoulder and started circling Devon's head.

"I wouldn't expect you to understand given your limited knowledge of neural networks and quantum states, but suffice to say, E-Squared doesn't have much visibility into the state of their game. If they want to know something, it's easier to comb through the forums or send a GM to play through content than it is to query a database."

"Okay..." Devon said. "So in terms of how to keep your condition secret, I guess your biggest problem is that people will start to notice that you aren't logging out?"

Hailey chewed her lip, not totally sure how many of her problems to lay on Devon at once. "It's a little more complicated, but at least for tonight, that's something of an issue. Think you can help cover for me?"

"Yeah, no problem," Devon said. "I'll tell those guys we swapped our turns standing watch because you had to log suddenly. If you can handle staying out here, that is."

Hailey shivered and glanced at her *Fatigue* bar. It was down to 85%, but it wouldn't drop much further until she could catch a nap. Sleeping in a swamp might not be the easiest prospect. Still, Devon's plan was probably the best answer. "I can make that work," she said. "But, hey Dev? There's one more thing. I'm not really sure how to put it, but when I agreed to this I didn't know that Valious was—"

Devon nodded. "That he was our boss and an actual employee of E-Squared. Yeah. I can see how that's an issue."

"I assumed the care facility would notify the company about my death, but they didn't, and that's one of the issues I'm dealing with. I hate to ask because I know you're..." What were Devon and Emerson anyway? They definitely hung out more than he did with any of the other gamers he'd hired. "Friends," she finished somewhat lamely.

A conflicted look crossed Devon's face. "I swear I won't say anything. I'm a shitty liar, but I don't think he's the most perceptive guy when it comes to body language or whatever."

Hailey nodded and swallowed and glanced toward the nearby swamp boundary. "I guess I'm going to go find somewhere to try to sleep, then," she said.

Devon abruptly stepped forward. Hailey stiffened at first as the other woman wrapped her arms around her, but she forced herself to return the hug. Devon wasn't exactly relaxed either, and when the embrace finished, she shuffled awkwardly. "Thanks for trusting me, Hailey. We'll figure it out, okay?"

"Yup," Hailey said, trying to sound more optimistic than she felt. "I'll see you when it's time for my watch."

Before the conversation could continue, she turned and straightened her shoulders and walked into the misty night.

Chapter Twenty-Two

HOLY SHIT. THOUGHTS about Hailey's situation were a whirlpool in Devon's mind. It was almost too much to fathom, the notion that her friend's entire life from here on out would be lived inside Relic Online. On one hand, it was like a dream. On the other, a curse. Whatever happened inside the game would be Hailey's actual reality. If the demons won, she could quite literally be locked in eternal torment.

And that didn't even get into the broader implications. When she stacked up the potential consequences alongside the moral dilemmas, the whole situation left Devon feeling like someone had shoved hand mixer through her ear and scrambled her brain.

Actually, that was a little gross. She grimaced, trying to forget that analogy.

Anyway, so much for the catnap she'd hoped to take now that she'd logged off while the other players took their turns standing watch. Trying to sleep now would be like trying to nod off in the middle of an earthquake.

She glanced at the makeshift curtain covering the window. It was mid-afternoon in St. George, not even close to dinnertime, but she had a feeling that Hazel's rescue would take most of the night. The pair of granola bars she'd had for breakfast weren't enough fuel for a marathon gaming session, but her stomach was churning as vigorously as her thoughts. She pushed back from the kitchen table and opened her pantry cabinet, scanning the shelves for something palatable. It was hard to go wrong with graham crackers and peanut butter, but the peanut butter jar had about two teaspoonfuls left. She shuffled to the freezer and peered inside. A frozen burrito was sure to send her straight to indigestion-land, but the contents of a box of frozen waffles looked vaguely edible. She opened the box, pulled out a couple of hockey pucks covered in freezer burn, and dropped them into the toaster.

As she was returning to the table to wait, someone knocked on the door.

Devon stood stock still, eyes wide. She glanced at her messages, but there was nothing from the apartment complex indicating that they planned to send a repair person to deal with her blind. Tiptoeing to the peephole, she peered out.

Oh.

What the...?

Crap.

Devon stared down in horror at her stay-at-home gamer attire, then glanced back out at Emerson, who was standing on the balcony with hunched shoulders, eyes flitting between her window and the door.

She tugged at the hem of her ratty T-shirt and looked at the faded text and graphic. Why did he have to show up when she was wearing a freaking bargain-bin shirt with that stupid donkey from Shrek pointing his butt out and mentioning something about ass? Not to mention, her sweatpants were just about the most hideous thing she owned. Frantic, she hopped to the coat hook on the nearby wall and yanked down a beige sweater-wrap thing with cuffs that had unraveled halfway up the forearms. Still, it was way better than proudly sporting a donkey butt shirt. She wrapped the sweater over her chest, dragged her fingers through the worst of her hair tangles, then scrubbed her cheeks with her knuckles in hopes of getting rid of any fabric imprints gained by lying on her couch while gaming.

With a deep breath, she ran her tongue over her teeth in a moment of sudden paranoia about stuck granola bits, then opened the door.

Emerson jumped, then coughed, then lost his balance and had to grab the railing behind him. He was wearing a zip-up sweatshirt with a windbreaker layer, and his pants had a crease that made her think he'd just bought them—she doubted he ironed his clothing. He clutched the handle to a paper bag in his right hand.

"I checked your network connection to make sure I wasn't bothering you while you were playing," he stammered before thrusting out the paper bag like a shield.

Devon blinked and accepted the bag. She shivered in the crisp winter air as she looked down at the sack. It was surprisingly heavy. "What's this? I mean..." She stepped back from the doorway. "Want to come in?"

Emerson glanced side to side as if worried he might be observed entering the home of a woman. "I—sure, if you don't mind. I don't want to impose. It's just, I felt..." He gestured at the bag. "I know how much Stonehaven means to you."

So this was a consolation visit? The same as when Tamara had shown up in the middle of the night with cookies? Devon waited for him to cross the threshold, then gently shut the door. She pulled out one of the kitchen chairs to offer him a seat, set the bag on the tabletop, and sat. When he glanced at her torso, she realized the sweater had fallen open to expose the donkey ass. Grimacing, she pulled the wrap tight again.

"So," she said. "I guess you were in town?"

He ran a hand through his hair, then squeezed the back of his neck. Devon realized that was a stupid question as he blinked, seeming to be sorting his words. Duh. Of course he was in town. The real question she'd meant to ask was whether he'd come just for her.

Emerson nodded, his eyes not quite meeting hers. "I thought you could use a friend."

"You were right. Thanks for coming," she said, realizing she meant it. A brief silence fell, and they both jumped when the toaster suddenly ejected the waffles.

Devon glanced from the counter to the table and back. "I was about to eat something. Do you want a waffle?"

Emerson flashed a smile. He'd been sitting with hands clutched together, but now he took a breath and untangled them, laying his palms on the table. "I grabbed some falafels while waiting to catch you when you logged off." His face twisted in an apologetic grimace. "Sorry if checking your network status is an imposition. I figured it was better than bothering you while you were in game. With everything going on with Stonehaven I mean."

Devon hesitated for a moment, then got up, checked that her sweater was still covering the donkey, and retrieved the waffles. The first bite tasted like sawdust, so she shuffled to the fridge in search of syrup or something. The shelves inside the door held an old jar of pickle relish, some Caesar salad dressing, and a squeezy bottle of tikka masala sauce that she knew was empty but had left in there as a reminder to order more. The other options for wetting down the waffles were milk or beer, but that would probably just dissolve whatever structure they'd managed to retain. As she started to reach for the pickle relish, she spotted a tub of yogurt. Much better.

Reclaiming her seat at the table, she realized she'd forgotten a fork, so got *back* up, fetched it, then tapped a glass of water.

During the whole operation, Emerson watched her quietly, not in a creepy way, but with tension in his posture like he was worried about disturbing her routine.

"Sorry about the curtain. My complex is supposed to be sending someone to fix the blind." Devon didn't know whether makeshift window treatments were something you were supposed to apologize for, but at least it gave her something to talk about.

Emerson glanced at the clothing hanging over the top of the broken blind and blinked as if noticing the decor for the first time. "It doesn't bother me," he said.

An awkward silence fell, which Devon first tried to cover by shoving a bite of waffle in her mouth. But then she got worried about making chewing noises, so she slid the plate of Tamara's cookies closer to him and pulled off the tea towel covering them. He smiled in gratitude and shook his head. "Still digesting the falafels." Then it seemed to occur to him that a conversation about digestion maybe wasn't the suavest topic, and he grimaced.

Devon swallowed with some difficulty since she hadn't chewed enough, then washed the bite down with a big swig of water. She set her fork down, deciding to wait for a few minutes before trying again.

"I didn't know you already had cookies," he said. "I mean, of course, I didn't know since you don't keep a webcam trained on your kitchen table. I mean"—he turned his hands over and raised his palms as if shrugging—"I thought you could use some comfort food and stuff." He gestured at the paper bag, which still stood unopened on the table.

Devon glanced at him, then stood and peered inside. She stuck a hand in and fished out a chocolate bar, then a quart-sized tub of ice cream, then a small bouquet of flowers, the stems wrapped in what looked like a hotel washcloth that had been soaked in water and stuffed into the vase.

"I was worried about spilling on the way over," he explained.

The outside of the ice cream container was wet with condensation. "I better get this in the freezer," she said. On the way over, she noticed that it sloshed a little.

Grabbing the flower vase, she dribbled in some tap water, then returned it to the table. The washcloth could come out later. Finally, she sat again. Emerson was shifting between looking at her expectantly and staring at his hands, which were once again clasping each other for support.

After a moment's hesitation, Devon reached out and touched his hands. She waited until he met her eyes, then she smiled. "Thank you. Really. It's about the nicest thing anyone's ever done."

"Really?" he asked, blinking. The corners of his mouth twitched in a shy smile. "I mean, I feel somewhat responsible for Stonehaven. If I were better at social engineering or straight-up manipulation, I can't help thinking that I could have talked some sense into Bradley about his idiot plan to leave Zaa active."

"It's not your fault he's crazy."

"Still."

"You want water or anything?" Devon said, dredging up memories of her mother's fumbling attempts at hospitality when people had come to one of their series of run-down apartments. Except it was rarely water that her mother had offered. Vodka, usually.

He shook his head. "I know you probably weren't planning to be offline for very long. Not with everything going on."

Devon stiffened, realizing that she'd lost track of time. She glanced at the clock in her interface and ran the mental math on what that would mean for the in-game passage of time. "I have a few minutes, but not much longer. We're camped on the southern edge of the savanna, heading into the swamp to rescue Hazel. I guess the demons have been building something down there." She sighed. "I'm trying to be optimistic, but it's hard to imagine winning this thing."

Emerson's eyebrows drew together. "You think it's that bad? Really?"

"I dunno." Devon pressed her lips together because all of a sudden, she was having a hard time controlling her emotions. "I mean—shit. It just all-around sucks. If it were just a game and the demons were to overrun the continent, I guess your company could wipe the game state and start over. If another title didn't swoop in and capture the player base while everyone was pissed off that they kept getting gibbed within seconds of spawning."

"Uh, gibbed?"

"You can pronounce it like jibbed, too. It's not really an RPG term. I had a brief stint playing shooters."

"Oh..kay?" Emerson said. "You're kinda speaking in an alien tongue." He shrugged and smiled crookedly, seeming surprisingly comfortable with his lack of knowledge. Maybe he was finally settling into the fact that he'd shown up at her apartment uninvited, and that Devon hadn't been annoyed or anything. Even though the whole attraction thing was now in the mix, Devon couldn't help thinking back to their conversations at other times, how they'd both been keen to skip the small talk and get to discussing something real.

"So, shooters are those games where you basically...shoot at things, I guess. It's a little more complicated because it depends on the game whether it's just shooting—lots of times there are different roles. Some people are responsible for planting explosives or driving a tank or whatever. Sometimes the games are realistic war simulators, and sometimes it's like space marines versus weird aliens. Anyway 'shooters' is kinda short for first-person shooters, but most people just call them FPS games when typing. Of course, since advanced VR took over, everything is in first person since you're shoved into the game with full sensory immersion. The experience just isn't the same if you're not inside your character."

"Got it," he said, then grimaced. "I don't think I'd be a big fan of VR shooters. Getting shot to bits isn't on my bucket list or anything."

Devon found herself smiling. "Says the guy who probably holds the Relic Online record for the highest number of deaths before level 10."

"That's different," he said with a timid laugh.

"Yeah, I know. Anyway, gibbed is basically a term for getting killed, but it comes from the gory explosion where people get reduced to chunks of meat. It's technically short for giblets. That's why there's the whole gibbed or jibbed thing. Giblets with a 'g,' pronounced like it's got a 'j.' *Anyway*, you don't need a gamer grammar lesson from me."

He smirked. "I'm always glad to learn something new."

Devon pulled her plate back over and cut off a bite with the edge of her fork. As she started chewing, Emerson's eyes went distant. He was probably checking something on his implants.

"I get what you mean about the difference between Relic Online and normal games," he said. "Wiping the game state would be like..." He shrugged. "You know."

"Like mass murder. At least, that's what I think since the NPCs have their own thoughts and desires and stuff."

Emerson nodded. "Sentience. It sounds kind of arrogant to say it, seeing as I'm sorta responsible for configuring and training Veia to create the content. But I can't help feeling like it's true."

"I wish more people got it."

"Maybe they do."

Devon shrugged. "Maybe. I guess I haven't been paying attention to the buzz. But there's so much AI all around us, and it all seems smart, but we're pretty much conditioned to think of it as machinery. Like the autocab driver or whatever. You have to befriend the NPCs in-game to really see how they're different."

"You know what I think...I think there are other players out there that think like we do about the NPCs. But it's kind of like, if the story hit the media, there would be a big political mess from people who are scared of AI taking over the world. That or Bradley would find some other way to try to monetize things in a way that would ruin the NPCs' lives. So those players probably keep quiet with their opinions."

His comment about Bradley reminded Devon of Hailey's concern that E-Squared would try to use her situation for profit, which brought the whole thing with Hailey back to the front of her mind. Which made her feel suddenly awkward talking to Emerson because she knew that it was going to be a major problem to try to hide her friend's status from his avatar.

Especially considering that Emerson had recently asked Devon for help tracking down the issue with the failed salary payment into Hailey's account. The truth was, if Hailey really wanted to keep her condition hidden, she and Emerson couldn't be playing in the same area. And if Devon didn't want to screw up and give away her friend's secret, she would have to cut off contact with one of them. Even if she agreed to keep lying for Hailey, she just didn't trust herself to keep the guilt off her face.

The waffle felt dry as it slid down her throat. Devon took a deep drink of water.

"Guess it's about time for you to get back," Emerson said. "I really didn't mean to distract you. I know how important it is for you to be online and doing what you can to fight off the demons."

Devon sighed and nodded, relieved that he'd been the one to raise the topic again. She didn't want to have to kick him out, but the reminder of Hailey's situation along with her worry for Stonehaven had sent her nerves into overdrive.

She grabbed the chocolate bar and peeled away one end of the wrapper. Breaking off a square, she offered the bar out to him. Emerson shook his head. "It's a gift."

As they stood from the table, his nervousness seemed to return full force. All of a sudden, his fingers started rubbing against the base of his palms, and then he ran a hand through his hair again.

Yeah...goodbye time. How was this supposed to work?

"So how long are you in town?" she asked.

"Actually, I took a little time off work. Feeling kinda disillusioned, you know? So I was thinking that if you're up for...I dunno...grabbing lunch or dinner or maybe figuring out a place where we could log in at the same time...I thought it might be nice to hang out a little."

Devon's pulse sped up, and she wasn't sure whether it was excitement or terror. She swallowed while trying to piece together a response, then took a couple of steps toward the door.

"I—yeah, that would be nice. Can I drop a line when I get my character back from the swamp? I have a feeling it will be kind of a marathon session until then."

Emerson exhaled in obvious relief. "I'd like that."

At the open doorway, they stood awkwardly in the afternoon sunlight. After a couple of seconds, Devon opened her arms for a hug. Emerson stumbled a bit when he tried to step forward, and he pretty much collided with her, jamming her back into the corner of the door jamb.

"Sorry," he said, quickly jumping back. "You okay?"

"I'm fine. No problem," Devon said even though the knobs of her spine hurt from being scraped. To spare him further embarrassment, she stepped forward this time and quickly wrapped her arms around his upper back. As he returned the hug, his Adam's apple bobbed against her forehead. Not sure how long was appropriate to maintain the embrace, Devon held on in hopes he would give her a cue. As time stretched on and neither of them moved, she gave a quick squeeze, which he returned. Still, he didn't let go.

A door down the terrace opened, and the guy she always ran into in the laundry area stepped out with a backpack in hand. He had a bandanna tied around his head. Heading out for a hike? Either way, she let go of Emerson and stepped back, glad someone had come along to rescue them.

"Talk soon?" Emerson said, his cheeks a bit flushed as he stepped away.

Devon nodded. "I'll message you. And thanks again for thinking of me."

Chapter Twenty-Three

"WELL SHIT," SOME guy behind Ashley said as the first ranks of the marching army reached yet another sheer drop where the Skargill Mountains fell away into a chasm that might as well have been bottomless. The speaker had kind of an annoying voice—nasal and somehow conniving. She could forgive or ignore the way people sounded in real life, but this guy must have gone through the same character creation system as everyone else, which meant he'd chosen something obnoxious on purpose.

Par for the course when grouping up with the kind of people who wanted to be in Nil's guild. Or rather, the kind of people that wanted to *stay* in Nil's guild. Even the name was dumb. Blood-soaked Blades, BBs to people who were too embarrassed to say the name aloud. If anyone who knew her from other games heard about the outfit she'd joined up with for Relic Online, they'd probably laugh their asses off. Her explanation that it had been the only PvP guild with any power early on wouldn't matter. Of course, it was still the only guild with power because of the whole momentum thing. Anyone who wasn't an actual asshole but who still liked to PvP was stuck joining the BBs if they wanted a chance at taking down worthy objectives.

Anyway, the situation wasn't permanent. She'd approached a couple more players lately, people she'd been grouped with who'd kinda made it known that they didn't agree with Nil's plan to go after the Stonehaven people again. Especially not the way Nil wanted to do it, where they'd start by taking out the NPC defenders and whatever fortifications were present, and they'd end by killing the players slowly and repeatedly. Nil was seriously obsessed with this vendetta thing, and it kinda turned Ashley's stomach. Seemed she wasn't the only one, and these other two players, a level twenty-seven Conjurer and a level twenty-five Knight had pretty much agreed to split off when Ashley founded a new guild.

But it was slow going recruiting people only when she'd grouped with them long enough to get a feel for their opinions on Nil. Not just a feel for them, actually. She needed to know their discomfort with the guild leader was strong enough that they wouldn't decide to tattle on her.

Ashley had no illusions about what it would be like when she betrayed Nil. In game, there would be wars between Nil's people and her new guild. Out of game, the harassment tactics that the BBs had been using on that livestreamer, Hailey, would be turned on her instead. Ashley needed powerful allies, characters with the levels and gear and play skill to stand against Nil. And she needed guild members who knew how to deal with doxers and hackers, ideally on defense only, but on offense if things got bad.

So, for now, she had to keep her head down and do her best to make sure she stood out as an indispensable part of Nil's army. The promotion to lieutenant would get her the authority to start organizing groups where her small core of allies could start watching for like-minded players. She'd have a chance to interact with other leader-type players, people with the gear and skill she needed to build out her fighting force.

All of which meant going along with this attack on the allies and followers of that player, Devon.

"Are you complaining?" Nil said with a snarl, his elven features twisted as he looked at the nasally voiced player who'd cursed upon seeing the drop. "Because it sounds to me like you're complaining."

Ashley closed her eyes, hoping that the other dude would just let it go. Apologize if it came to it. If Nil threw him over the cliff, chances were fifty-fifty that the guild leader would then decide that they needed to camp and wait for the guy to respawn and run back to the group. At which point Nil might throw him off again. It was stupid and a waste of time, but Nil preferred to rule with cruelty and fear than intelligence. Probably because he didn't have enough of the latter.

"Just wishing we were there already. That bitch Devon and her friends need to die," said Nasal-Voice.

Ashley cast a glance over her shoulder, careful to keep her disgust for the guy's attitude off her face. Calling female gamers bitches, especially after losing to them, was the classic mark of Nil's kind of person. It was also a sure giveaway of someone with insecurity issues and not a lot of friends. The nasal voice came from a toon decked out in caster gear—that was a surprise, actually. She'd expected a melee class. People with his kind of attitude usually preferred to be close enough to smell someone's fear as they killed them. She checked his class. Another Conjurer. That was even weirder since that class required a ton of play skill. Getting max combat effectiveness required excellent situational awareness and deep knowledge of how to combo various conjurations depending on the enemy's strengths.

"Yeah, with you there," Nil said, apparently pleased by the answer. "These detours suck balls."

Ashley hadn't realized she was still staring at the Conjurer until Nil turned away and the other character's true feelings showed on his face. The guy actually curled his lip in disgust at the guild leader, but when he realized that Ashley was watching, his eyes widened in fear. Ashley had a moment of panic as well when she realized that the guy had known exactly the right thing to say to Nil. So he was smart. If he thought she might rat him out, he might preemptively try to undermine her.

She fixed his face and character name—Fiall—in her mind, hoping to talk to him in private ASAP. It would have to be in-game and out of earshot of other guild members—knowledge of out-of-game contact information was limited by the guild hierarchy. Lieutenants could contact peons, Nil's inner circle could contact lieutenants and peons, and Nil could contact anyone. All designed to prevent the kind of coup Ashley hoped to pull off, of course.

Anyway, since it looked like they'd be marching for quite a ways to find a point where the chasm was narrow enough for the Mages to portal people across, Ashley guessed she might be able to get Fiall alone. She hoped.

For now, she shrugged as if to say that his reaction to Nil didn't bother her. Fiall examined her for a moment, then turned aside.

"Nil," someone else called from the rear ranks of the march. Having swollen to over three hundred people, the army was bigger than any guild she'd been in. It often took a good ten minutes for the people in the back to arrive at a stopping point.

"What?"

"Got more news from the inside. Info on the current defenses and weak points."

"From Jeremy or someone else?"

"Still just Jeremy. He said he hasn't had any luck finding others ready to turn coat. But he said that Devon recently entrusted him with some more responsibility, so it will be even easier for him to open up vulnerabilities."

Nil's face looked even more angular when he grinned. "Nice. I can almost taste the victory already."

Ashley closed her eyes. Just one more conquest with these people and she could go her own way.

Chapter Twenty-Four

"ALMOST MAKES ME wish we were getting ambushed by demons," Magda muttered as she stepped forward to take up the lead. Swamp water sloshed around her knees, and strands of trailing algae dotted with clumps of scum and rafts of dead insects wrapped her leather pants. From up on her *Levitation* cushion, Devon looked down with sympathy, but she knew better than to say anything. Speaking would just draw attention to how comfortably she floated above the muck.

"Me too," Torald said. "I keep thinking tadpoles are swimming in my boots. I'm worried I'm going to take them off at the end of this and find tadpole jelly under my feet."

"Ew," Hailey said.

"I know, right?"

"I swear you people are the whiniest group I've ever traveled with," Greel muttered. "Marching in your perfect starborn bodies, formed from the aether as adults with no past injuries to pain you in the night, no twists in your spine earned by a brutal goblin attack when you were just a child..."

Devon grimaced at the man's words. Greel rarely talked about his past. The fact that he was bringing it up now meant he was probably in enormous discomfort. Shoving her hand into her *Sparklebomb Backpack of Subpar Holding*, she summoned her inventory screen and started scrolling through the contents. She stared at the *Jungle Energy Potion - Major* until a tooltip appeared explaining that the potion would reduce *Fatigue* and discomfort. Unfortunately, the variety of potions Hezbek had concocted from jungle ingredients tasted awful—like, dead-rat-barf awful—and so far, Hezbek hadn't discovered a savanna version. Still, next time they stopped, she'd discreetly offer it to Greel. Maybe the pain relief would be worth the disgusting taste.

"Is there anything I can carry for you, Greel?" Torald asked. "My manpurse has plenty of space, and I don't feel the weight."

Out of the paladin's line of sight, Devon shook her head as she prepared for the lawyer's outburst. There was a reason she planned to offer the potion discreetly. But to her abundant shock, Greel didn't bite Torald's head off. Metaphorically or by chewing through the paladin's scalp and thick skull with a hundred slices of his razor-sharp fighting knives. Instead, he just shook his head, adjusted his pack, and kept sloshing forward.

"We all have our burdens," the lawyer said. "Some of us just manage to bear them with a modicum of stoicism."

"A what?" Magda asked.

As if on cue, Bob swirled out from behind a decaying log. "He means—"

"Shut up, Bob," Hailey and Devon said at once.

"Well, fine. I guess I'll go where my vocabulary is appreciated." The wisp gave Hailey's nose a sullen boop before it faded off into the mist. This time, Devon felt no jealousy. She wasn't on the quest to become Champion of Ishildar anymore, so she didn't need a guide. But if there was a chance that the wisp could help Hailey navigate her situation, Devon was more than happy for Bob to try.

Hailey smirked as the last glow from the wisp melted into the swamp mist. "Anyway, we may get lucky and get ambushed by demons while trudging through the swamp. Ever think about that?"

"Shut. Up," Magda said, turning a fake glare on Hailey. Everyone laughed, but the tension in the air was unmistakable. Devon peered into the surroundings, wishing for clear sight lines, but the curtains of moss and tendrils of mist closed in on the view, hiding everything more than fifty to one hundred feet away. She shivered and pulled up her mini-map.

The Grukluk Swamp was about as wide as it was deep, stretching from the Noble Coast northward to where it butted up against the savanna. The Argenthal Mountains bounded the swamp on its eastern border, the range gentling from its jagged northern spires to rounded humps that struck out into the Noble Sea as a chain of islands that resembled a giant sea serpent's spine. West of the swamp, a massive bay carved a chunk from the continent. The coastline there was a morass of mangroves that Hazel had noted as largely impassable during an earlier scouting trip. At the head of the bay, three rivers flowed into the sea, though only the easternmost watercourse was fully mapped, starting with tributaries in the savanna, passing the site of the Drowned Burrow, and joining into a mid-sized river that once again divided into a branching network of streams at its delta near the bay.

Of course, looking at the layout of the landscape as a whole was a nice distraction from the buzzing, biting insects and the worry of demon ambush, but what Devon really needed to inspect was the notations Hazel had made regarding the current situation in the area.

The party's location appeared on the map as a little green blip. So far, they'd traveled around thirty percent of the distance between the savanna and the coast. The Fortress of Shadows—or rather, the sunken temple that was now a deserted ruin—lay almost directly east of their position with the demon installation sandwiched between. Between the installation and the savanna, the scout had sketched an almost straight line running north-south. Hazel had called this a *Bridge Road,* which Devon had been assuming meant there was some sort of causeway raised above the level of the swamp. Normally, that would have been a much better choice for their route south, except that Hazel had also written *(unfortunately, demons)* along the line.

As for the installation, more details had emerged now that they were close enough for it to show up on a zoomed-in map. Alongside a sketch of what looked like an Egyptian step pyramid were the words *Black Fortress, can't approach. Major demon presence.* None of that sounded good, but that was where the quest marker indicated Devon should go. She'd briefly considered rescuing Hazel first, then checking out this fortress-installation thing. But that would mean backtracking for at least a couple hours, not to mention putting Hazel and her ostrich in danger. Besides, they weren't planning to try to attack the fortress or anything, just check it out.

Just as she was about to close her map interface, she noticed a toggle that let her view historical position information. She grimaced when she saw the snaking course they'd taken through the swamp. They must have walked twice the distance they needed in terms of straight-line progress.

"Okay, guys," she said. "We need to start heading almost directly east. Anybody have the *Sense Heading* skill? I know it's a challenge, but we've been weaving back and forth a ton."

"I know it's a challenge," Greel parroted in a mocking voice. "Do you? Because it seems to me you're just floating over all the submerged logs and tangled sticks we have to weave around."

Devon's nostrils flared as she took a deep breath. Maybe she wouldn't give him that potion after all.

"I'm just hoping to save you the effort of—"

"Hey, guys?" Hailey said, cutting Devon off. The woman was pointing into the swamp ahead. While they watched, a dark mass curled forward from the swamp, writhing between the trees and snuffing all light save for a purple glow that pulsed in the darkness every few seconds.

"Uh. Doesn't look very welcoming," Torald said.

Devon shook her head as she checked the map again. No, they definitely hadn't reached this installation thing, and yes, the dark fog stuff *definitely* stood between them and their goal.

"Well," she said, "I guess we should buff up."

***

As the party moved deeper into the murky darkness, the group members walked closer and closer together. Devon started to worry that she'd step on someone's head if she didn't watch her feet as they paddled on her *Levitation* cushion. She cast a tier 1 *Levitation* spell over the top of the higher-tier version to lower her max height. The previous spell effect ended gracefully, lowering her to within just a few inches of the surface of the swamp water. Of course, then she felt vulnerable without the minor advantage her height had gained, and she grimaced as she glanced side to side at the nearly featureless surroundings. Trees grasped at them, extending skeletal limbs from the darkness like some kind of creepy-ass Halloween ghouls. Ghouls shedding their gray-green skin in the form of desiccated strips of bark and scrappy sections of hanging moss.

It was the kind of situation that brought out the worst in people's personalities. On edge, Devon's friends snapped at one another over things that otherwise would have passed without comment. Ahead of her in line, even intrepid Hailey walked with hunched shoulders, her head turning neither left nor right as if looking at the surroundings would make them real by the acknowledgment.

So far, they'd been marching through the darkness for about twenty in-game minutes. Torald took the lead, his platemail shining faintly in the murk as the magic from the group's collection of buffs danced over his body's surface. He held his sword before him as usual, still not seeming to tire despite the effort it must have taken to maintain such a massive weapon in the guard position, but something in the set of his shoulders made Devon feel even iller at ease. Ordinarily, the man looked, even from behind, as if his chest were puffed out beneath the steel plates defending his torso. Now, Devon got the uncomfortable feeling that inside his armor, he walked with shoulders hunched over a collapsed chest like he'd just taken a blow to the gut.

She considered asking him whether everything was okay but decided that her perception of her friends was probably just skewed by the oppressive surroundings. To quiet her nerves, she pulled up the map again. They'd probably covered around half the distance between where they'd entered the miasma and the supposed location of this demon-built fortress thing. Just another twenty minutes or so to go, then they could check out the installation and beat a quick retreat toward Hazel's position.

As Devon made the mental gesture to dispel the map interface, a shriek from one of her party members sent a frigid bolt down her spine. She slapped for the hilt of her dagger while sidestepping to try to see around Hailey, who'd stopped short at the scream. Ahead, the bodies of her friends were a tangle of shadows accented by the wavering lights from the buffs and the dull glints of armor buckles and blades. She couldn't tell what the hell was going on until Greel streaked past her, his eyes white-rimmed and his lips drawn back from his teeth. The expression on his face was one of utter terror.

"Shit!" she yelled. "How many?"

"I don't know! I don't see...ugh..." Torald's response trailed off in a sort of low groan. Still, Devon heard no sounds of combat, no thunks or grunts or screeching of demons. Frantic, she dumped mana into casting a *Glowing Orb*. When it materialized in her hand, she threw the ball of light forward, squinting to get a picture of the scene. Magda was still standing, the druid's head whipping back and forth in search of a target, and Hailey remained stock still, her spine rigid. Torald had gone down on a knee, the water now reaching almost to his hips, and he'd planted his blade point-down in the muck. His head was bowed.

There wasn't an enemy in sight.

Light glowed around Hailey's hands for a moment, then winked out. Her cast bar flashed and vanished too fast for Devon to read the name of the spell she'd started to activate.

"Damn it," Hailey muttered. "Wrong thing."

"Can someone tell me what's going on?" Devon said as she yanked open her combat log.

> Greel has been afflicted with *Fear* with a duration of 45 seconds.
>
> You successfully resist the *Fear* effect. (95% chance due to *Bravery* score of 10)
>
> Magda successfully resists the *Fear* effect. (-1 charge on *Nature's Resilience*, 2 charges remaining)
>
> Torald successfully resists the *Fear* effect. (45% chance due to the passive resistance vs evil)
>
> Faced with evidence of the power of his deity's nemesis, Torald is afflicted by *Weakened Resolve*.
>
> Hailey begins to cast *Dispel Illusions*.
>
> Hailey's spell cast was canceled.

Crap. Devon hated *Fear* effects. They weren't as bad as *Confusion*, which usually caused players to start attacking their friends, but *Fear* really, really sucked.

She whirled, trying to track Greel's headlong sprint. If they lost him out here, they might never find him again. Fortunately, the man was trying, unsuccessfully, to clamber into one of the nearby trees.

Hailey's hands began to glow again, and this time the cast bar remained active, steadily filling as the timer expired. Moments later, the *Recognize Falsehoods* buff appeared in Devon's interface.

Greel went rigid as the spell struck and then, stock still, he stared at the tree he'd been trying to climb. The lawyer pulled out his blade and hacked off a twig as if to punish the offending tree. As Devon cast another *Glowing Orb* to illuminate the scene, Greel turned, red-faced, with hands balled into fists.

"Just so we're clear, my loss of courage there was a result of unnatural magical influences."

Magda breathed a sigh of relief. "Thanks, Hailey. My *Nature's Resilience* spell has an hour refresh timer. I thought we were hosed."

Lips pressed into a straight line, Hailey nodded. "Don't thank me yet. Refresh timer on that buff is longer than the duration. If we're not out of the influence of whatever caused that *Fear* spell in the next 30 minutes, I won't be able to do anything."

Still down on a knee, Torald shook his head. "I'm afraid I may be unable to advance any closer to our enemy's stronghold. My companions will have to carry Veia's light to the evil-doers without me."

"Uh..." Magda said. "I don't think attacking a demon fortress without a tank is such a good idea."

"Pardon me, but I was under the impression this was a scouting mission," Greel said. "I know that starborn can be foolishly hasty in the decision to initiate combat, trusting their automatic reincarnation to remedy any ill effects of the misguided act, but—"

"We're not attacking, Greel," Devon said, cutting him off. "But if a fight were to happen *to* us, I assume you aren't volunteering to soak up all the damage."

The lawyer grumbled something about speaking precisely if one had a certain meaning to convey but otherwise remained quiet.

Devon examined her friends' faces in the wan blue glow from her orb. After a moment, Torald staggered to his feet, but he swayed and left his blade partially submerged in the water. That alone was proof that he couldn't lead the group any deeper into the murk.

She glanced at her quest log again, but the mission to investigate the installation was still one of the requirements for completing the quest. Shaking her head, she shared the map pin for Hazel's approximate location with the group, something she should have done in the first place.

"Okay, you guys. There's no point in all of us going forward here. Whether it's a group of five or just me, we won't be taking out the demon force occupying the installation. As Greel pointed out, this is a scouting mission only. With the way you guys slosh through the water, you're more likely to alert the enemy of our approach than anything. Head on to Hazel's position and wait for me."

Hailey blinked, fixing Devon with a hard stare. "What happens if you die? You're our taxi out of the swamp."

"I guess if I haven't turned up by nightfall to teleport everyone to Ishildar, try making your way back north. I'll get another group together and meet you at the ruin where we camped." Of course, just the thought of fighting her way south through the savanna again sent a wave of exhaustion through Devon's limbs. She'd do it if she had to, but maybe the next time she would bring a real off-tank.

"I hate to leave you here in the depths of enemy territory," Torald said. He tried to straighten up, but his armor seemed too heavy for his frame.

"If it helps, I won't tell your paladin friends that your chivalry and valor were overcome by something so simple as a heinous debuff," Devon said.

He smirked. "You know me too well. Fair enough." He glanced at the remaining party members. "Shall we head out before Hailey's spell expires?"

Greel snorted. "If only our fearless leader would have thought of this *before* we marched through oppressive darkness for half an hour. Let's get out of here."

Chapter Twenty-Five

ADVANCING ALONE, DEVON decided to stick with the tier 1 *Levitation* so that she remained near to the ground. If she encountered a group of demons, she was pretty much screwed regardless of her height advantage. Better to stay inconspicuous. To further lower the chances of getting jumped, she cast a *Simulacrum* of herself and set it marching around twenty paces ahead of her. If she had the bad luck of running into demons, the decoy might buy her a chance to escape.

Plus, as stupid as it seemed, the presence of the illusion made her feel a little less alone and therefore, a little braver.

As she continued toward the fortress, the terrain grew gradually higher, and patches of boggy earth emerged from the still water of the swamp. The air even felt a little less humid, but it was also eerily quiet. Devon certainly didn't blame the frogs and insects from leaving the region; even if it weren't for the demon infestation, living in perpetual darkness would kind of suck. But the silence made her feel as if every rustle of her *Raiment of the Keeper* and creak of her leather armor could be heard from miles away.

She'd just checked her map again when she spied a line of what appeared to be green-burning torches and stopped short. Devon dropped to a crouch and dispelled her *Simulacrum*, hoping it hadn't drawn the attention of any demons near those points of light. She held her breath while waiting for an alarm to be raised. After maybe five minutes with no movement and no sound from the vicinity of the flames, she took a deep breath and picked out a path where she could move from tree to tree and stay in relatively good cover while approaching the lights.

As she neared the row of torches, she realized they were placed atop a long raised platform. Moments later, it dawned on her that she'd come upon Hazel's so-called *Bridge-Road*. The causeway, in other words. Hazel had mentioned a significant demon presence on the road, but the raised surface was currently deserted. Devon checked her map. She had indeed intersected the line of the causeway a short distance north of the location of the fortress, having deviated from her original bearing by a small amount. Still, it would be good to get an idea of how well-traveled the roadway was, so she settled in to watch and wait.

After maybe half an hour, she heard something approaching from the direction of the fortress, the thud of footsteps along with what sounded like the creaking of cart or wagon wheels. A few minutes later, the wagon appeared, a massive thing crafted from dark wood and pulled by a team of the most gargantuan hell hounds she'd seen in the game. The hounds yipped and snarled as the driver, a level 27 Demon Thrall, cracked a whip onto their backs. To either side of the conveyance, a guard of six more thralls escorted the wagon, and the apparent foreman of the hauling team, a level 30 Demon Ravager, brought up the rear.

Using the trunk of a tree to disguise her form, Devon stood to her full height in hopes of glimpsing the contents of the wagon. Strangely, it appeared to either be empty, or the load was so small she couldn't see it over the sides of the wagon bed. As the small caravan moved past her and headed north into the darkness, she sat back on her heels to think it over. Whatever they were transporting, it seemed that the cargo was probably being sent from the savanna region to the fortress only. This wasn't a two-way supply route.

Not long after, another wagon appeared in the opposite direction. Even without looking inside, Devon could tell her theory had been confirmed. Whining and sweat-soaked, the hell hounds rolled their eyes and strained against their harnesses, and the demon with the whip struck twice as hard and often. The guards seemed more alert, but Devon might have been imagining that. When the Ravager boss was a few paces past her, Devon once again stood to get a glimpse of the cargo. Unfortunately, between the darkness and her distance from the causeway, she couldn't quite figure out what she was seeing. It *looked* like the demons were transporting a pair of massive black cubes—glass from the player camp?—but she couldn't be sure. She shrugged as the procession vanished into the darkness, then she slowly retreated from the causeway. Once again, she summoned her decoy. She proceeded toward the installation, setting a course roughly parallel to the demons' roadway.

The fortress emerged so gradually from the darkness that she didn't notice it at first. As Hazel had sketched, it was indeed shaped like a step pyramid. The laden wagon had arrived at a dark opening that seemed to be the gate, and the Ravager was barking orders at a group of demons milling outside the structure. The ground around the pyramid stood above the water, though in the dim light, she couldn't tell whether the demons had constructed the foundation platform or whether they'd built on the natural high point. Either way, a good hundred yards of barren terrain stood between the nearest cover-lending tree and the rise of the pyramid. She wouldn't be able to get very close, but she could still get a little closer and gather whatever information was available.

Devon crept forward, eyes pinned to the massive structure. Only a few of the green torches burned on the surrounding platform, just enough to throw glints off the glassy surface of the pyramid itself. The structure also seemed to glow from within, hints of deep purple leaking between the dark streaks as if the walls were ever-so-slightly translucent.

She stopped when she'd reached the final rank of spindly swamp trees.

You have discovered: Ziggurat of the Damned (60% Complete).

Among the highest tier of demonic military installations, a completed ziggurat has a wide sphere of influence that can counteract any defensive bonuses conferred by a Veian Temple.

Ziggurats are notoriously difficult to build because they require a large supply of glass blocks quarried from an area where earth or sand has been molten by hellfire and infused with bones of incinerated mortals.

Unfortunately, it seems that the demons recently encountered just the necessary conditions.

But at least you gain 100000 discovery experience. Good job.

And also:

Quest objective complete: Investigate the demon installation near the Fortress of Shadows

Well, crap. There went any hope Devon might have nurtured about hiding, indefinitely, within the protection of Ishildar's Veian temple. She glanced at one of the guards standing near the base of the ziggurat and used *Combat Assessment*.

Demon Elite - Level 35
Health: 4659/4659
You are unlikely to survive an encounter.

Perfect. Not only would the completion of this building eradicate her best defense, but also, she didn't have any hopes of attacking and winning.

This scouting mission really wasn't going well.

As Devon started to retreat, a deep voice tore through the swamp. "Betrayer! I sense you."

Devon froze and, without thinking, laid a hand on her chest as if to ask, "Me?"

"Ezraxis." The voice practically dripped hatred. "Once, you came to me to learn. I taught you the power of blood. Guided you in your quest. And then you betrayed our god."

Yep. He was talking to her all right. Devon glanced behind her to keep from tripping over something as she continued her retreat. When she returned her gaze to the installation, she grimaced as she saw a massive figure emerge from within the ziggurat. She didn't need to use *Combat Assessment* to recognize the monster, but she did it anyway.

Archdemon Gaviroth - Esteemed Vessel of Zaa's Will.

As Torald had reported, there was no further information about the NPC's level or health or challenge rating. Which basically meant she could probably die by just *thinking* of attacking him.

"Worm," the demon roared as she took another step back. "Reveal yourself, and you will be spared a small fraction of the torment that is your inevitable punishment."

"Hmm. No. I think I'll decline," Devon mouthed into the thick swamp air.

As if in response to her silent words, the demon drew himself up even taller. He was a collection of shadows more than a physical form, the darkness writhing in sickening patterns. Great horns of smoke towered above the demon's head.

"Your defeat approaches," he shouted, the reverberation causing puddles of water to ripple. "Perhaps you can hide now, but you cannot hide from the inevitable."

Devon had nearly reached the point where she could no longer see the fortress or the archdemon through the dark miasma surrounding it. She quickened her retreat until the lines of the ziggurat and the dull green glow of the torches disappeared entirely, and then she turned and set a straight course for Hazel's location.

People who liked to try to sound wise always said that knowledge was power. But at this precise moment, Devon was kind of wishing she could forget what she'd just learned.

Chapter Twenty-Six

THE SOUND OF dishes being washed filtered from the diner's kitchen. A faint haze hung in the air, smelling of cultured bacon sizzling in its smoke-infused fat. The restaurant was full enough to cover any awkward silences, but that had rarely been a problem when Emerson spent time with Devon. He found her gaming stories endlessly fascinating, but more than that, he appreciated the glimpses of what lay beneath the outer shell she showed the world. Of course, back when he was recruiting for his team of pro gamers, he'd hired a PI who had delivered a brief overview of Devon's life—the years after her mother had kicked her out when Devon was sixteen, anyway. Thinking of those days, he couldn't help a flush of embarrassment and guilt over the violation of privacy. But done was done, and mostly he felt grateful for the opportunity to get to know her for real, now.

Spread between their cups of coffee, tiles for the classic game, Settlers of Catan, were laid out in a rough hexagon. Devon leaned forward, examining the board, and a strand of hair escaped from where it was tucked behind her ear. She twisted her mouth in an expression of concentration, then traded a few resources from her stockpile. Blinking for a moment, she then nodded. "Veia's turn."

Emerson lifted his tablet to acknowledge her words. The board game had been his idea, something to look at besides the insides of their coffee cups and each other's faces. Not that he minded looking at her face, but he'd never really figured out exactly how long eye contact was supposed to last before it started to make the other person uncomfortable.

Of course, as he'd quickly browsed through the stock at the downtown game store, choosing his purchase based on the picture on the box, he hadn't bothered to read the number of required players. Turned out, Settlers of Catan required at least three. That was one benefit of being the creator of a general AI. He'd forked another instance of mini-Veia, detuned her processing capacity to bring her down to the level of an intelligent human, and handed her a copy of the game's instructions.

Of course, it might have been a slightly better experience to have chosen a game that didn't require a third player, but Devon seemed to be having fun. And she didn't mind the slight awkwardness when Emerson held a little wireless camera over the board at the start of Veia's turn, nor the interruptions when the AI used the audio feed from his implants to tell him how to move her pieces.

As for the game itself, Emerson was having a great time. He'd played a couple of times in college, but he hadn't really remembered the rules. Devon, it turned out, had never played, but that didn't stop her from picking up the rules faster than he'd managed to remember them.

Also, as far as he could surmise, she was absolutely destroying both him and his AI. That was pretty awesome.

Emerson picked up the dice and rolled for Veia, then grabbed the resources that the roll earned him and his AI. "So after you saw this ziggurat building, things went smoothly?"

Devon nodded. "When I found Hazel and the rest of my group, they were sitting around a small fire. They'd screened the area with a mesh of branches, but Hazel had scouted the peninsula well enough to know there weren't any demons nearby anyway. She'd caught a string of some sort of catfish-type species, and everyone was happily sucking the flesh off the bones. I'm pretty sure she and Zoe could have lived out the rest of their lives there."

"Except then you wouldn't know what the demons were building."

"And I'd be short Stonehaven's best scout and forager, not to mention a friend. The ostrich I could probably do without, though."

"Did you teleport back to Ishildar once you found them?"

Devon shook her head. "Not yet. When I get back home and log in, we'll gather up, and I'll port us to the city. But we figured that Hazel could instruct those guys in which mushrooms make good forage and stuff. Plus, Greel is trying his hand at fishing. Might as well do what we can to help with the food situation while we're somewhere that isn't paved over with ancient flagstone."

Emerson nodded. See, that was the thing with Devon. Whereas he spent much of his in-game time trying not to get lost or tripping over his own sword, she thought ahead and made plans and balanced what seemed to be endless priorities. It was no wonder that she had examined the rule set for Settlers of Catan and immediately formulated a strategy that was obliterating him and Veia.

"If you're done mooning over the woman, I'd like to conclude my turn," mini-Veia said into his skull.

Mooning over? Where had the AI picked up that expression? Some 1960s family television program? Sighing, he lifted his tablet again to signal to Devon that their competition wished to make her move. Though she sent her move requests to his implants, the AI was mirroring them in text on the tablet's screen. It had seemed like a good idea so that Devon could double-check the moves he made as Veia's proxy, both to avoid mistakes and—he'd insisted—so that he couldn't accidentally cheat for himself.

Of course, maybe he could provide her a little more competition if he *did* cheat. Was it boring to be so much better at something than your opponents? Emerson paid Veia's building costs and placed a new settlement for the AI. Then he rolled for himself and started his turn.

As he sorted his resource pieces into different little groups, running through different options for using or trading them, Devon abruptly sat up straighter. Her eyes went distant as she started reading something from her implants' interface.

"Shit," she said.

"What?"

"A message from Tamara. Apparently, Torald contacted her offline because someone from the former player camp contacted *him* offline because Prince Kenjan said his home is under attack."

"Wait, who?"

Devon hesitated, then shook her head and blinked as if making a sudden realization. "You haven't met Fabio...?"

"Like, that romance novel guy?"

"Yeah, him. Only not him. He's a Skevalli NPC." She paused, and a look of distinct discomfort settled onto her face. "He...hmm. Well, the short explanation is his parents—the king and queen of the vassal society, that is—sent him to Ishildar with the mission to convince me to marry him."

Emerson felt his face go slack. "Uh...wait. You're getting married?" He couldn't bring himself to ask the real question that jumped into his mind—did that mean they would...er...consummate the relationship?—partially because he was embarrassed for thinking of it first thing, and partially because he didn't want Devon to think he was a perv or a jealous would-be boyfriend or anything like that.

She shook her head, an almost-violent motion. "No way. I mean—no. No way. When I finally got the truth out of him, I explained that there was zero chance of that happening. But I did agree to deal with a basilisk problem they're having as a way to prove to the king and queen that we don't need a marriage to cement the alliance."

"So the basilisks are attacking?"

Devon's face was abruptly somber. "That's the thing. No. It has nothing to do with basilisks or harpies or any of the problems the Skevalli have been dealing with until now."

"What then?"

She pressed her lips together and unfocused her eyes as she reread the message. "It doesn't make any sense to me, but according to Tamara, Torald said the Skevalli are being attacked by players."

"Yikes. You should go," Emerson said.

She glanced at the game laid out between them. "I'm really sorry," she said. "This was a great idea. Really thoughtful." After a moment's hesitation, she reached out and grabbed his hand. Her skin was so warm. Emerson fought the urge to cling.

"If you want, I can take a picture of the board, and we can set back up another time."

Her mouth twisted in a smirk. "You really want to finish this particular game out? You know you've already lost, right?"

Emerson laughed and shrugged. "Okay, fair point. Maybe we should just start with the rematch."

Devon lifted her purse strap from the knob on the back of her chair and started digging through the contents. "Mind if I leave a little cash with you for the bill? I should get online as quick as I can."

This time, Emerson reached for her hand. Unfortunately, he missed and ended up grabbing a fold of her purse before resetting his aim and managing to catch her thumb. "I got it. Seriously. Go."

She spent about two seconds seeming to consider an objection before nodding. "Okay. But next time's on me."

Next time. That sounded nice. Emerson realized he was smiling in kind of a dazed grin sort of way, and he swallowed and stood. After shifting his weight between his feet a couple of times, he held out his arms for a hug. Devon leaned against him and squeezed her arms around his chest before stepping back and, without making eye contact, stood on her tiptoes and kissed his cheek.

"Bye," she said as she whirled for the door.

The turn was quick, but not quick enough to hide the blush in her cheeks.

Chapter Twenty-Seven

THE CROAKING OF frogs on Hazel's peninsula was so loud Devon had to work to be heard over them. "Everyone ready?"

Magda took a deep breath as if savoring the rot-smelling air. "Affirmative. Prepped for evacuation from the Dagobah System, admiral."

"Huh?" Hailey said.

Devon shook her head. "It's nothing. Star Wars joke."

"Oh." Hailey did a subtle eye roll thing as if to suggest that references from a movie that was, like, almost one hundred years old were just not that cool. "Anyway, yeah, ready."

Torald seemed to have paid closer attention to Devon's body language after she'd logged back in because he nodded quickly with a set jaw. Devon noticed that his hand was still cupped as if he were considering drawing his sword. By unspoken agreement, neither had mentioned the rumor about the attack on the Skevalli home. Better to get back to Ishildar and collect the facts before involving the other group members who, given the strong personalities present, would probably just delay the return trip by expressing their opinions on who had attacked and why and what Devon should do about it. Right now, Devon just needed them to click 'Accept' when she cast the group teleport.

Devon made quick eye contact with Hazel and Greel, and when neither objected, she made the mental motions to activate *Journey*. Soon after, the group rematerialized on the polished floor of the open-air Veian Temple—now that Devon was a city manager, she could actually travel there quickly. Devon counted to five to make sure she'd caught her balance, then turned to face Temple Square and the ramshackle refugee camp her followers had set up.

"Er...did you decide to put on a toga party, or what?" Hailey asked.

"Or maybe Neanderthal spring break?" Magda added.

Devon stared at the scene on the north edge of the square where a bunch of newcomers wearing leather body wraps, off the shoulder even, were milling around in what appeared to be a dazed sort of shock. As she was considering that Hailey wasn't that far off the mark with the toga party comment, a griffon swooped in. Prince Kenjan, once again stripped down to his loincloth—for the speed buff, she gathered—jumped off Proudheart's back and helped a pair of teenaged passengers dismount from where they'd ridden behind him. The adolescents shuffled into the group where most of the adults looked up long enough to acknowledge their presence before returning to their previous state of shell shock. Fortunately, though, someone nudged a middle-aged woman who touched her husband's shoulder. The couple hurried over to the new arrivals, and the small group fell into a family hug.

Prince Kenjan watched for a moment before turning back to Proudheart.

"Kenjan, wait," Devon called. She hurried out from the center of the temple and trotted across the square. The man stepped to put the bulk of his griffon between him and his people as she reached him, granting them a modicum of privacy.

"What happened? I heard it was a starborn attack, but that doesn't make any sense." As if to verify her statement, she glanced around the square. Her quick estimate was that about half the population of the player camp was visible. Some were sparring in the center of the square, some were huddled in small groups and talking, and others were working with NPCs on a variety of crafting tasks, mostly those that didn't need much in the way of components. No one looked like they'd recently returned from a raid on their own allies, and the number of people logged in seemed about right, if not a little high given that it was the middle of the day and most people had work or school obligations.

Proudheart blocked her view of most of the newly arrived Skevalli—she gathered that these people were probably the commoners who lived in the settlement on the chasm floor—but from what she could see, no one actually looked injured. So maybe it had all been a miscommunication.

When she brought her gaze back to Prince Kenjan's face, though, that hope quickly faded. Something terrible had happened; it was obvious in the anguish written over his features.

"For centuries, my family held our lofty perch. Chasm View's height together with the ability to escape into the cliff-side cracks and caverns meant that we could focus our efforts on defending our people on the chasm floor. Any problem with harpies and their ilk has been easily solved by sending the youngest and oldest of the royals into the stone depths while we of hero age harried them from our mounts." He shook his head. "We never imagined that attack would come from above and in such force. Such brutality."

She blinked. "I still don't understand. Who came?"

He shook his head. "Strangers. Starborn. So many of them. I was on my way to deliver the news of your refusal of my offer of marriage—and the promise you made to prove our alliance in other ways. I arrived as the last of the attackers were using some sort of magic to teleport from our home back to the high plateau." He swallowed. "We'd always assumed that the uplands would remain the desolate wilderness they've been since our arrival. Travel over the tops of the Skargills was considered so impractical as to be impossible."

A picture was coming together in Devon's mind: a player raid deciding to travel through the Skargills, hunting whatever NPCs they could find, not thinking that the humans, especially, had lives and consciousnesses all of their own. A deep, searing emotion flooded her chest, a mix of rage at their ignorance and willingness to murder for the sake of XP colored with self-loathing over the knowledge that she hadn't been so different from them less than a year ago. Granted, the NPCs in other games didn't have the quality of awareness that they did in Relic Online. Avatharn Online mobs were simple machines, programmed to fight back when attacked and, in the case of the friendly NPCs, to hand out human-scripted quests.

Could people really not see that things were different in this game? Or maybe they could, and they just didn't care.

Regardless, the presence of other players in the region could be a big problem. Even if she could reach out and ask for their help in defeating the demons, that would have to be a last resort. How could she subject Kenjan to allying with people who had mercilessly attacked his home?

She met his eyes. "What happened to your family?" She assumed that all the royals were advanced NPCs, meaning that if they were killed, they could at least be resurrected at a shrine or temple.

"I..." He clenched his jaw as his voice broke. "They're gone. Slaughtered in the tea room, the nut oil spa—surely the children would have been murdered in their playpens if not for their birth buffs. Our griffons were killed and cut up for parts. Maybe if I'd come back sooner...I am—was—the best fighter among us."

Quest failed: Nobody's Boy Toy
So, the idea was you prove to the king and queen that you would protect the Skevalli without being bound by marriage. Nobody's feeling very well-protected right now. Also, the king and queen are no longer around to bear witness to your heroics.

"Wait, and you can't resurrect?"

"Resurrect?"

Did he really not know? She opened the settlement interface and flipped to the population tab on the royal settlement.

Settlement: Chasm View
Population: 6

Basic NPCs
4 x Children

Advanced NPCs:
King Kenjan
Grandmother Valin

Okay, so yeah, he was advanced—and a king now. And apparently, there was another survivor. But before she could ask him about that, a memory sprang to mind. After she'd claimed Ishildar as a base and had been able to look at the populations of the vassal settlements, Chasm View had listed...what...forty-something? It must have been a complete massacre to reduce the number to six. From what she'd gathered, most of the people living there had been Kenjan's extended family. It took her a moment to figure out what else was bothering her about the population number, but when she realized the issue, she felt sick to her stomach.

A settlement with a population of around forty was capped at the Village designation. She might not remember all the specifics of Stonehaven's progression, but she did recall that her cap of advanced NPCs had been seven during that period. Even if resurrection were an option for some of Kenjan's slaughtered relatives and friends, it would only be a small fraction.

Swallowing hurt, like someone had rammed an avocado pit down her esophagus. She shook her head slowly. "I just checked with the...special ledger that's available to me as the Keeper. Prince—King Kenjan, I am so, so sorry." She didn't know what else to say. Words didn't seem adequate.

He seemed to wrestle with his emotions for a moment before managing to speak in a relatively even voice. "What matters now is that I do what I can to protect the people that depend on me. They're too vulnerable in Vulture's Rift, especially if the"—his control slipped, and his cheek trembled—"if the attackers find their way to the bottom of the chasm. I'm able to rescue one or two people at a time, but Proudheart will need to rest soon."

"How many are left?" she asked, realizing as she spoke that she could check the population tab for the settlement. Pulling it open, she saw there were over five hundred total citizens of Vulture's Rift. Kenjan had probably brought just thirty or so to Ishildar. "Never mind. I see."

"Then you can see why I must mount up and head out."

"Wait..." She glanced around, assessing the players who were more or less idle. "Is it possible to reach Vulture's Rift on foot? I can't let you try to rescue every one of your people singlehandedly." Of course, if she were able to help him bring five hundred more people here, she had no idea how they'd be fed. Maybe she could also send some dwarves to help carry supplies.

"The way is difficult, and the risk of attack by basilisks and king sidewinders is ever present, but it's a journey of about half a day if all goes well."

"Then let me organize a group of fighters."

He inclined his head, and his shoulders sank in obvious relief. "I see now why Veia above blessed you with the Keeper's mantle."

> **King Kenjan is offering you a quest**: Lead the Skevalli to safety
>
> **Objective:** Skevalli population relocated to Ishildar.
>
> **Reward:** Redemption and more responsibility. Yay.
>
> **Accept?** Y/N

*You know you've missed escort quests. Especially when the NPCs walk **So. Freaking. Slowly.** Yup...and if you auto-follow and grab a soda, for sure that's when the attack will come. Have fun!*

Devon accepted without hesitation. Once the entry was in her log, though, she couldn't help wondering if the rescue was just a distracting side quest. Because really, what good would it do to bring a bunch of Skevalli commoners into Ishildar where they would likely either starve or be murdered by demons once the Ziggurat of the Damned negated the defense offered by the Veian Temple?

"You look...conflicted," King Kenjan said.

She sighed and decided to be honest. "I'm just not sure they'll be any safer here. I wish I could have more confidence."

"And if I'm not mistaken, you feel responsible for carrying each of the burdens singlehandedly."

She shrugged. "Guilty, I suppose."

You know, there is a little concept that most people have grasped by the time they reach adulthood. It's called delegation.

Devon brushed away the popup, but not without considering the words. Okay, so maybe she could stand to hand off some responsibilities. She'd done a decent job building up her NPC leadership, but right now, she needed more help from players. It had been a step in the right direction to allow Jeremy to start advising her on strategies for base battles. But she needed to go further.

Kenjan seemed to sense that she was working through possibilities in her head, and he stood quietly, arms hanging, fingers lightly curled near his loincloth. When she glanced at him, he nodded as if understanding that she'd made some decisions. "If you wish to send another as leader of the group traveling to Vulture's Rift, I'm sure it will be the best choice for all of us," he said.

She touched his arm. Reflexively, he flexed his bicep and abs, then sighed. "Sorry," he said. "Habit."

"It's all right," she said. "Will you rest while I sort out responsibilities for the coming days? Proudheart looks like he could use some..." What did griffons eat anyway? "...meat?"

Kenjan smiled faintly. "He needs a chance to hunt, that's true. And after that, some time to digest, or he'll get cramps. Thank you, Keeper Devon. We are fortunate to have you guiding us."

Devon nodded in gratitude at the compliment, even if she didn't feel like a very good leader right now. She patted Proudheart's sleek flank then turned and walked away.

Chapter Twenty-Eight

You create: 1 x Field Rations

Ashley licked her fingers to keep from burning them, pinched a scrap of leather as added protection, and quickly tugged the jagged plate of iron from the fire. On it, a mush of oats, ham, and rehydrated vegetables steamed. Ash puffed as the makeshift platter dropped off the edge of the fire ring. The cloud swirled before coating the already-unappetizing meal in a layer of gray.

She grimaced. A pot with a lid or even some kind of skillet with curved sides would really be nice, but the whole evil-alignment thing did cause occasional problems. The idea of raiding NPC villages for the supplies she needed was usually a sound one—she hadn't paid a copper for her armor or weapons. But attacks against villages were usually pretty freaking hectic. Not the sort of situation where she stopped to consider what kind of kitchenware she should steal. Oh, and NPCs typically weren't walking around their homes carrying bags of holding she could loot either, so it wasn't like she had a lot of free inventory space.

Anyway, she'd fashioned the cooking plate from a looted scrap of platemail. It worked okay, even if her food was usually burned on the underside and cold on top. And often, like today, seasoned with ash or dirt.

The platter was still too hot to touch, so she grabbed a stick and used it to push the meal farther from the fire. While waiting for it to cool, she sat back on her heels and watched the camp. Already, around half the guild had logged out, so the usual sparring and contests of stupidity—who could last the longest without a heal after taking an arrow to the eye socket, who could eat a hot coal without screaming—had settled down to a few arm wrestling competitions. At the next fire over, they'd been passing around a skin of in-game alcohol, and the results were predictable. Half the people surrounding the blaze were passed out and drooling, and the other half were involved in some inane argument about real-world sports teams.

Fortunately, something in Ashley's expression had seemed to dissuade anyone from joining her fire, so she didn't have to deal with the kind of crap that Nil's followers considered fun. Especially tonight, she just wasn't in the mood. She would rather have logged out and left her character hungry, taking the hit to her *Fatigue* tomorrow, than deal with their shit.

The truth was, the attack on the griffon people's camp just wasn't sitting right with her. Sure, it had been a decent break from the monotony of constant marching, detouring around one chasm after another and wondering whether they'd *ever* reach the Stonehaven area. Last time they'd attacked, they'd come in through a sane route, following an ancient roadway that approached the jungle basin through a notch in the mountains that bounded the region to the east. That had been fine. Like, maybe two days' journey from the Eltera City region. But according to Nil's inside informant—Jeremy was the name she kept hearing—that approach was currently unusable. Plus, it would destroy their element of surprise.

Anyway, yeah, the attack on the cliff-side camp had been a change of pace, but it had left her feeling...off. Maybe because there'd been old people there? The kids, of course, had been invulnerable. Pretty much a rule of this game world, and Ashley was grateful for that. Some gamers might laugh at her for being squeamish about murdering young NPCs, but she had a feeling most people would share her discomfort. It was a common decency thing.

Of course, Nil had bitched about their invulnerability buff. No surprise there.

Regardless, maybe it *was* the presence of elderly NPCs that had left her feeling so unsettled. They hadn't been *old* old. Not like wheelchair-bound or anything. More like powerful-tribal-elder old. The kind of mobs that usually summoned totems that nuked the crap out of a party. At least, that's what it had seemed like. But no amount of elder wisdom could deal with a raid force ten times larger than the entire population of the camp. The NPCs living in that village just below the canyon rim hadn't stood a chance.

Maybe that's what was bothering her, actually. It didn't have anything to do with the age of the mobs. The issue was that they'd gone in and slaughtered the camp for the sake of it. Ashley's experience bar hadn't even budged, and as for loot, a couple of people got some jars of nut oil that were supposed to give a buff, but only if you ran around half-naked.

It was weird. This kind of thing hadn't ever bothered her. They were just NPCs. They'd literally been created so that players could fight them. But still. Maybe the immersion was getting to her, blurring her notion of reality. Maybe she was spending too much time inside the game, the added hours causing her to lose touch.

She sighed as she carefully tested the temperature of the iron plate with a fingertip. Her meal was cool enough to eat, so she grabbed the plate by the edges and lifted it onto her lap before scooping up a bite on her index and middle fingers. As she sucked the food off her fingers—silverware: another thing it was hard to justify consuming an inventory slot for—a shadow appeared at the far side of her fire. Her eyes widened when Nil stepped into the light.

"Not drinking tonight?" he asked, slurring his words a little. He had some sort of flask in his hand, and he raised it as if in a toast.

She shook her head. "Not tonight." Ashley never drank in-game alcohol, but mentioning that seemed like it would just antagonize him.

The guild leader sneered and dropped lazily into a cross-legged seat. He picked up a stick and poked the fire, sending a swirl of sparks toward her face. When she cringed and leaned backward, he just laughed.

"So, what did you think of the little raid today?" he asked.

Ashley swallowed and tried to look casual. Was this a trap? Rather than answer right away, she scooped another bite from her plate and sucked it off her fingers.

Fortunately, Nil liked to hear himself talk far more than he liked listening to others. After another quick swig from his flask he glanced at the stars overhead, he took a deep breath and pointed at her food. "Tier 1 cooking recipes suck. If you're going to make your own food, you should at least level up the skill."

Ashley felt her lip twitch in annoyance and hoped that his drunkenness and the relative darkness covered it. She needed to stay wary here because this was exactly the kind of thing Nil did when he was pissed off at someone. Saunter up acting all buddy-buddy, make some idle conversation, then curse them with some disgusting damage-over-time spell. Usually an insect swarm, but sometimes he cast this thing that made people start sprouting fungus everywhere. Then, if they actually fought back, he'd call in his lackeys to hold the person down while he cut their heart out or something. The man was sick, honestly.

Of course, the only reason he might be pissed off at her was if he'd gotten wind of her plan to splinter off and start a new guild with a hefty chunk of his followers. And if he'd actually heard that, she didn't think he'd confront her now when half the guild was offline. He would want an audience for whatever punishment he'd cooked up.

"Trade skills aren't really my thing," she said with a shrug. "Takes forever to skill up to the point where they give decent buffs or gear upgrades. Just seems like I'm better off leveling if there's no good PvP opportunities."

"Well, you do you." He shrugged. "Anyway, yeah, so I wanted to know what you thought of the attack. It was fun, right?"

She shrugged. "I guess. Just wish the mobs would have been a little harder."

"See!" He grinned and pointed at her with the gnarled stick thing that was his casting focus item. "That's what I thought. It seemed like a stupid distraction from our actual goal. But I try to be a good leader and shit and people were bored with this goddamn endless walk. So I thought, fine. Let's take a couple of hours and clear the camp."

"Okay..." she said, still wondering why the hell he'd decided to come sit with her.

"And I heard that people have been bitching and even talking about joining another guild. Though if I find out who is actually saying that kind of shit, they're freaking out of this organization so fast they won't even have time to beg for forgiveness. Anyway, yeah. I figured it couldn't hurt to kill a few things. Raise morale. But then I hear, just this evening, that news of our freaking raid got to Devon and the Stonehaven peeps."

"What? How?"

"I don't know. Those griffon freaks were just some random mobs out in the middle of nowhere, but word came from our informant that the attack screwed up a whole bunch of plans. Jeremy said he'd deal with it, but he's pissed, and he said that if we go off script again, he's done helping us. Freaking control-freak, right? After this is over, I think I'll have to show him how this power dynamic actually works. But for right now, we can't lose his info, or we're going in blind."

"Yeah, sounds sketchy to lose him as an ally now," Ashley said. She still had no clue why this conversation was happening. He'd just mentioned the rumor about people leaving the guild. So maybe he *was* trying to bait her into some kind of confession? Still, that really wasn't his style—frankly, he wasn't smart enough to try that kind of thing. Maybe this little chat was the typical leader thing where they were internally freaking out but couldn't show it in front of their followers, so they chose someone off by themselves to lay their woes on. It wasn't like she was trying to pull the woman card or anything, but it *did* seem like this kind of crying-on-a-shoulder thing happened to her more often than it did the male gamers she knew.

"Exactly. You know, sometimes of all the people in the guild, I feel like you really get where I'm trying to take this thing. It's like, I don't even have to explain my logic like I do with all those other shit heads." He took another swig of liquor. "You sure you don't want some?"

She shook her head. "Screws with my combat reflexes, even a day later."

He smirked. "I feel you. And yeah, we're actually close enough that we might drop into the Stonehaven area tomorrow. Could be we hit our first resistance if shit goes sideways. But it's kind of the same issue as you eating those field rations. I get that grinding out a tier or two in cooking is boring as hell, but with the time compression stuff, we basically spend more time in game than we do in the real world. Even more if you subtract the out-of-game time that you're sleeping and shit like that. So maybe you should consider relaxing a little. You know, enjoy the experience and shit."

Ashley almost wanted to record the conversation to count the frequency of swear words in Nil's speech. It was like he used them for punctuation. "Maybe I'll have a swig or two after we take out the Stonehaven peeps," she said.

Nil smiled and (ew) winked at her. "Maybe we'll put back a few mugs of ale together. Just you and me."

Oh. Gross. Was he actually into her? In-game character to in-game character? Ashley was tempted to leave the guild now. She probably would if she could roll up an alternate character, even if it meant starting over at level one, but the company was still restricting avatars to one per player. She really needed to get offline before she barfed up her dinner or something.

"Ah, shit," she said, fumbling for some excuse. "I gotta log. Roommate just messaged me about my stupid dog. If I don't walk him, he'll pee all over the carpet. You'd think my roomies could just take care of it, but they're lazy jerks."

Nil dropped back onto an elbow as he took another big swallow of whatever swill he was drinking. "Tie the mutt up outside next time. Or better, if he can't hold his pee, you should just give him to a shelter or something. That shit's annoying."

Ashley gritted her teeth to keep from saying anything else. Instead, she waved a pair of fingers while mentally pressing the logout button. What an asshole.

Chapter Twenty-Nine

AS HE READ the message, Emerson's first thought was to wonder how the heck he was going to tell Devon the news. His second thought was: what the hell? He could have *sworn* he'd seen Hailey's avatar online sometime in the last day. Was he confused? Misremembering?

He reread the note.

To whom it may concern:

Thank you for your inquiry. It is with deep sadness that we at Horizons Long-term Care are writing to inform you that Hailey Landers lost her battle with a devastating illness on January 3rd, 2058.

Please cease sending pay stubs and other company communication to this address.

Sincerely,
Horizons Administration

He shook his head again. There had to be some sort of mistake. January 3rd was ten days ago. Yeah, the more he thought about it, he was *sure* he'd seen Haelie the Seeker-class character at least once since. He distinctly remembered walking with Devon, spotting Hailey on a bench, and commenting on how Bob was spending more time with the other woman than with Devon.

But her unexpected death—unexpected to E-Squared, at least—would explain the issue with the failed payment and HR's inability to contact the woman.

He'd been getting ready to log in. Already, he'd laid a set of hotel towels on top of the bed because he didn't want to get under the way-too-warm covers and wake up in a sea of his own sweat, and he definitely didn't want to lie directly on top of the hotel comforter which was probably never washed and was likely infused with cellular material from the last one hundred guests. But now he needed to pace, so he got up and started walking a circuit of the small room.

The best explanation that covered both the notice of Hailey's death—again, he caught himself shaking his head in disbelief. Could she really have been that sick?—and the continued presence of her avatar in the game world was that her login had somehow been hacked. But that was a huge stretch. Authentication for the game was based off hardware keys that were literally implanted in the players' skulls. Technically, the control module could be removed and implanted in another player. It was one of the few pieces of the Entwined hardware system that could be sterilized and refurbished if you weren't squeamish about that stuff, but the installation required an Entwined-licensed surgeon, and Emerson assumed that a random person coming in with a set of parts and asking for full implantation would raise a few flags.

Unless there were also some black-market installers out there? The tech seemed awfully new to have spawned its own illegal industry, but then, Emerson had never been all that savvy when it came to darknets and shady characters.

So...maybe?

He paused and flicked aside the curtain. The hotel room looked out over a small park with native desert plantings. Despite the mild, mid-afternoon temperatures, the park was deserted. Most people were probably at work or in school. He considered going down for a little fresh air and a chance to clear his head, but decided that would just be putting off an issue in need of urgent investigation.

Maybe he *had* misremembered his last Hailey sighting. That would be the easiest explanation to deal with, even if it meant that he would still have to break the news to Devon. The alternatives were a bit thornier. If Hailey were online, he'd have to verify that the letter about her death wasn't some mistake or messed-up joke. And if *that* still pointed to the possibility of hacking, he guessed it would be time to alert corporate security.

Of course, the downside there was that the hacking of one of his players might put undue scrutiny on his other recruits. Not what Devon needed to deal with given the other burdens she was shouldering.

Emerson sighed and headed back to the bed. He straightened the towels and made sure there were no gaps in the protective barrier, lay down, and activated the Relic Online icon.

Chapter Thirty

AFTER TALKING TO King Kenjan, Devon had tried to dig straight into helping out with the organization efforts in the square, but she'd soon felt panic welling up and had fled the area. For just a few minutes, she'd needed to be where she couldn't glimpse the faces of the Skevalli refugees, wouldn't see the worried expressions worn by her Stonehaven followers. After a short break, she could head back, retake control of her emotions and confront the tasks at hand. But for now, she needed to escape and take stock.

She'd chosen a street at random, a narrow avenue that wound a gentle course through the city, taking her past building after half-ruined building. The structures seemed to loom over her. Empty windows were like dark pits, and the vacant courtyards seemed forlorn, a drastic change from the bright sense of awakening she'd imagined she'd felt from the city just a few days ago.

She ducked into one of those empty courtyards where water had just begun to trickle over the lip of a three-tiered fountain. Leaves and twigs floated in the pooling liquid and formed swirling rafts. Devon stood over the water and scooped out the dead foliage. She shook the soggy mess off her fingers, then hugged her arms over her chest.

Just *one* of the problems facing the Ishildar region would be enough to keep her from sleeping at night. Together, they conspired to grind her up and spit her out before destroying everything and everyone she cared about in the game. Stonehaven was occupied, the Skevalli royal settlement was the site of a recent massacre, and Ishildar's only defense, the shield created by the Veian Temple, was threatened by the construction of a freaking ziggurat that Devon and her people had no hopes of destroying. Oh, and the Stonehaven evacuees had fled with only what they could carry. If they didn't figure out a food supply soon, the population would starve before the demons had a chance to finish them off.

Of course, Devon's worries weren't limited to Stonehaven and Ishildar. She could *still* barely fathom the issues with Hailey's condition and what it meant for the woman's interaction with Emerson, not to mention the woman's future existence.

For that matter, why was Devon even thinking about spending more time with Emerson? He was her *boss*. The problems there were huge. But it had been *so long* since she'd found anyone interesting, much less someone who kinda seemed to like her back. ...If she wasn't being a moron to think so, anyway.

Regardless, the dating issue was the kind of situation she *knew* she needed to think through logically, figure out if hanging out with him was worth the risk. But by the time she logged out every day, she barely had the mental capacity to feed herself, not to mention handle the other real-life stuff like getting her stupid blind fixed. Figuring out whether she should get into a long-distance relationship with her supervisor seemed way beyond her capabilities at this point.

Dropping her forehead onto the heel of her hand, Devon retreated to a small stone bench. The seat was tucked into a corner between buildings, and woody vines still clung to the walls even

227

though their foliage had dropped off when she'd banished the Curse of Fecundity. Even so, the vines softened the burbling echoes of the fountain, wrapping her in a peaceful almost-silence. If she could just stop herself from thinking, she might be able to chill here for a few minutes and forget her problems. But she couldn't.

So she might as well get to work on solving whichever of them she could.

First, she pulled open the settlement interface and tabbed over to examine Ishildar's details. Beneath the overview that listed the population as zero, but with 543 temporary inhabitants—should she reassign her Stonehaven people to Ishildar? Would the game do it eventually?—there were pages and pages of information about the city's structures. She blinked and hit a toggle to reduce the info to headers only.

Thinking back over the couple of weeks during which she'd sent scouts criss-crossing the city in search of potential advantages against the demons, she sighed. Too bad she hadn't thought to claim management of Ishildar *before* ordering a random search. The settlement details might not tell her where each of the buildings were, but it would probably offer way better hints on the capabilities than the haphazard scouting had.

But done was done. At least she could remedy the oversight now.

First, though, she expanded the fortifications section and checked progress on the construction.

Completed:

7 x Stone Guardian

2 x Watch Tower

1 x Archer Platform with Screen

Required for advancement to Fortified Camp:
1 x Bulwark - 90%
1 x Watch Tower - 10%
3 x Archer Platform with Screen - 15%

Good. Jarleck once again had things in hand. She couldn't help shaking her head at the list of completed defenses. It was hard to say what defense tier the Stone Guardians actually belonged to, but she could bet it would take a bunch of in-game years to build something up to that level. Kind of ridiculous when compared to the actual fortifications status. The ancient, sprawling metropolis of Ishildar was on its way to becoming a Fortified Camp, the lowliest of defense tiers.

Next, she skipped to the resources section. Devon winced. Things were not looking good there; even if they dropped to half-rations, something she would need to institute today, there would only be enough food for around three days.

Okay, so a concerted effort to secure resources was a priority. Devon made a mental note and moved on.

The main area of interest in Ishildar's details was its structures. At least, that was her best guess on where clues to the city's power would lie. The Veian Temple was great and all, but its apparent shielding effect couldn't be the only reason the city had been prophesied to be a beacon of light in the fight against the demons. She flipped to the section with the most advanced buildings and scanned down until she spotted the Temple's entry. A tooltip appeared.

<u>Veian Temple</u>
The most advanced structure dedicated to the creator goddess, Veia, this temple can entirely prevent intrusion by the forces of evil. The barrier created by the temple is indestructible by ordinary means. Only a Zaa-dedicated structure of equivalent advancement can counteract the shielding.
Radius: 5 kilometers

Okay, well that was good and bad. The defensive shielding was way better than she'd realized. The demons couldn't physically reach them inside the city. Except for that whole equivalent-Zaa-structure thing. The temple description confirmed that if Archdemon Gaviroth successfully finished the ziggurat, the shield would be nullified.

She quickly scanned the rest of the list of upper-tier buildings, but once she realized there were at least seven or eight pages of them and that most were listed as partially ruined, she shook her head and closed down that tab.

Priority number two to be weighed and addressed: sorting through the list of building descriptions and finding what might be useful.

She ignored the tabs for the vassal settlements for now; the status of Chasm View was too depressing, and she pretty much knew the situation at Vulture's Rift—around five hundred people were waiting to be evacuated. The felsen settlements wouldn't have changed much unless one of them had come under attack, and if that had happened, she would've been informed.

That left Stonehaven.

Devon curled her hand into a tight fist around a handful of her Keeper's cloak. Pressing her lips together, she opened Stonehaven's tab.

92% contested. She didn't really need to look further than that, but some sort of morbid curiosity made her scan the list of structures. Only the Shrine to Veia remained fully under her side's control. Uncontested but besieged on all sides. She cocked her head while scanning the rest of the list. For some reason, the Inner Keep was still just 70% contested. Devon had a sneaking suspicion that the demons could have taken it by now if they wanted. The parties being teleported through to the shrine certainly wouldn't head for the keep if they were making strikes into the settlement—it was too far away. The next closest building to the shrine, if she remembered right, was the Tailoring Workshop, and that was 100% under demon control.

Archdemon Gaviroth must have figured out that the Inner Keep held special significance for her. She supposed it wasn't that hard to surmise seeing as she'd chosen the upper floor as her personal chambers. The demons probably wanted to take the keep last, a final, devastating blow.

Jaw clenching, she forced herself to take another hard look at the list of everything she'd built. Then she closed the settlement interface.

Time to call a meeting.

***

Familiar faces formed a semicircle around Devon. She stood on top of a short flight of stone steps outside a building that might have once been a residence for one of Ishildar's aristocratic families. Or maybe it had been a guildhall for one of its artisan groups. Either way, its rooms were now vacant, and through the doorway behind her, rubble could be seen where portions of the upper story had collapsed into the lower.

Right now, the building seemed kind of like a metaphor for everything she'd hoped to build. But that was just negative thinking, and the war wasn't over. Not yet, anyway. She took a deep breath.

"I'll be brief. There's too much to do for you guys to waste time listening to a pep talk or inspirational speech." She paused to let that sink in and then launched into the meeting agenda. "I've been kind of a control freak, but at this point, I've got to hand over some responsibilities."

She glanced at King Kenjan who stood, somber-faced, at the fringe of the gathering. The man had once again donned the clothing she'd given him, probably still thinking that the tunic and trousers had the ceremonial significance she'd claimed. Given everything he'd been through today, she felt a little guilty for lying to him about that. But at least the loincloth wouldn't be a distraction for anyone here.

She gestured toward him. "You've all heard about what happened to Chasm View, I assume." She paused and glanced around the gathering. After receiving nods of acknowledgment, she continued. "We still don't know who attacked or why they chose Chasm View. But we'll figure it out. Chen?"

The teenager jerked, startled. Out of reflex, he reached for his sword before realizing what he was doing and dropping his hand to his side. "Yeah?"

"I need you to do two things. First, can you get some bots running? I want something that crawls the Internet for anything mentioning the attack or the Skargill Mountains."

Chen's brows drew together, and he scratched at his hairline. "Sure. I think I can do that. Are you interested in just public mentions? Or do you want me to have a go at some password-protected sites?"

"Whatever you think you can do without raising alarms. I don't want you to get in trouble."

"Okay. And the other thing?"

"I need you to start crunching data. Everyone here should have combat logs from our altercations with the demons. If they don't know how to find the proper files, please help them figure it out and send them to you. I want to know about any combat advantages we might have. Any gap in the demons' abilities or chinks in their defenses. Can you do it?"

She really hadn't needed to ask since the answer was made obvious by the delighted grin on the boy's face. "Totally on it," he said with a bit of a swagger.

Devon turned to Owen, acknowledging Hailey with a quick glance. "Owen and Hailey, I need you to start by looking through the settlement interface for information on Ishildar's potential strengths. If you find anything listed, head out and use the Pattern and your truth-seeking to figure out how we access that power. I know there's something here. We wouldn't have had quest lines for a hundred-plus players that led to supporting me as Keeper otherwise."

Hailey cocked her head. "The settlement interface? Oh." Her eyes went distant as she focused on her interface. "When did this show up?"

"When I got a clue and finally accepted management of the city. Believe it or not, it was Tamara who made me realize this was a base battle and that Stonehaven wasn't the only point we can control."

Hailey raised her eyebrows at Tamara at the same time that Torald draped an arm over the woman's shoulder and squeezed. A wide smile spread across Tamara's face.

Devon nodded at Hazel. "If you hadn't been traveling with Zoe and your windsteed, would your *Stealth* have been high enough to avoid demon attention?"

"Yes, of course," Hazel said. "But I couldn't abandon them."

"I know. I was only asking because Hezbek needs potion components." She targeted the scout and shared the quest. "Can you help her?"

Hazel nodded and gave a quick salute. "Of course, Mayor."

Devon turned her attention to Grey, Stonehaven's lead hunter. "Our defenses don't matter if we starve behind them. Can you think of any region where the hunters can secure food without traveling through demon-controlled territory?"

The hunter pressed his lips together while thinking. "There might be wild game in the Argenthal foothills. And maybe we could try scouting the Skargill chasms."

Kenjan cleared his throat. "When we bring the citizens out from the Vulture's Rift, we can do the scouting. Traditionally, my people have subsisted on nuts and berries and the occasional roc egg when we find an unoccupied nest, but there may well be meat sources we've overlooked."

Devon nodded. "Good. We will instruct your people to forage on our way out from Vulture's Rift."

"We?" Dorden asked, picking up on her choice of pronoun.

Devon took a deep breath. "Yes, we. I'll be leading the party that will escort the Skevalli to Ishildar. King Kenjan's people suffered great losses today. Though we will never replace some of his beloved friends and family, there were a few advanced citizens among the losses at Chasm View." She popped open the vassal settlement interface to double-check, then flicked the window away. "Vulture's Rift has a Shrine to Veia, and as far as I know, I'm the only one who can use it."

Kenjan cocked his head, undisguised hope in his eyes. "Is this related to the resurrections you mentioned?"

Devon nodded. "I can't promise anything, except that I'll try my best." She ran her eyes over the crowd. "I'll be taking Dorden, Heldi, Greel, and Bayle." It would be just like old times, just her and her NPC followers out on a mission. She needed that right now because she needed to be reminded that it was the people of Stonehaven that mattered. Buildings could be replaced.

"And as for Stonehaven?" Jeremy asked.

"That's exactly what I was going to cover next. We can't win Stonehaven back. We can't even come close given our current situation." She ran her eyes over the group then gestured toward Jeremy. "I recently handed over some of the management of the base battle to Jeremy. While I'm away, he'll continue to hold that responsibility. Please take his orders as if they were my own."

She waited as the gathered leaders shifted, the information settling in and becoming part of the new order. "Jeremy, I want you to stop organizing attacks of any sort through the shrine. It's a waste of resources. From now until I return from Vulture's Rift, I want you to focus on two priorities. We need groups of players attacking the demons from the edges, but only picking fights we can win. This is about gaining experience and levels and nothing else. That's one priority. The other is more important. Demons are quarrying glass blocks from the remains of the player camp. They're using them to build a structure that will obliterate any chance we have of surviving. However you see fit, I need that supply chain disrupted. Get with Hazel for a map update that will show the route where they're transporting the blocks."

A hush fell over the gathering until finally, Hazel raised a hand. "Sorry, Mayor Devon, but just so I understand, you're saying we give Stonehaven up?"

It hurt, like a fist to the ribs to hear it stated so plainly, but Devon nodded. "That's what I'm saying."

Chapter Thirty-One

"HEY, SO ABOUT those priorities..."

Devon stopped at the sound of Jeremy's voice and turned while waiting for him to catch up. She'd been walking with the group of NPCs she'd chosen for the escort quest, and when Jeremy reached to them, she nodded to Dorden. "I'll meet you in the Veian Temple in an hour. Grab what you'll need for two or three days out, okay?

"Aye, lass, sounds good," Dorden said, nudging Heldi with his elbow. "We'll just say goodbye to our wee lad and grab some trail rations."

Devon waited until the group, including King Kenjan, had moved out of earshot, then turned back to Jeremy. "They're putting on brave faces, but they can't be taking the decision to abandon Stonehaven very well. I figured we could at least spare them from listening to us talk about it."

Jeremy laid a hand on her shoulder, and Devon tried not to jerk in surprise. He wasn't usually the touchy-feely type. "It was totally the right call, you know. I'm guessing it's hard on you, too."

"Yeah, you could say that."

"But that's not actually what I wanted to talk about. It's about the new agenda."

"Oh?" Devon shifted her weight to her other hip. "Do you have another suggestion?"

As he dropped his hand from her shoulder, a small wrinkle formed in his brow, just barely peeking out from his fringe of perfectly styled hair. "You know the former player camp is clearly visible from the walls of Stonehaven."

"Yeah, I know."

"That's what I'm saying."

"Huh?"

"I know you know, so that's why I can't quite figure out why you want to attack the supply line. Stonehaven's walls give a good view of the savanna pretty much all the way to the swamp. But since the bulk of the demon forces are centered in and around Stonehaven, why go for the supplies? Why not attack the rear installation? The ziggurat or whatever."

Right. She hadn't explained the conditions surrounding the ziggurat. "Sorry. I forgot to mention that there's a fear aura surrounding the place, and the guards are like ten levels higher than us."

"Oh," Jeremy said with a grimace.

"Yeah, exactly."

He tugged at his velvet cape as if thinking. "But it's not actually critical that we attack near where the player camp was, right? It would be okay if we, say, tried to disrupt the supply inside the swamp where their leaders can't see us in action? I mean, no reason to *try* to provoke a whole demon army into attacking our little raid parties, right?"

Devon smirked. "Yes, please disrupt the construction in the least-idiotic way possible."

Jeremy laughed. "Okay. Don't be an idiot. Got it. Thanks, Dev. I figured you had a reason for staying away from the ziggurat. Just wasn't sure what it was."

For a moment, the space between them felt like it had during the better times in Avatharn Online. Jeremy could be an ass, and the new troubadour class certainly hadn't made him *less* annoying, but there was a reason they'd grouped together for so long, the relationship spanning different game worlds.

"You know, I really appreciate your help here," she said. "The number of things I'm juggling had just gotten to be too much. And the stakes are too high for me to fail by trying to do it all myself."

Jeremy seemed to have been on the verge of saying something, but he shook his head as if reconsidering. "It's a ton of pressure, Dev. Not sure how you've held up this long, actually. But for what it's worth, I think you've done a crazy good job. I'm just glad I can help out."

"Thanks, Jeremy," she said. "I should have started leaning on you guys for help sooner. Anyway, speaking of responsibilities, I better get ready to head into the Skargills."

Again his brow wrinkled, but he once again seemed to shake off the thought. He doffed his hat and gave a ridiculous bow. "Be safe," he said before hurrying off.

Chapter Thirty-Two

HOLY SHIT. OKAY. Yes. Hailey—or Hailey's avatar anyway—was still playing Relic Online.

Hidden in the shadows of the pillars making up the outer boundary of the Veian Temple, Emerson watched as the woman—or maybe it was a man in control of her character now, he had no way to know—walked across Temple Square with Owen. Talk about bold...if Emerson had stolen hardware from a dead woman's skull, implanted it in his own, and then taken over her online identity, he certainly wouldn't be hanging out with her former friends. That was just begging to be unmasked as a fraud.

But this mystery hacker didn't seem worried; they must have spent a hell of a lot of time observing Hailey to be able to slip into her identity this way. Which was actually a clue as to their real identity when he thought about it. It seemed almost certain that the perpetrator was one of the subscribers to the woman's livestreaming channel.

Emerson made a mental note to grab the list of subscribers—he could probably use his E-Squared credentials to get the streaming service to send him the full data dump. And actually, he should probably check to see whether the identity thief had taken over the stream or whether they'd shut it down.

But for now, he had the opportunity to watch the thieving scum in action. Fumbling through his interface, Emerson found the controls to start recording video of his session. It might be important if this went to court.

Hailey and Owen stopped near the base of the marble steps leading up to the temple proper, then their faces went blank, their eyes distant, as they started examining their user interfaces.

Emerson crept closer, hugging the pillars. He scanned his list of abilities just in case he had something to help him eavesdrop, but the Frenzy class was more focused on frontal assaults than subterfuge. Still, he managed to pick up fragments of their conversation. They seemed to be looking through details about Ishildar and discussing whether they might be of use against the demons.

Emerson shook his head. It wasn't like he'd hoped that there would be a flashing hacker icon over Hailey's head or anything, but the thief's ability to fit in wasn't making this any easier.

He sighed. The truth was, the hacker theory was partially concocted out of self-preservation. Hailey Landers had been one of his star players, specifically recruited to help him train Veia into making clever content. If she'd willingly handed over her implants and identity once she found out she was dying, it wasn't exactly his fault, but it didn't say great things about his ability to judge character either.

He needed to alert E-Squared and the hardware company, Entwined, about the situation. But first, he wanted to gather more information. Because what if—okay, this was just occurring to him now, and maybe he should have thought of it earlier—what if it was her real-life details that had been "hacked"? As in, what if someone, a rival gamer or something, was trying to screw up her life by somehow tripping alerts to suspend her bank account and by sending a fake death letter to her employer? If Emerson reported her character as online after her supposed death, he could just be falling into this hacker's trap.

Pulling up an external window, he set up a task to scan for and analyze network traffic associated with Hailey's character. If his first theory were the true one—that Hailey had passed away and someone had stolen her game access, the hacker would almost certainly be using tricks to disguise the real-world origin of their network connection. That was cybercrime 101. But Emerson was exceedingly confident in his ability to divine patterns from what might seem to be random data. A deep analysis of the traffic was sure to tell him *something*.

Once the scan was configured, he stepped out from the shadows and descended the steps.

"Hey," he said. "Sounds like you're digging into Ishildar's details? Anything I can help with?"

Hailey's eyes went wide for just a fraction of a second. If he hadn't been looking for micro-expressions, he wouldn't have noticed it. But Emerson smiled, knowing he'd caught the emotional tell on camera. So yeah, theory number one was looking pretty solid. He wasn't too bad at this detective stuff.

Tragic circumstances notwithstanding, this investigation might actually be kind of fun.

Chapter Thirty-Three

STONE LEAVES, CHIPS of translucent agate long since fallen from the petrified trees towering over the ancient roadway, clicked and clattered under the party's feet as they filed through the forest. Dorden marched at the front, his warhammer slung over his back. The dwarf hummed to himself, a repetitive tune. Every once in a while, he sang a couple of words, usually having to do with ale, cheese, or beards. Evening haze filled the air, and honey-colored shafts of sunlight slanted through the trees, glinting brilliantly off crystalline twigs and shining through the thin blades of leaves still attached to their branches.

Even with Greel muttering and grumbling at the rear of the party, Devon could almost imagine they were on a grand adventure. Heading out to slay some baddies, explore a cavern or two, maybe come home with some awesome shiny loot. The notion kept her footsteps light; she needed this chance to group up with her friends and visit somewhere new, even if the end of the trip would find them at a settlement with a population grieving for their murdered royal family.

Near Ishildar, the roadway through the Stone Forest had been clogged with deadfall. Jumbled logs of onyx and jade and opal had crossed the path, forcing the party to clamber over or duck beneath the petrified wood. As they journeyed deeper into the area, however, the obstacles grew less frequent, and fewer leaves carpeted the track. Never short of theories, Greel mused that the change likely reflected the history of the place. After the fall of Ishildar, but before the petrification of the forest, the road linking the outlying settlements to the ruined city would have fallen into disrepair, the state worsening the farther the road traveled from the Skevalli hub city.

"So does that mean we're going to pass through the old Skevalli capital?" Devon asked.

Greel snorted as if this were the most idiotic question in the world.

"What?" Devon asked. "Seems like a valid question. If you'd prefer, I could go back to ignoring you."

"Look," the lawyer said, pointing into the trees.

Devon squinted through the fractured light, the faceted crystal branches creating starbursts from the rays of the evening sun. High above, she spotted what looked like wooden platforms built between the branches. No, actually, it appeared that the trees had been encouraged, long ago, to grow in a manner that created the flat perches. Now preserved in stone, the griffon landing sites would likely last as long as the forest itself.

> **You have discovered:** Parshinta, Ancient Capital of the Skevalli Vassaldom
>
> *You gain 100000 experience.*
> **Congratulations!** You have reached level 27!
>
> *(About time...)*

"What do you mean, 'About time?'" she muttered as she brushed away the popup. "It's not like I've been sitting around twiddling my thumbs."

"Pardon?" Greel asked. "Speaking nonsense again?"

Devon shook her head. "Nothing. So hey, think there's any reason to search through the settlement?" She projected her voice forward to include the rest of the group. Peering ahead, she spied more structures, some of which appeared to be crafted of the same limestone and marble used in Ishildar's buildings, and others which had been formed, at least in part, by training the foliage into desired shapes.

Bayle looked back and shrugged; more than the others, the ranged fighter almost always deferred to Devon when it came to adventuring decisions. Of course, ask her about crop rotations in Stonehaven's farm plots, and you could count on a full dissertation on the subject.

Dorden's rolling gait slowed as he glanced upward, taking in the surroundings. Behind him, Heldi had a hand on her crossbow. Not a bad idea to be ready for a potential attack—they still didn't know who had attacked Chasm View, or why. Devon rested her hand on *Night's Fang's* hilt as the party advanced.

"Ordinarily, I'd say aye, lass," Dorden said. "But I can't help thinking we'll get our fill of adventure in the Skargills. Basilisks, ye say?"

"According to King Kenjan. But he said that only the alphas have the *Stone Gaze* ability, and there hasn't been one of those spotted near Vulture's Rift in a generation. So I think we'll be okay, even without an antidote or a spell to cure petrification. The common type just has a temporary paralysis attack."

"Oh, just *temporary* paralysis," Greel muttered. "Well, that certainly makes me feel better about this venture."

The dwarf patriarch, however, turned with a wide grin splitting his face. "Ye answer like ye think I was looking for reassurance, lass. To tell the truth, I just don't want to waste time turning over rocks in a dead city when I could be cracking some reptile skulls."

Devon blinked. Were basilisks actual reptiles? She'd never really thought about it. The last time she'd encountered one in a game world, it had been kind of like a two-legged armadillo-rooster hybrid with lizard scales. So yeah, maybe?

Dorden's grin was infectious, and even Bayle started smiling as she glanced toward the north where the Stone Forest thinned near the foothills of the Skargills. Devon wanted to mention that, *Stone Gaze* or not, the basilisk threat *was* serious enough that the Skevalli commoners needed help from their griffon-riding royals to fend off the beasts. The cracking of their skulls might be a challenging matter. But she decided there was no reason to be a downer.

They'd entered the denser portion of the ruins of Parshinta, and she cast a faintly longing glance at one of the open doorways. Okay, so there might be loot inside some of the buildings, but then again, there might not. It wasn't like the Skevalli ancestors had abandoned their home in a panic. They'd probably taken their most valuable items with them, anyway.

"All right," she said. "Onward."

Dorden unslung his warhammer from his back and raised it in a cheer. "Time to show the beasties what it means to mess with a Stoneshoulder."

Beside him, Heldi sighed and shook her head. She cast Devon a long-suffering look.

Oblivious, Dorden turned back to the north and started stomping forward, a tune once again rumbling from his throat.

"Oh," he said, "speaking of creatures and turning to stone, did I ever tell ye the story of the search for Agawen's silver vein and the cave troll that interrupted us?"

"Fool man," Heldi said. "Ye know that's not true about sunlight turning those monsters to stone."

"Aye, but many still believe it."

"Only because people like ye keep telling tales that say that's the truth."

"Shush, woman. I'm talking here!" Dorden raised his hammer again as if to punctuate his words.

Heldi rolled her eyes and shrugged at Devon as if to suggest she'd tried.

"Anyway," her husband said. "It was me, Gonavan, Elshwill, and Bombli, and we'd heard a rumor from a traveling bard that Agawen's lost silver strike might be found in the cleft between the Wyvern's Tooth and Olwen's Knucklebones. So we packed up our rucksacks and laced on our boots. Drank a few horns of ale and headed out to make our fortune."

***

An hour later, the group reached the edge of the Stone Forest, and Dorden was still talking.

"So when we heard it again, and this time I said 'Bombli, ye beardless fool, cave trolls don't come out in the daylight. Quit yer yellow-spined whining and go peek over that ridge.'"

"Wait," Greel said. "I thought we already established that cave trolls don't turn to stone when struck by the rays of the sun. If you were to walk in the sort of circles in which you talk, we'd be back to Ishildar by now."

Dorden raised a finger. "Patience, friend. I never said anything about *why* I told 'im that the monsters stay hidden in daylight."

"But that's just it. To suggest that, as a race, trolls of the cave-dwelling variety eschew daylight appearances is utter nonsense. There are innumerable accounts of the monsters waylaying travelers during their noon-time meals. Frankly, I'm beginning to wonder if this tale is a fabrication."

Devon had been wondering the same thing, but she wasn't about to give Greel the satisfaction of knowing it. Whether the story was true or not, at least Dorden's recounting had given her something to listen to besides the lawyer's complaints.

"Maybe we should just let him finish before we reach the Skargills." As she spoke the words, she cast a wary eye toward the stony ridges that knifed from the terrain ahead. The rock was jagged and ruddy, and in the darkening light now that the sun had set, streaks of what she assumed was iron oxide looked unpleasantly like blood shed by adventurers who had tried to ascend the severe crags. Between the ridges, dark gashes opened in the foothills—the entrances to the infamous chasms, she surmised. According to Kenjan, it was usually safest to travel through the chasms at night. She'd already conveyed that information to the group, but so far none of them had thought to ask why. She hoped the answer wouldn't cause their courage to falter. Just thinking about his explanation made her shiver.

"In any case," Dorden said loudly, "the *reason* I mentioned that myth about cave trolls was because otherwise Bombli would never pull 'imself together and go see what all the infernal bellowing was about. So I mentioned the daylight thing, and I questioned whether his beard was real or the product of a Zongi witch doctor's potion, and pretty soon, Bombli was marching up that ridge and muttering to himself about how his first whiskers sprouted before he was belly-high on a mule." Dorden chuckled to himself at the memory.

"Ye might notice that nowhere in this tale is me dear husband volunteering to investigate the strange sounds himself," Heldi commented.

"Woman! I seem to remember asking ye to shush. And it was important that someone stay back to guard the rest of the group."

"Gonavan and Elshwill," Heldi said with a smirk. "Now I hadn't yet come to the Stoneshoulders at that point, but since those two were graybeards when I arrived, it makes me think they would have been warriors in their prime at the time of this story."

Dorden growled. "At this rate ye'll be cooking yer own meals for a week once we return, me traitorous spouse."

Heldi just laughed.

"Anyway," Dorden said, "it was a fine thing I had the wisdom and foresight to suggest it should be Bombli who investigated the noise." He paused and turned, raising an eyebrow as if waiting for someone to ask *why* this choice was so wise. When no one did, he shook his head in disappointment and continued anyway. "Because the whole point of this story is that the bellowing and hollering wasn't a cave troll at all. Ye see, Bombli wasn't much for bathing. Said it interfered with his natural musk. We all felt sorry for the lad, so we didn't tell him that his problem with the ladies likely had more to do with the unfortunate composition of his face than his particular odor. And though his efforts to avoid cleansing were little help with the dwarven lassies, turned out his scent bore a strong resemblance to that of a female yak in heat. All that racket we'd been hearing was a group of bachelor yaks fighting over who would have the right to the fair lady they thought they smelled. When Bombli appeared on the ridge top, and the wind carried his scent down into the gully beyond, well ye can imagine the stampede. Never saw a dwarf run so fast. Not even Bodenir when he stripped down and lathered up with that nut oil ye so kindly gave us."

Silence held for a moment, but when Dorden started laughing, a deep rumble that rose from his chest, Devon couldn't help herself. It *was* pretty funny—if not quite the story she had expected. The rest of the group joined in the laughter as they continued forward, but as they passed the final tree and gazed out over a barren stretch of ground between their position and the nearest chasm mouth, the chuckles petered out to silence.

"So where is Bombli now?" Devon asked. The yak-smelling dwarf definitely wasn't among the group of Stoneshoulders who had joined her village. Thankfully.

Dorden sighed. "Miss that fellow, I do. Unfortunately, the memory of being chased by a herd of horny yaks gave 'im nightmares. He got 'imself frightened of going outside after a while, and a few months later, he announced he'd be heading to the lowlands—an area too warm for wild yaks to graze, ye see. He said that he figured one of the hill clans could use a dwarf with hard-rock mining expertise."

"Think he ever found a woman to appreciate his musk?" Devon asked.

Dorden laid a hand on his belly as he laughed. "We can only hope, eh?"

"Well then," Greel said, a slight edge in his voice. He gestured toward the mountains. "Shall we?"

Another silence fell. Devon eyed the nearest chasm. The floor of the rift was already lost in shadow, dusk-cloaked cliffs rising on either side. She'd never been particularly bothered by tight spaces, but something about the hemming walls made the gap between them seem ever more ominous.

Everyone jumped when a piercing shriek came from behind a large boulder. Hands flew toward weapon hilts, and both Heldi and Bayle had arrows nocked before Proudheart strode forth with a well-oiled Kenjan on his back.

"The quickest route lies through the second chasm to your right," the Skevalli king said. "I suggest keeping your weapons at the ready because there have been strange happenings lately. I can't say for sure what we'll find."

Chapter Thirty-Four

THERE'D BEEN ABOUT a five-year window—back before Devon's mom had kicked her out but after Devon was old enough to ride public transportation alone—when she'd spent most weekends out on her own. Usually, that had meant taking her crappy tablet somewhere downtown, a library or coffee shop that allowed freeloaders, and playing old flatscreen games. She couldn't afford time in a VR pod back then, and the games industry had already pretty much abandoned regular viewports, but at least it had been an escape from her mom's drunken rants and the stacks of unwashed dishes piled from one end of the apartment to the other.

Sometimes, though, even that hadn't given her enough clear headspace to make it through another week at whichever crappy public school, online or physical, she'd been enrolled in at the time. Just being surrounded by walls made her think of the peeling paint and decaying plaster that encompassed her home life, and on those days, she'd hop a bus out past the outskirts of the city. When they'd done stints in Vegas, that had meant cruising to Red Rock Canyon National Conservation Area where sandstone peaks the colors of orange and strawberry sherbet baked under the desert sun and stray burros lived wild. Near St. George, she'd head to Zion National Park to walk along the river where it carved a channel between canyon walls thousands of feet high.

The trek through the chasm reminded her of those times, and especially of the side trails she'd explored, heading off angry and alone to find a spot to stab at the sandy ground with a stick and imagine what it would feel like to escape her life. She remembered the smells of those lonely side canyons, the faint ammonia scent wafting from vertical cracks in the stone where rodents made their nests. Midday, the sun-warmed rock gave off an odor like an empty, preheated oven. Mornings and night, moisture rose from deep in the sand while dew painted the hardy foliage, bringing the smell of life from what had seemed to be a dead land during the heat of the day.

Of course, now when her nose picked up the unmistakable smell that meant something was nesting in one of the deep clefts in the stone, Devon didn't stop to see if a cute little packrat might poke its snout and whiskers from the crevice. She'd rather avoid whatever might live deep in these cliff walls.

They'd been trekking through the gash in the mountains for about half an hour, and their progress had put them well beyond the foothills. Although the canyon walls would grow even taller as they advanced, already the sky was nothing but a narrow strip of cold stars. If someone were to drop a rock from the rim, it would probably take thirty seconds or more before it landed on the packed-clay floor of the chasm.

Of course, thinking about something tumbling from the rim made her worry about larger rockfalls. If someone above knew her party was down here and that person had the means to knock free a cascade of stones—not a tremendous stretch given the variety of magic spells in the game—there'd be no escape. Once again, she thought of the player party that had attacked Chasm View, and she glanced at her messenger app to see if Chen, who she'd recently added as a contact, had anything to report from his investigation.

Nothing.

Well, at least the choice to move through darkness meant that someone up top would have to detect them by means other than sight. And since only her close allies knew she was journeying through the chasm maze to reach Vulture's Rift, it wasn't like anyone would be looking for her party. Her working theory about the raid on Chasm View still made sense. It had almost assuredly been conducted by players out exploring and adventuring for experience and loot. The only thing that made her question that theory was the reported brutality of the attack.

It wasn't that Devon lacked for enemies. Members of the griefer guild that had attacked Stonehaven a few months ago probably still hated her and her player allies. But the Skevalli royal settlement was so remote—it was a huge stretch to think that the griefers would both know about her relationship with the Skevalli *and* decide to travel all the way into the Skargills just to screw with her plans.

Anyway, the real danger lay in the enemies they might find in the chasm bottom. Hand gripping her dagger's hilt, she squinted into the darkness ahead. Kenjan and Proudheart walked at the front of the group, the griffon's wings folded tight to his sides. The griffon's tail twitched as he stalked forward, feline rear paws silent against the ground. Now and again, Devon heard the click as one of the animal's front talons scraped a stone embedded in the chasm floor, but for a beast with a twenty-foot wingspan, Proudheart was remarkably quiet.

Quieter than Dorden, anyway. Bringing up the rear, the dwarf clattered and grumbled, his armor squeaking when it wasn't clanging against stone. Fortunately, Kenjan had assured them that *Stealth* wouldn't make the difference between making it through the initial stretch of chasm or not.

Whether they'd make it through the gateway chasm and into basilisk territory depended on whether they ran into a certain dreadful beast that Kenjan had called a Rift Spinner, and if so, whether they could escape with their lives.

She squinted harder, scanning up and down the walls around a hundred feet in front of Kenjan. Nothing yet.

She just hoped their good fortune would last.

***

"Uh…" Bayle said.

"Yeah, uh…guys?" Dorden echoed.

"What?" Devon asked. "What is it?"

"I guess I'm not the only one who feels watched," Heldi said.

"No. You are definitely not the only one," Greel returned. The lawyer's shoulders were hunched more than usual, and his head whipped side to side as he scanned for enemies. Devon searched the area as well, utterly confused. What were they even talking about—oh. She hovered her attention over the debuff icon that had appeared in the corner of her interface.

You are afflicted by: Watched.

You feel watched. (Obviously)

"Try to spot the glowing eyes," Kenjan said in a tight voice. "We must know how many."

"The eyes?" Dorden growled. "What's this about eyes?"

Devon grimaced. So yeah. She hadn't found the right opportunity to warn the party of the potential they might run afoul of a Rift Spinner. Mostly because Kenjan had been so fervent in his hope that they wouldn't encounter any.

"We may have some sort of gargantuan human-spider hybrid to deal with here," she said, attempting to keep her voice casual. "They're called Rift Spinners. But if there's just one set of glowing eyes, it's probably not a nesting brood mother, so we should be able to fight or escape."

Greel whirled and stared at her.

"And if it *is* a nesting brood mother?"

"Let's just hope it's not," Kenjan answered from up ahead.

"There." Bayle already had an arrow nocked, and she aimed it at a point around fifty feet up the cliff face. Devon peered, and the sudden flare of a pair of glowing red eyes momentarily overwhelmed her darkvision. She squinted as the spell adjusted, then winced as what appeared to be another two dozen sets of glittering eyes emerged from the darkness.

"Blasted boreholes," Dorden said. "Not sure I can count that high."

"I'm pretty sure you can't," Heldi agreed. "But only because you'd run out of fingers."

"So the groupings of eight eyes..." Greel said. "I'd like to assume the Rift Spinner young are more spiderlike than human, and that each cluster represents only one enemy." The lawyer was trying to sound cavalier, but the trembling in his voice gave him away.

"Given their distribution, I'd like to say yes," Kenjan said. "But the truth is I don't know."

"Wait. How can you not know?" Greel said. "Are you not the literal king of the intelligent race that peoples this region?"

"I don't *know* because the only information my people have about Rift Spinner brood mothers comes from our investigations of the aftermath."

"Aftermath?" Bayle asked.

"Yeah. Such as when we go in search of a lost scouting party and find their greatly damaged remains near the broken egg sacs of the hatchlings. As far as I know, we are the only living souls to have seen a brood mother. So at least there's that."

"Yeah," Devon muttered. "At least there's that." Speaking in a whisper she continued, "Hey game, shouldn't I get some kind of achievement or something?"

Like a consolation prize for utterly failing to reach the followers you are supposed to escort?

"Yeah, like that. And technically I haven't failed yet, thank you very much."

Up above, the brood mother made a hissing-shriek sound. Devon shivered as the thing's young responded with a chorus of insect-like chittering. Single-player games—and the save points that came with them—were sounding pretty darn nice right now.

A soft glow surrounded Heldi's hands as the dwarf woman began to cast her damage shield. The spell fired, surrounding Dorden with a shimmering field, and his wife immediately began casting another.

"Not for me," Kenjan said as he swung up to Proudheart's back. "Save your mana."

"Wait," Devon said, too late because Heldi's cast bar vanished as the words left Devon's mouth. "Kenjan, you have the second highest hit points after Dorden. I assumed you and Proudheart would off-tank."

"Just try to hold out," Kenjan said as Proudheart spread his wings and began running away down the chasm. "Whatever you do, don't anger any more hatchlings than necessary."

"Uh, wait. You're leaving?" Devon called.

"Does that man truly intend to abandon us?" Greel asked, incredulous.

"Veia willing, I'll see you again," Kenjan called as his mount lifted into the sky.

Chapter Thirty-Five

"THIS EXPEDITION HAS certainly gone well," Greel said. "Thank you so much for bringing me along. I can't imagine what useful things I might otherwise have done with the remaining years of my life."

The lawyer aimed a kick at another Rift Spinner young as it sprang from the cliff face, fangs extended and dripping poison or ichor or saliva or something else gross. Greel's boot heel connected with the attacker's thorax, sending the Spinnerling sailing across the chasm. The monster smacked the chasm wall with a wet sort of crunch, but a quick *Combat Assessment* told Devon that Greel had only knocked off around a quarter of its health. Though momentarily dazed, the thing righted itself and started scuttling forward on legs disturbingly similar to a toddler's chubby limbs but with weird barb-like growths all over the flesh.

At least Greel had been right about them being more like spiders than humans at this stage—fighting spiders with creepy baby heads would probably give her nightmares for years. As it stood, the things were still disgusting: brownish-black in color with light fur coating their bodies, eight limbs jutting from a vaguely human-like torso, and a spider's head.

Of course, their human head wasn't entirely absent; on the larger of the Spinnerlings—those which had had more time to mature,

Devon assumed—a bulge on their torsos marked where the human skull would soon burst free. Dorden's first hammer strike had split the chest of an attacker, granting the party a glimpse of *that* little surprise before the dwarf had freaked out and smashed the Spinnerling to a pulp.

It seemed like, after the human head emerged, the spider version deflated and withered. At least that's what Devon gathered after spotting a flapping lump-thing on the back of the neck of the Spinnerlings' charming mother. Mama dearest—sporting a woman's torso and head, eight grasping arms, and a fat spider's abdomen— was above the party now, shrieking and hissing and leaping between the chasm walls. Every second or so, she shot out a strand of web from the spinnerets inside the bottom of her bulging butt. Devon could see the mother's plan. The Rift Spinner held the upper ends of the strand, likely for further weavings. The other ends attached to the cliff faces and chasm floor, forming the beginnings of webbed barriers ahead and behind the party.

She was fencing them in.

For all her hissing and squealing, the brood mother didn't attack. She didn't need to, not when she had dozens of children happy to sacrifice themselves for the cause. Six or seven of the things were swarming around the party now, striking with barbed legs and razor-sharp fangs. As Greel delivered a karate chop with the blade of his hand, the blunt trauma splitting the flesh of a Spinnerling's torso, the mother squealed in anger. Her glowing red eyes seemed to burn into Greel for a moment, but a shout from Dorden brought her attention back to the tank.

Mama hissed and shot out a thick strand of web. Dorden yelped when the silken rope snared his warhammer and yanked it from his hand. Devon's eyes widened as their tank's weapon flew high over the party. Quickly, she canceled her cast, a *Freeze* spell she'd aimed at a Spinnerling and instead slammed mana into a *Flamestrike* targeting the lasso. The strand burned for a full second before finally parting and dropping the dwarf's weapon to the chasm floor. Dorden bellowed and ran for the warhammer, and the brood mother turned an angry stare on Devon, her lips pulling back from creepy teeth/fang things.

"Oh no ye don't," Heldi shouted.

In one quick motion, the woman snapped off a crossbow shot, skewering one of the Spinnerlings through the eye, then started casting her damage shield to protect Devon.

As the buff landed, another four Spinnerlings dropped from the walls and aimed leg strikes at the party members. A chitinous barb caught Devon in the back of the knee, and she staggered forward as pain flared and a chunk of her hitpoints fell away. Dorden roared and snatched up his hammer, then dropped it again as the smell of burning flesh and a puff of smoke leapt from his palm. Crap. Devon hadn't considered that her *Flamestrike* would leave his weapon too hot to touch.

Kicking the Spinnerling that had attacked her knee, Devon shook her head in frustration. They needed to get control of this fight, keep the mobs' attention on the tank so that Heldi could focus her heals and shields on one person and everyone else could focus on burning the attackers down. Problem was, there were so many Spinnerlings, with more arriving by the minute. Dorden's methods for grabbing mob attention didn't have a wide area of effect, and the brood mother moved her focus around too easily.

Of course, without a weapon, the tank couldn't even grab the attention of a single Spinnerling.

Gritting her teeth, Devon first cast *Freeze* on the Spinnerling targeting her, then summoned a *Wall of Ice* near the warhammer, temporarily blocking the advance of two more Rift Spinner young while—she hoped—cooling Dorden's weapon enough that he could grab it. The spell managed to trap the pair of the Spinnerlings in the frozen wall while leaving their hindquarters exposed, and Greel sprang, whipping out knives for a double backstab. The juvenile Rift Spinners stiffened then died.

> *You receive 2300 experience.*
> *You receive 2500 experience.*

"Nice aim," Devon called. "Keep it up, and we might stand a chance." Not that taking out two of the Spinnerlings would make much difference. At least twenty remained, many still clinging to the walls above, which prevented anyone from taking their best advantage of area-of-effect attacks.

They really were hosed. But admitting it wouldn't help anything.

"Frankly, you're delusional," Greel muttered as he launched a flying roundhouse at another pair of enemies. "All I can hope now is that you remember how to perform your resurrection magic at the Veian Temple. And that you have the wits to figure out what sacrifice Veia will demand."

Devon rolled her eyes but otherwise ignored the comment. She focused on the brood mother and tried another *Combat Assessment*.

> Rift Spinner Brood Mother - Level 31

Health: 5632/6123

Resistances: unknown

Weaknesses: unknown

Well, crap. Devon had hoped that between her *Flamestrikes* and the arrows Bayle kept firing at the brood mother, they would have knocked off at least a quarter of the monstrosity's health. Survey says: no. Not even close. The level difference surely didn't help, but there had to be a boss mob mechanic at play, making it even harder to damage the thing.

In the chaos caused by the theft of Dorden's warhammer and the newest Spinnerling adds, Devon had lost track of the web barriers the brood mother was constructing. She glanced along the chasm toward where Kenjan had taken flight—some help he'd turned out to be. The exit was now nearly sealed by a web of thick silk strands. So much for any hope they had of fleeing. The web pretty much guaranteed they'd die here.

Of course, maybe she could try to burn a hole through the web. It had worked with the lasso, though slowly. Or...actually, that gave her another idea. After verifying that the ice had sufficiently cooled Dorden's hammer—yup, he was back to laying about with it and slowly losing hitpoints despite his wife's healing efforts—she focused on the web ahead of them and cast *Phoenix Fire*. Slow-moving flame sprang into existence at the base of the barrier and began to crawl up the strands and spread across the silk net. Devon tensed and waited while the firelight crawled up and across the chasm, creating a burning lattice, brilliant against the night. As the Rift Spinner gave a laughing hiss and sent another strand down between the burning web and the party, suggesting that she would just rebuild, Devon took a breath and cast *Conflagration*, her most destructive spell, but one that required a source of flame to combo off.

The web exploded in blue and purple light, sparks arcing between strands. Lightning raced up the ropes still connected to the mother's abdomen, and in a disgusting and satisfying couple of seconds, the brood mother's belly glowed from within as her spinnerets ignited inside her body. The creature screamed and howled in pain and frustration. When she'd recovered enough to turn her rage on Devon, she aimed her butt straight in Devon's direction, but no silk shot out. Devon smirked and tossed a *Combat Assessment* at her.

Rift Spinner Brood Mother - Level 31
Health: 4742/6123
Resistances: unknown
Weaknesses: Lightning

Now *that* had done some damage. Around 900 hitpoints removed in one hit, and as a bonus, Devon had uncovered a weakness to lightning-based damage. Unfortunately, the trick wouldn't work a second time, seeing as the Rift Spinner no longer produced silk and her connection to the remaining barrier had been severed in the blast. When the brood mother's silk organs had exploded, the dangling strands connecting to the other web had fallen to hang somewhat haphazardly from what was now a rather tattered-looking barrier. Devon fixed the location in her mind, keeping a mental note of its distance from her position. She wanted to keep it in range of her *Phoenix Fire* just in case some miracle would allow her to take advantage of the combo in another way.

But for now, she delivered a kick to a Spinnerling that, while focused on Dorden's bellowing form, was too close to comfort. The enemy stumbled as one of its legs folded in the wrong direction, and Devon dashed away before it could retaliate. Jaw clenched, she cast a *Glowing Orb*. When the ball of light manifested in her hand, she threw it against the wall, sending wild shadows moving over the scene.

A tearing sound came from the cliff overhead.

Devon whipped her gaze up. She moaned in dismay as, disgorged by a new set of ruptured egg sacs, dozens more Rift Spinner young poured down the cliff toward the party. The chittering of the hatchlings swelled to a roar, filling the chasm and echoing along its length. The enemies on the ground seemed to draw strength from the appearance of their siblings, and all at once, they leapt at Dorden.

The dwarf's hitpoint bar flashed as his health dropped perilously low. 15% or less. Heldi bellowed in frustration and cast another heal, but the arachnids were all over Dorden now, and his health dropped despite his wife's effort.

Devon glanced again at the web blocking their retreat. Well, this had been a glorious waste of time. But she could always spare the party the misery of being legged to death by dozens of grotesquely half-human spiderlings. Might as well go out in a blaze of glory, dragging their enemies with them.

"This way," she shouted as she started for the web, the casting motions for *Phoenix Fire* already dancing on her fingertips. A fraction of a second before the spell launched, a shadow passed overhead.

"Leave the web!" Kenjan's shout rolled through the chasm.

Devon stopped short, the spell fizzling on her fingertips as Proudheart swooped down from high between the chasm walls. Wings pulled tight to his body, the griffon streaked toward the tattered web. Devon shook her head, utterly confused. Did Kenjan intend to use the web like those hook things that snared fighter jets when they landed on aircraft carriers? Didn't seem like the brightest idea. And anyway, what good was Kenjan going to do at this point? He might as well save himself.

The wind whistled over Proudheart's wings as the griffon opened them and converted the energy of his dive into horizontal motion. He skimmed past just inches above the top of her head, the downdraft from his wings flattening her cloak against her back. She smelled the griffon's feathers and the scented oil that Kenjan put in his hair. Mouth agape, she watched as Proudheart sped straight for the barrier, not even bothering to brake.

Maybe Kenjan had actually lost it, gone mad after the murders of his family and the failure of their party to reach Vulture's Rift and rescue his remaining people. Or maybe he'd had the same suicidal thought as she had, deciding that the whole blaze-of-glory thing was the best way to go.

Well, if not a *Conflagration* spell, maybe she could take out a load of Spinnerlings in some final AoE attacks, even if the splash damage would hit the party too. Turning back to the party, she insta-cast a lightning-based *Shadow Puppet*. While her minion rose from the earth, a keening shriek echoed through the canyon. She yanked her gaze up in time to see a massive winged creature streaking between the walls. Light from her *Glowing Orb* glinted off massive talons and a gargantuan beak, and a hint of oily iridescence rippled in the bird's plumage.

Devon's jaw went slack a second time as the bird—what was it anyway? An eagle?—swooped down and skimmed, as Kenjan had, over the top of her head. She ducked and spun in time to see Proudheart pull up so swiftly that she could scarcely imagine the G-forces. Strands of Rift Spinner web fluttered in the wind caused by Proudheart's passage. A second later, the other bird-thing slammed into the web; it hadn't stood a chance of matching the griffon's maneuver. The silken ropes strained and stretched as they caught the giant creature, and the bird thrashed in the net's sticky grip.

Devon snapped off a *Combat Assessment*.

Chasm Roc - Level 40

Feared by all who fall beneath its shadow, the roc is the top predator of the Skargill Chasms. Only one other creature has been known to contest the roc's supremacy, and then only by trickery, not by prowess. Rift Spinners, a spider-human hybrid, have been known to spin webs between the chasm walls for the specific purpose of ensnaring rocs as a food source for a brood of Spinnerlings.

All around, the chittering grew silent. Stillness gripped the floor of the chasm for a moment, and then the Rift Spinner young burst into motion, scurrying not toward Devon's group, but heading straight for the captured bird. The brood mother shrieked in dismay, howling at her children to warn them of the trick, but the Spinnerlings paid her no heed.

"Focus on the mother," Kenjan shouted as he came through in another flyby. "If we can figure out a way to disable her spinnerets, I think we might just stand a chance of survival."

If only they could disable the spinnerets, huh? Devon grinned as she cast a second *Glowing Orb* and matching *Shadow Puppet* and sent her minions streaking toward the brood mother.

"Care to take back those negative comments you made earlier, game?" she asked aloud.

Fine. Yes. Good job. As long as you stop gloating and start fighting.

Devon smirked and slammed the brood mother with a *Flamestrike*. 2000 hitpoints down, 4K to go.

Chapter Thirty-Six

EMERSON WAS PRETTY awesome at this detective stuff. Not certified-private-investigator level, but seriously, that had been kind of a brilliant move to suggest he help with the investigation into Ishildar's structures. His presence was *definitely* making imposter-Hailey nervous, and that behavior alone was enough justification for his continued investigation.

Not only that, but he'd also just gotten a response to his request for a secondary confirmation of the poor woman's death from the care facility. According to some nameless administrator at Horizons Long-term Care, yes, as reported previously, Hailey Landers had indeed and regrettably passed away. The message went on to ask if he would be willing to come pick up Hailey's remaining belongings. Apparently, the facility was not allowed to donate or destroy anything that belonged to a deceased patient without waiting for two months for the possessions to be claimed.

Clearly these people needed some lessons in compassion and tact. But anyway.

While following Hailey and Owen as they strolled down one of Ishildar's wide avenues, Emerson focused on his messenger interface and composed a reply asking, as tactfully as he could manage, what had become of Hailey's body. If—or maybe he should say *when*—his theory panned out, he and the company would certainly need to learn how the woman's implants had been stolen. It seemed unlikely that care facility staff were involved with the theft. Not because they seemed to be great people or anything, but because this was some serious high-tech crime. The skill sets just really didn't line up. So that was a mystery: how had the culprits managed to waylay her body between the care facility and its final destination?

At the next street corner, Hailey and Owen stopped to consult the settlement interface. As Emerson drew to a halt behind them, a message came in from Devon. He grinned as he read it.

"So Hailey," he said, then waited for the woman to acknowledge him. "Did you get the latest note from Devon?" Of course, he knew full well that Devon and Hailey had never stayed in touch through any kind of out-of-game messaging, but he was pretty certain the hacker wouldn't know that.

"No," she said, blinking and looking moderately annoyed. Her expression quickly changed to something resembling concern, but Emerson had already spotted her true feeling.

"Is everything okay?" the imposter asked.

"So far, so good," he said, watching the woman's eyes as he spoke. "I guess they had a scary fight with some sort of spider woman, but Fabio rode to the rescue by distracting the spider's young with the species' natural prey. The party was able to finish off the mother, and now Fabio thinks the young will die off without her to bring in more food. Devon's party just arrived at Vulture's Rift, and Devon is getting ready to rez the Skevalli royalty."

"Well, that's good, I guess. Thanks for the update."

Owen was looking back and forth between Hailey and Emerson, apparently perplexed as to why Emerson seemed to be addressing this information to Hailey alone. Emerson didn't blame the guy, but he wasn't about to tell him about the investigation, either. This kind of thing was delicate, and not everyone could pull off the kind of incognito research Emerson was managing.

Also, he had to admit that he sorta liked the idea of being the one to single-handedly gather the evidence and unmask the criminal. He couldn't help imagining the look on Devon's face when he explained how he'd managed it. Speaking of, he ought to check on the other threads of investigation that he had active. While Hailey and Owen fell back into a discussion of which structures they should physically visit and investigate next, Emerson opened a secure communications pipe to a virtual machine that he'd assigned to analyze network traffic for patterns matching Hailey's connection.

Emerson's eyebrows raised upon seeing the results.

Now *this* was interesting. He'd known this hacker must be pretty savvy to hijack the authentication process, and that he (or she, if he wanted to be equitable) likely had the backing of a hardcore criminal organization. Arranging an illegal and specialized surgery to install the implants didn't seem like the work of a single, rogue actor. Regardless, Emerson had expected multiple layers of obfuscation on the network traffic, and he'd prepared his analysis to deal with that.

But he hadn't expected his search to turn up *nothing*. Not a single query had come back with more than ten percent confidence that it had detected traffic from Hailey's avatar.

He narrowed his eyes as he stared at the side of the imposter's face. Clever or not, the thief would not evade him indefinitely.

Emerson would just have to up his game.

Chapter Thirty-Seven

TURNED OUT, WHEN five hundred people gathered together and stared at Devon, hoping she wouldn't screw up, it wasn't so easy to concentrate. Facing the Shrine to Veia that stood in the center of Vulture's Rift, Devon swallowed. This shrine was constructed differently than Stonehaven's, with gnarled and age-polished timber tied in a tripod by twisted-fiber ropes. Supported in the cradle of the tripod was a red-hued stone slab a couple of inches thick. The stone was about one foot by two feet wide, and the dried remains of offerings from the past—bunches of herbs mostly—still scattered its surface. Leaves of agate from the Stone Forest and shiny fragments of metal dangled by strings and leather cord from the legs of the tripod.

She took a deep breath. All right, so it was pretty clear where she'd place the items that would be sacrificed to bring back Kenjan's family. Veia demanded meaningful offerings as payment for bringing advanced NPCs back from the dead. Unfortunately, Devon didn't have much in the way of spare possessions.

She searched through her inventory and finally landed her attention on the empty clay pot that Hezbek had given her on her first day in the game. The gift had come with a quest popup offering Devon the opportunity to train in potion making. At the time, Devon had declined and asked for a raincheck, but she'd held onto the pot, thinking she might as well keep her options open in case she wanted to get into crafting.

Of course, that had been months ago, and she'd now given up any delusions that she'd have time to grind out a crafting profession on top of her other responsibilities. But whenever she saw the pot, it reminded her of Hezbek's kindness and the relationship they'd developed since that first meeting. And now that she had inventory space thanks to the garish *Sparklebomb Backpack of Subpar Holding*, she'd taken to carrying the item around as a sort of good luck charm.

Glancing at the gathered crowd, she pulled the pot from her backpack and set it on the shrine's slab. A popup appeared.

Looks like you want to resurrect an advanced NPC.
Is this correct? Y/N

Devon sighed in relief. Okay, this might work after all. Of course, she only had the one pot, but maybe Veia would cut her a break and give her a two-for-one deal or something. After that, there had to be something else she could cough up to keep the process going. She selected 'Yes' and waited for the next interface screen.

And you really think that a Nondescript Clay Pot - Small *is a worthy trade for the king or queen of a vassal civilization? That's interesting.*

Devon sighed. "Come on, Veia. Work with me here," she muttered. "I've been too busy trying to save the mortal realm to accumulate a bunch of stuff, you know."

"Is everything okay?" Kenjan asked, moving close so his quiet words could reach her ears without alarming his people.

Devon glared at the shrine. "Bringing people back requires that I sacrifice items with deep meaning."

Kenjan looked at the pot. "Interesting choice."

"It's a long story."

"Must be."

"Anyway, the problem is that I don't have much. Most of the things I have saved are unidentified magic items that I hoped to get around to identifying."

"Perhaps one of them would work?"

She sighed. "Yeah, perhaps. Except I was storing them in a chest in Stonehaven's Inner Keep. Didn't think to grab them when we got invaded."

"I see. Hmm."

You know, the items don't necessarily have to be in your possession.

Devon's brow furrowed as she stared at the popup. What other items could Veia be talking about?

Look to your right, genius.

Devon blinked and flicked her gaze in the direction indicated. Kenjan stood to her right, once again clad in the clothing she'd given him. Wait...no. She shook her head in a tiny motion.

I think you're starting to catch on. Tunic, trousers, and your little clay pot for the Skevalli royal family.

"All right," she muttered. "But don't think this is over." She turned to Kenjan. "I hate to ask this of you..."

Literally.

She brushed the popup away as Kenjan's brow lowered in earnest concern. "Anything, my liege. After everything you've done for us, I will sacrifice whatever I am able."

"I believe the shrine will accept your ceremonial garb as a sacrifice."

Kenjan looked down at the shapeless tunic and fingered the hem. "Of course. I—of course."

He tugged the tunic over his head, but the neck hole got stuck on his ears. Devon was forced to step close and awkwardly help him out of the garment. When he started fumbling with the tie for the trousers, flexing his abs in apparent consternation over how to unfasten the knot, she turned away and let him deal with it.

A couple of long minutes later, Kenjan set the neatly folded garments beside her pot.

Okay, cool. For the magic to work, you must stand near to the individual who is sacrificing his treasured possessions.

Devon rolled her eyes but stepped sideways until she could smell the scented oil in his hair. In response, a popup appeared with five names listed. Among them were Kenjan's parents, King Jildan and

Queen Kiela. The entries were already selected, and all she needed to do was mentally press the 'Resurrect' button.

The shrine began to hum, and the crowd gasped as, in the empty space encircled by the Skevalli citizens, multiple clouds of light began to form. Within moments, five humans and—a nice surprise—five griffon mounts materialized in the center of Vulture's Rift.

The crowd cheered, and Kenjan swept Devon up in a hug, his oiled muscles pressing against her as they hardened when he squeezed. Devon squirmed, but he didn't seem to notice her discomfort.

You know, even if this side trip doesn't end up helping defeat the demons, the entertainment is totally worth it.

***

"Aww, now look at them," Queen Kiela said as she laid a hand on her husband's shoulder. "No matter how much Kenjan complained about doing his core workouts, it was the right thing to make him continue."

"Wait. No." Devon finally wriggled free of Kenjan's muscular grip. "We aren't—I mean, your son didn't need to convince me to marry him to cement our alliance."

The queen gave her a knowing smile. "It's good of you to say that. Better to start your lives together with a foundation built on more than duty. But whether you might have been persuaded to come to our aid without my son's charms or not, what matters is that you did come. As prophesied, you have dragged the king and I from the very halls of Veia's Palace, restored us to life when our people need us most." The woman's face sobered. "But I fear things must move forward without delay. The two of you must formalize your union this very afternoon. You won't want to delay for preparations and feasts, because the final chapter is surely upon us. You must make haste to the Throne of the Ancients to seize the lost power of Ishildar."

"Mom," Kenjan said, "we're not getting—"

"Wait," Devon said, interrupting him by placing a hand on his arm. "What's this about a Throne of the Ancients?"

The queen cocked her head as if confused. "You are the Champion of Ishildar, are you not? We have long known that a time would come when a hero would rise to bring Ishildar's power to bear against the greatest threat the mortal realm has ever seen. And we've also known that one of our firstborn sons, heir to the Skevalli throne, would need to offer himself to you as our dear Kenjan has. Ishildar and the Skevalli people must be joined forevermore to ensure our continued survival." At this, the queen beamed another proud smile at Kenjan. Devon noticed that his inspection window once again titled him Prince Kenjan rather than King.

"This throne... It's within Ishildar?"

"Where else would it be?" Queen Kiela asked, blinking. "During the centuries when our ancestors paid fealty to the city, the Keeper sat upon the throne, using the city's spirit to bring protection and prosperity to all her citizens and vassals."

Veia is offering you a quest: Do I need to spell this out for you?

So, sounds like this little side trip has been worthwhile after all. Maybe hope isn't entirely lost.

Objective: Locate the Throne of the Ancients

Reward: The world might not end in fire after all.

Accept? Y/N

Devon quickly accepted the quest. She and Kenjan shared a glance during which the queen and king looked on as if it were the most romantic thing in the world.

"I've got things handled here," Kenjan said. "Between your friends and my parents and cousins, we can escort everyone safely back to Ishildar."

"What about the basilisks?" After defeating the Rift Spinner Brood Mother, the party had enjoyed an uneventful trek to Vulture's Rift. But Devon figured they'd just gotten lucky.

"I asked around, and it sounds like something scared off the nearby nest of those beasts," Kenjan said. "Ironically, I suspect we can thank the Brood Mother. Regardless, my family has always defended our tribe against this threat. You've brought back our strongest fighters. Together with these fine combatants"—he nodded at the dwarf couple, Greel, and Bayle—"I feel confident we can escort our people on a route that avoids the remaining Spinnerlings."

"You're sure?" Devon laid a hand on Kenjan's arm, which prompted a chorus of *awwws* from the gathered Skevalli.

He nodded. "And don't worry. I'll clear up this little misunderstanding by the time we arrive at Ishildar."

"Thanks," she said. "And just so you know, I do think you're great. It's just the whole starborn/non-starborn thing."

He smiled crookedly and flexed his abs, probably without realizing. "I don't feel bad. And honestly, it will be nice not to have to weigh each of my meals before eating to ensure I won't get a paunch."

The king and queen were staring at them in confusion. Devon guessed by the distance that although they couldn't hear many of her and Kenjan's words, they had to know something was going counter to their expectations.

She acknowledged them with a nod. "Your people will be in good hands on the return journey to Ishildar. I can see that much. I'll be teleporting back, and I've got room for a handful of passengers if you wish to send any."

The queen laid her hand on the king's lower back, just above the waist of his loincloth. She looked faintly dismayed but seemed to be trying to hide it. "I...yes, the elders would certainly appreciate the assistance. But may we offer you anything first, Liege? A meal perhaps?"

"Actually, if your elders can handle a temporary burden, we could really use a boost to our food stores. As much as they can carry would be great."

"I—sure." The queen blinked and then glanced at one of the villagers. "Please bring forth the nuts and berries."

Chapter Thirty-Eight

THE RESOLUTE DETERMINATION that had filled Devon's followers in the days after the evacuation from Stonehaven was gone, and an air of gloom now hung over Temple Square. While she stared out over the crowd, Devon tapped each of her fingertips with her thumb, a nervous habit. It seemed something had changed in her absence, and she had a feeling that an unpleasant surprise was waiting.

She motioned for the Skevalli elders to lay down the sacks of nuts and baskets of dried berries and gestured toward their gathered kin. With grateful wheezes and the cracking of joints, the grandmothers and grandfathers deposited the supplies on the polished floor of the Veian Temple and shuffled off.

Devon hurried to the stairs leading into the square. On the top step, she scanned the gathered refugees until she spotted some of her leadership in a small cluster. Jarleck appeared to be deep in conversation with Hezbek, Hazel, Torald, and Jeremy.

Her jaw clenched as she hurried over and noticed the state of her friends' gear. Torald's platemail was so dented that it *had* to be leaving bruises when he moved, and Jeremy's velvet court garb was in tatters. The bellows of the troubadour's accordion hung out of the frame, looking to Devon like the instrument had been disemboweled.

When Devon caught Jeremy's eye, her friend's shoulders sank, and he shook his head. Once she drew within earshot, he nudged Torald, who turned and shrugged, showing his palms.

"No luck taking out the glass supply, I guess," she said.

Both men shook their heads. "We chose the most thinly guarded position on the supply line," Jeremy said. "Came at them with a full raid force thinking we might disrupt the transportation, then press back toward the player camp and figure out a way to damage the supply itself."

"And?" Devon asked, her eyes flitting back and forth between the players.

"Dude," Jeremy said. "We don't have a prayer of halting work on the ziggurat. I think the supply wagons were trapped to send out an alarm signal. We managed to take out the guards—not without losses, of course—but the moment we tried to damage the wagon and the glass block, it was like the whole savanna came down on us. I think we might have killed a two or three demons for every player that dropped, but when you're outnumbered fifty to one, that hardly matters. Even when we formed up and tried to retreat, they just overwhelmed us. And with the death penalty causing us to leave behind random items when we respawn, now we're even weaker."

Just then, Devon noticed that Torald's greatsword was conspicuously absent. He seemed to follow the direction of her gaze and nodded, once again showing his empty palms.

"Shit," she said.

The men nodded.

"Mayor Devon?" Hazel asked quietly. "I'm afraid it gets worse than that."

Great. Devon took a breath and focused her attention on the little scout. "Go ahead."

"Well, I did manage to find the ingredients for Hezbek's potions. Went ahead and gathered enough for quite a few batches."

6 x Quest complete: Component gathering, now with DANGER. (repeatable)

"If you wish to choose which potions I brew with them, we can speak later," Hezbek said.

Devon shook her head. "It's fine. Your judgment on these things is always great." She turned back to Hazel. "And?"

"Well, I couldn't help thinking about how I made things harder on you by taking Zoe into the swamp and then getting trapped with her, so I thought I could make up for it by scouting for real. After I'd gathered what Hezbek needed, I took a detour to the south to check out progress on the ziggurat." The little scout pressed her lips together as if reluctant to deliver the news. "Unfortunately, I doubt disrupting the supply line for a little while would have saved us in any case. The building was 92% complete."

Devon's eyes widened. So fast? "How long ago was this?"

"Just yesterday evening."

She ran the math in her head, estimating the rate of construction based on the 60% completion stat Devon had gathered when she'd first scouted the installation. It was drawing toward evening already. If she wasn't mistaken, the ziggurat would be completed...tonight.

"Crap," she said, running her hands through her hair. "All right. Hope isn't entirely lost. Anyone seen Owen and Hailey recently? I have a lead on how we can finally use the city to win this thing, but I need their help to locate the structure."

Torald's brow furrowed as if he were trying to recall something. "Yeah, actually. I saw Owen at least. He came through about an hour ago, said he and Hailey had split up to cover more ground."

"Do you know which way he headed?" Devon cursed herself for not getting his messenger contact. Her avoidance of out-of-game contact was not worth the consequences. After this, whether it made her uncomfortable or not, it was time to get over her aversion.

Torald shook his head. "He just said he was going to check out some structures to the north, and that Hailey was heading southeast. He also mentioned that your friend Emerson had nominated himself an unofficial helper and that he'd tagged along with Hailey despite the woman's hints about working faster alone."

Devon sighed. Great. Just what they needed right now, Emerson spending enough time with Hailey to notice that the woman never logged out. Put together with the failed payment to her bank account, their boss was going to start to think something strange was going on. But at least his presence with Hailey gave her the means to contact the woman.

She opened up her messenger interface and selected his contact.

"Hey," she subvocalized. "Where are you guys? I think I might know how to win this, but I need Hailey's help."

There was a delay of just a few seconds before Emerson responded.

> *I'm not far. About ten blocks east, two south. I can see one of your Stone Guardians. Guessing it can see me, too.*
> *But, Dev, there's something up with Hailey.*

Oh no. He'd figured it out. Or at least, he knew she was no longer the ordinary player avatar she'd been. The pressure of the situation started to press in from all sides, squeezing the air from her lungs.

Devon closed her eyes and forced herself to take a deep breath.

"I'll be right there," she subvocalized, closing her eyes as she wrapped her hand around the *Greenscale Pendant* and activated *Ishildar's Call.*

Awareness of the Stone Guardians sprang to life in her mind. She felt their ponderous bodies and ancient, alien minds. Through their perception, she became aware of different areas of the city, the peace that still filled the streets despite the threats beyond Ishildar's borders.

Through one of the golems, the Guardian nearest Temple Square, she perceived Emerson pacing in front of...what was this? It seemed that there'd been a recent collapse of a building facade, and the man was stalking back and forth in front of the caved-in entrance, stopping now and again to peer through cracks between the fallen stones. He occasionally called something through the gaps, though the Stone Guardian's perception didn't pick up the words.

Was Hailey inside? Was that the problem...she'd been trapped in the structure when the wall collapsed? But that didn't make sense. If Emerson were concerned for her safety, he would have said so.

All right. The man wasn't far from Temple Square. If it turned out she needed to enlist help in digging Hailey free from the rubble, it wouldn't take more than a few minutes to run back and gather more people. But until she knew more, Devon didn't want anyone else involved.

She glanced at Hezbek. "Can you let Tom know that I've brought back food? I'm sure being reduced to half-rations hasn't helped our people stay strong. Since it sounds like we face a battle within the day, everyone should eat their fill."

The medicine woman nodded, a grim look on her face. "It will be done, Keeper."

Chapter Thirty-Nine

HA. EMERSON TOTALLY had the hacker now. Yes, this evildoer could disguise network traffic with all their fancy tricks, and they must've done something to change up the regular patterns for Hailey's avatar. But the game still had a notion of three-dimensional geographical locations for every object, NPC, and player in the world—it was a requirement for displaying and simulating the world and conveying the game state to the players' minds. And for the information about players' actions to be hooked up to the correct visual representation, network updates also included tags to identify the entity who was performing the action.

Ergo, since he was in Hailey's avatar's vicinity *and* he'd managed to trap her in a small geographic location, all he needed to do was analyze the information sent to his implant regarding nearby world state, and it should be trivial to isolate information relevant to Hailey's connection.

Pretty darn clever, honestly.

He smiled to himself as he peered through a small crevice between blocks which he'd managed to bring crashing down with his berserk-style charge. Hailey was inside glaring at the destroyed wall. The chamber beyond was only about ten feet square, probably a storeroom from Ishildar's glory days.

"I can see you, you know," she said. "Seekers can look through walls, remember?"

Aww crap. He'd forgotten that and had assumed that the hacker would figure he'd run off to get help.

"And I *also* can detect when enemies and people I'm not grouped with are activating abilities. I know you brought the wall down with one of your Frenzy attacks. Seriously, what gives, dude?"

He grimaced. Worse and worse. Though if he thought about it, maybe it didn't matter if the hacker knew Emerson was onto him or her. The edge in Hailey's voice continued to indicate nervousness, maybe even outright fear. Within the next half an hour, Emerson should have everything he needed to back up an accusation. And seeing as the worst this thief could do was log out, an operation that *definitely* left network fingerprints, the evildoer was pretty much toast.

His lip twitched as he pinned the thief with an icy glare. "All right, scum, we might as well stop pretending then, huh? I know what you did, you despicable cretin."

Hailey was silent for a moment, a bewildered expression briefly flitting across her face before her lips curled up in a snarl. "What the hell, Emerson? Don't know what your deal is, but would you stop staring at me like that?"

Emerson was about to ask whether his steely gaze was actually making her regret her unscrupulous life choices when Hailey's hands and eyes began to glow. A bolt of energy shot from her fingers and impaled him through the eye.

You have been afflicted with: Crippling Self-Doubt.
Combat effectiveness reduced by 15%.

"Ow," he said even though it didn't hurt. "Jerk."

He cupped a hand over his eye as he stepped back from the fallen wall and glanced at the output from his network analysis. The sooner this was over with, the better. Unfortunately, there was still nothing matching network patterns associated with Hailey's avatar, or for that matter, traffic that indicated player communication. The analysis bot should have picked up *something* by now.

How was the hacker managing it? What had he missed?

The sound of a deep sigh traveled through the rubble, surprisingly audible given the situation. "Look," Hailey said. "Despite your unforgivable treatment of me, I know enough about you to understand that is not your usual behavior. Given that you seem to be accusing me of some sort of crime, and since I have no clue what you're talking about, I think there must be some sort of misunderstanding."

Emerson slowly removed his hand from his eye and rubbed it with a knuckle. When he blinked a few times, he still saw the purple ghost of her spell's light, but his vision didn't seem to be damaged. Fists clenched, he stared at the rubble. Would a hacker actually admit to doing something wrong? No. But he knew the type, and their usual posture was one of defensiveness or aggression. This attempt to reason out the situation kinda *did* sound like Hailey. The results of his network analysis didn't point to a hacker either—after further data processing, the analyzer had finally managed to isolate information about a mobile entity in the proper geographical location, but there was no player-facing network connection associated with it. It was like he was looking at the pattern for an NPC. But obviously that didn't make sense.

"Hey. What happened?"

He whirled at the sound of Devon's voice, and his knees went a little weak with relief. He could really use some help puzzling this out. But quick on the heels of that emotion followed the realization that he'd have to tell her, here and now, that her friend had died. Unless...what about his theory that this was some kind of harassment? It still wouldn't explain the network weirdness or Hailey's suspicious behavior, but everything else lined up. Somewhere along the line, he'd heard players mentioning that Hailey had been the target of malicious internet comments from the griefer guild that had attacked to Stonehaven. The more he thought about it, that could make sense after all. Maybe she hadn't actually been nervous about his presence. Maybe she'd been—justifiably, perhaps—annoyed that he'd been disrupting their investigation.

He swallowed, totally at a loss for words as his thoughts whirled.

"Hey! Is it Devon? Are you there, Devon?"

Devon turned toward the rubble heap. "Hailey? What's going on?"

"Your friend here collapsed the wall and trapped me, and he's been accusing me of some kind of crime. Or of something nasty, anyway. He hasn't actually been clear."

Emerson cringed as Devon turned her gaze on him. "Emerson? There's got to be a misunderstanding here, right?"

"Well I did knock down the wall, but I can explain."

"Dev, can you get me out of here? I dunno...*Levitate* the blocks away or something?"

Devon blinked as if she hadn't thought of moving the rubble that way, then nodded. As her hands began to glow, Emerson dashed forward and grabbed them. "Wait."

The light faded, and for a split-second, Devon actually looked nervous. The expression was eerily similar to that which Hailey had been making for the last few hours.

"You're doing it, too," he said, gesturing at her face.

"Doing what?"

"Looking nervous."

"Uh, well, my friend's trapped and I don't understand why."

Emerson took a deep breath. "Listen for just a sec. I thought Hailey's account had been hacked and that the person was pretending to be her character. I figured I must be making the hacker nervous because of my position with E-Squared. But now I'm starting to wonder if I was just horribly confused in some way. Is there something you're not telling me?"

Devon stared at him like a confused kitten or something, her wide eyes blinking. She chewed her lip and glanced at the fallen wall.

"Tell me what you think of Bradley Williams," she said abruptly. "I mean, really I want you to tell Hailey. So you might want to face her."

"Uh...why?"

"Just trust me for a second."

The thing was, he did trust her, so Emerson slowly turned to face the rubble. "I think Bradley Williams is misguided and that he's had too much power for too long and that he's horribly out of touch with the needs of the game world."

"Okay, and how is he with people... I mean, does he have humanity's best interests in mind?"

Emerson snorted. "No. Bradley Williams has Bradley Williams' best interests in mind."

"And if there were something you knew, even if it related to Relic Online's technology—if you knew about something that would be terrible for Bradley Williams to find out, what would you do?"

He turned a confused look on Devon. "Didn't we already go through this with Owen? We only told him what we thought would be best to keep Owen and the rest of the player base safe."

"I know," Devon said. "But could you please just answer the question specifically? If you knew something that could be hurtful in Bradley Williams' hands, would you tell him about it because he's your boss?"

Emerson grimaced. "What? No. Definitely not. The truth is, lately I've been so disgusted with him that I want to quit working for E-Squared. Except if I do that, there's no one around to protect the players. There's no one around to make sure that you guys keep your jobs." He swallowed as he looked at Devon. Okay. Time to take the plunge. "Don't think I haven't seriously considered it, if only because of...because of us. I know it must be kind of nerve-wracking to think about dating your boss, Devon—I mean, not that I'm assuming anything. We can absolutely just stay friends if that's what you prefer. But anyway, yeah. No, I mean. I wouldn't tell Bradley something that could be harmful. The guy's pretty much a sociopath."

Devon seemed to need a moment to master her emotions. "We can talk about that other stuff later, and for what it's worth, you're not an idiot for thinking that I might be interested. Right now though, I really need Hailey's help. We have kind of an urgent situation going on."

She turned toward the rubble and stepped closer. "Hailey? What do you think? I'll follow your lead here."

She pressed her ear to one of the gaps so that Hailey could speak quietly. Emerson couldn't hear the other woman's words, but he could guess they aligned with Devon's hopes based on her nods. After a moment she turned back to him. "Okay, so this really isn't a subject for a super quick conversation, but that's all we have time for. So..." She paused while glancing around the scene, and gestured to a bench. "Hailey hasn't been hacked. She's the same, somewhat short-tempered gamer she's always been. So I'm going to let her out, and then we'll explain as best we can. Can you trust me on that?"

"I...sure."

Emerson shuffled to the bench while Devon once again began making the casting motions for *Levitate*. He felt exhausted, like he'd been hit by an emotional rogue wave or something. Or maybe by an emotional landslide like when a dump truck raises one end of its bed and lets a bunch of dirt and rocks fall out.

Anyway. Like some sort of clever metaphor that left him feeling kind of flattened or pounded or something. He was glad he wasn't in charge of creating content for this game, that his AI managed to come up with all the quest text and stuff because describing things was *hard*. But deciding to trust Devon was easy. So he took a seat on the bench and waited.

Chapter Forty

"WHOA," EMERSON SAID, his gaze distant. "I mean, jeez. Yeah, I can see why it's complicated." He turned to Hailey. "Are you sure? As in, you still feel self-aware and not like some sort of automaton just slaved to whatever pattern this...arcane AI cooked up?"

Hailey raised an eyebrow. "Um, well... I mean, if I were just a machine following some pattern, but I had enough meta-perspective to realize it, wouldn't that make me self-aware anyway?"

Emerson's mouth twisted as he pondered this. "Yeah, I guess so." He blinked and shook his head as if still trying to come to terms with the situation. "Crazy stuff. And that's without even considering that this whole situation was made possible by an emergent, self-creating AI." He glanced at Bob, who had arrived during the explanation and now perched on Hailey's shoulder.

Yeah, that was something Devon hadn't put much thought toward, given everything else that had been occupying her mind lately. It didn't surprise her that Emerson latched onto it, being an AI programmer and all. As much as she wanted to give him the time to process and ask more questions, a demon army would soon be marching into the city unless she could find this Throne of the Ancients and figure out how to use it to save the world. So, enough chitchat.

"Sorry to interrupt, but back to the war against the hellspawn," she said.

Her friends turned to look at her, their expressions quickly turning businesslike. Hailey spoke first. "I know you were hoping for results, but the truth is, Owen and I weren't making a ton of progress for a variety of reasons." She glanced at Emerson, who blushed a little. "So we decided to split up and work through the high-priority structures methodically. The settlement interface doesn't show locations for the buildings, so we're trying to cover ground quickly by walking the streets and using our discovery experience notifications to know whether the structures are on the important list."

"Well, the good news is I know what we're looking for now. Have either of you checked out something called the Throne of the Ancients?"

Hailey shook her head slowly as her gaze went distant, no doubt due to her focus on the user interface. "I think I remember—yeah, there. It's in the uppermost tier of buildings, but looks like neither of us has found it."

Devon felt her shoulders slump a little. Damn. "Okay, well then—"

"Devon."

She turned at the sound of Owen's voice, and couldn't help feeling a pang of guilt at the sight of his haggard appearance. Dark circles surrounded his hollow eyes, and his monk's garb hung off a skeletal frame.

"I guess someone from the square told you I was looking for you guys?" she asked.

Her guildmate looked perplexed for a moment, then shook his head. "I finally have something from the pattern. I saw the currents change, the shifting of potential. It happened late morning."

Devon's pulse quickened. "That was around the time Queen Kiela mentioned the Throne of the Ancients," she said.

Owen's eyes widened, and his face took on more color, heightening his feverish appearance. "Yes! That's it. If you can pull the threads together, join with the light by weaving them at the nexus—"

"Okay, great," Devon said, cutting off the obscure explanation, "so can you tell me how to find it?"

He cocked his head and stared at the ground for a while. "No...it seems that you're the only one who knows how to find it. The rest of us are just bystanders."

Uh. That wasn't very helpful. How was she supposed to single-handedly locate a single throne in the middle of a giant ruined city?

In the back of her mind, she still felt the plodding thoughts of the Stone Guardians. Could they help? As she focused on the nearest and gently asked it to approach, a popup flashed to life in her vision.

> **Ziggurat of the Damned** has been completed.
> Benefits conferred by the **Veian Temple** are no longer active.

She staggered as the buff icon, *Ishildar's Blessing*, faded from her interface.

Crap.

"Run to the square," she said to Emerson. "Tell them the demons are coming."

Chapter Forty-One

"ALL RIGHT, PEOPLE," Nil said. "I detected a few failed authentication attempts on our private forum. So I've wiped the history for now, and from here on in, we're sticking with the radio silence out of game. I mean it. Not even a PM to your mom, okay? The only communication allowed is through those of us in contact with Jeremy. The latest word is that we'll be attacking within the next hour or two, so don't be assholes and idiots. Now let's keep moving."

Ashley sighed as she rolled over in the grass. The whole stupid raid group was, at the moment, belly crawling across this endless grassland because this Jeremy guy had insisted they avoid going through the old ruined city to reach their target. Apparently, Devon had some way to sense things that happened in the city's borders, so it would just give the whole operation away. So after they'd come out of that godawful chasm and plateau area, they'd detoured around the eastern edge of Ishildar, skirting the Argenthal mountains. Now they had to approach through the fricking grassland, where there was jack-all for cover unless you were under twelve inches tall.

Or unless you belly crawled.

Regardless, they'd nearly reached the area that had been uncovered on her map the last time the guild had attacked

Stonehaven, so Ashley could finally get a notion of their distance to the goal. Just a mile or two, which was a crappy amount of belly crawling, but she assumed that once they moved into the shadow of that cliff that protected Stonehaven—finally gaining some cover—they'd be able to cross the ground more quickly.

She couldn't *wait* for this expedition to be over with. Already, she imagined the look on Nil's face once, after he'd promoted her to lieutenant for executing things so perfectly on this raid, she turned around and used the promotion to recruit the final people she needed for her betrayal.

It was going to be awesome.

Even if she had to massacre Stonehaven's NPC citizens and torture Devon and her player allies by spawn camping them for a couple of days.

As she crawled forward, she noticed that Nil had stopped moving. He seemed to be watching her as if waiting for her to catch up.

"Need something?" she said as she drew even with him.

Sharply cut features and a twisted mouth remained still for a long pause while he stared at her. "You take this as seriously as I do, don't you? I can tell. It's like...you're so intense. I like that."

She clenched her jaw. Was she going to have to deal with him talking to her all the way to their destination?

"Thought you might want the honor of advancing by my side," Nil said. "It's the best way I know to thank you for your loyalty."

She swallowed back bile. Yeah, seemed so.

Chapter Forty-Two

TOO LATE.

Even as Devon focused on her Stone Guardians and directed them to march for the southern border of Ishildar where they could, maybe, buy the defenders just a little more time before the demons overran the city, the words ran through her mind again and again.

Too late, too late. Too late.

But she kept trying anyway. The demons wouldn't take the city without a fight, battling the best resistance she could muster.

She put all her concentration to the task, focusing her perception on what she could see from the vantages of her golem defenders, desperately looking for tactical advantages she could use. Even so, she couldn't shut out the sight of Owen, Hailey, and Emerson standing in a tight group near her physical body. They spoke in clipped tones, and Hailey kept asking the same question over and over. Was there nothing they could do to help Devon find the Throne of the Ancients? And every time, Owen shook his head in response. It was up to Devon now, he kept saying, his facial expression inviting no argument.

Okay, but how? Scouring a vast city alone, how was Devon supposed to find the throne at all, much less locate it before the demons obliterated her people? She didn't even know where to start.

Stonehaven has been captured. The settlement's status is no longer contested.

If the forces of Archdemon Gaviroth remain in control for forty-eight hours, their claim to Stonehaven will be considered confirmed. Thereafter, any who wish to challenge for possession must first contest and then capture the settlement.

Devon closed her eyes and shook her head. She'd known this was coming now that the ziggurat was complete, but still, the confirmation was a gut punch. Back when she'd told Jeremy to stop teleporting strike teams into the hamlet, she still believed she'd find a way to keep the settlement's ownership contested until she could reclaim it. Despite the odds, she'd imagined she'd unlock Ishildar's secrets and ride to Stonehaven's rescue. But now...now she expected the loss would be just the first of many today.

Devon had never been a quitter, though, and she certainly wasn't about to give up now. Focusing the eyes of one of her Stone Guardians, she peered out over the savanna, her vantage improved by the golem's height. Unsurprisingly, the gates of Stonehaven were now open. A column of demons marched from the settlement, the orderly procession passing under the heavy portcullis at the main palisade gates, along the corridor between the settlement's inner and outer walls, through the curtain wall gate, and over the drawbridge to the open fields in front of the walls. There they were forming large companies and standing in strict formation. Looking at the rigid order, the flawless discipline with which the demon army now conducted itself, Devon couldn't help but wonder if all the screeching and howling and apparent chaos among the ranks had been some kind of trick. Had the disorder been designed to make her and her followers believe they stood a chance? Or maybe the completion of the ziggurat and the capture of Stonehaven had allowed the army to level up in some fashion.

Anyway, with dark pennants flying and an aura of evil blanketing the demon force, the scene was enough to make Devon want to log out and give up. But she would never forgive herself for abandoning her people in the face of that horde, so she clenched her jaw, straightened her shoulders and sank her awareness deeper into her connection with the Stone Guardians, commanding them to stand firm no matter what came.

That's when she felt it, a faint pulse that flowed into the guardians. Energy surged into the golems in a regular cadence like the slow throb of an ancient heart. Devon grasped after the sensation, trying to wrap her human awareness around something that was distinctly *other*. Bringing all her concentration to bear, she tried to put herself into the mind of one of the stone giants, and when she did, she perceived that the pulse was rejuvenating the guardian's animating essence. Each infusion was like a jolt of caffeine or maybe a sugar rush from too much chocolate. Only not so jittery. But anyway, she got the sense that, without the steady influx, the golems would slowly wind down and then simply stop, returning to the inanimate rocks from which they'd once been formed.

And that, at least, explained why the constructs remained vigilant and strong within Ishildar's boundaries, but once they had ventured into the savanna during the first battle with the invading demons, their energy had quickly begun to fade.

As she focused, she could sense that the pulses traveled from *somewhere* to each of the golems. Abruptly hopeful despite the odds, she closed her eyes and followed the paths of energy, groping after them with a sense that seemed to be anchored at the very base of her skull. It felt as if the awareness sprang from the same place where shivers originated before traveling down her spine and out through her body. The harder she concentrated on the sensation, the faster her perception traveled along the lines of energy, and where they converged near the center of the city, she felt the place as a fizzing, popping tingle, a nexus bursting with potential.

> **Quest Updated:** Do I need to spell this out for you?
> **Objective Complete:** Locate the Throne of the Ancients.
> **New Objective:** Actually, this one probably doesn't need to be spelled out, either. Godspeed.

Still huddled together and speaking in desperate tones, Devon's friends turned and stared expectantly when her eyes flew open, and her spine went rigid.

"I know where to go. It's probably four or five miles. Did anyone bring a bike during the evacuation?"

Everyone shook their heads.

Damn. If she had to make her way on foot, even at a run, it would take too much time, and her *Fatigue* might hit max before she arrived at the throne. And she couldn't pull her golems away from their position on the front line. She really needed a mount or a speed buff or something.

All at once, the solution came to her. Gritting her teeth, she waved to her friends. "Never mind. I got it."

300

She whirled and ran for Temple Square, and once she reached the open area, she veered for the quadrant filled with Skevalli refugees.

"I need your best nut oil," she called.

Chapter Forty-Three

VAGUELY, CHEN WAS aware of the activity around him, the panicked shouts, the scrape of steel against scabbards, the calls of archers from their platforms asking for tallies of arrows and updates on the demons' approach.

But the information that lay open before him, right now, was even more alarming—or at least, it was more horrific because the threat didn't come from some distant demonic AI. If Chen was right about this, Devon had been betrayed by one of her closest friends, someone they'd both known and trusted for half a decade.

Splayed across Chen's vision were spreadsheets of user handles, correlated forum comments, and the real trove, a dump of logs off a private server that had been scrubbed just minutes after he'd managed the download. And no matter how many ways he analyzed the web of data, the spider in the center was his guildmate, Jeremy.

The thread Chen had followed to this point started with a single comment from someone using the handle Devious. Posting on a forum catering to the PvP and griefer communities, the commenter had asked for contact information for the player group that had attacked Stonehaven a few weeks ago. The message claimed that the poster had information that would be of high interest to the group. A posted response said that someone would be in touch via private message.

After that, the trail disappeared into PMs for a few in-world hours, but then it popped up again in the chat log from the private server.

Devious (guest) has joined the chat.

Devious: Thanks for the invite.

Nil: Well, don't get too comfortable. I assume I don't need to introduce myself. But just in case you're clueless, I'm leader of the Blood-soaked Blades.

Devious: Good for you. What I care about is finding the people that attacked Stonehaven.

Nil: ... You're here by invitation, dude, and your IP address has been recorded.

Devious: Does that mean it was the Blood-soaked Blades who attacked? Help me out here.

Nil: Not like I have anything to hide. Yeah, we're the raiders. So what do you want? We're not taking applications from random shits on the internet.

Devious has changed his name to Jeremy.

Nil: lol. Well, whether that's your real name or not, you're still a random shit. Nice try, but you still aren't getting in. Applications are by invitation only. We recruit based on in-game talent.

Jeremy: I'm not looking to join.

Nil: Oh? Come to make threats, then? Because that's a pretty stupid move. Remember what I just said about having your IP address?

Jeremy: I came to propose an alliance. A deal, really.

Nil: hahahaha what?

Jeremy: Actually, it's more like me telling you how to actually win against Stonehaven.

Nil: You think you can tell the most powerful PvP guild in the game how to fight?

Jeremy: There's a reason I switched my name. I assume you've seen the livestream that Hailey made of our fight against the bog serpent queen back in Avatharn Online, I mean. I know you guys found out about Stonehaven from following her stream, so I assume you've seen her highlights reel.

Nil: If by following, you mean we were telling that bitch exactly what we thought about her in the comments section.

Jeremy: ...

Nil: Anyway, I guess I'm supposed to recognize you as Jeremy, the planar priest from that recording. Or at least, that's who you're pretending to be.

Jeremy: I don't expect you to believe me just based on my handle. Messaging you a sensory stream clip I took from inside Stonehaven recently. I'm talking to Devon. You know that sense streams can't be forged, I assume.

Nil: Not yet anyway.

Nil has marked himself as away.

Here there was a break in the chat log of perhaps five minutes during which Nil was likely immersed in the sense stream.

Nil has marked himself as active.

Nil: Okay. Seems legit. I still don't see why your information will help, though. Unless you know something about demolitions that we don't. Planning to plant a charge under Stonehaven's wall for us?

Jeremy: Let's just say that Devon is vulnerable right now. Extremely vulnerable. I can give you information on her weakness and help coordinate your attack.

Nil: All right, cough it up.

Jeremy: Sorry. First, we'll need to talk about what I get out of the deal.

Nil: Let's take this to a PM. This channel is visible to all my lieutenants. You've still got some trust to build here, but if we come to an arrangement, I'll decide who needs to know the details.

Chen's jaw tightened as he reread the exchange. He almost felt like he was going to puke due to the disgust he felt for Jeremy. Yeah, Chen's relationship with the man was complicated. As tank and healer in their previous game, they'd spent enough time together to get plenty annoyed with one another. The responsibility they'd shared for the group's safety had honestly become too much for Chen, leading him to choose a non-tank build for this character. Just being around Jeremy sometimes made him flash back to that overwhelming feeling of stress.

But they'd also worked side by side for five long years, sharing a burden that people outside a virtual-reality MMORPG would probably never understand. They'd always, *always* had each other's backs, sharing the blame when the group got wiped out as easily as they'd shared the credit for a successful dungeon crawl.

But now, Jeremy had turned traitor on all of them. After the exchange on the chat server, there was additional evidence to indicate that Nil and Jeremy had reached an agreement. Scattered messages in the private chat and oblique references on public forums sketched out a history of the griefer guild's march through the Skargill Mountains.

Sometime yesterday, they'd dropped off the plateau and into Ishildar's basin. After that, they seemed to have adopted a strict policy of radio silence, because he couldn't find a single post from one of the handles he'd identified as a guild member, not even an unrelated comment.

They could be anywhere in the vicinity.

With the demon army marching in from the south, it might not matter whether the player raid added to his allies' troubles. But if Devon found a way to activate Ishildar's power, fulfilling the prophecy that she would make the city a beacon of light, she might be able to control the demon threat.

Chen doubted the prophecy accounted for a group of shithead griefers led to them by a friend-turned-traitor.

The only way they could prepare for the player offensive was to learn their attack plan. And to do that, Chen needed to find Jeremy and extract a confession.

Banishing the spreadsheets and chat logs, he stood and surveyed the square while pulling up a messenger window to update Devon. It sucked to tell her this way, but she'd recently left the square at a dead run—much to the shock of everyone present—stripped down to her underwear and slathered with glistening nut oil.

Even if Chen could catch her, it honestly wasn't the sort of situation where he'd be able to keep a straight face while explaining.

He started sub-vocalizing a message while pushing through the tumult in the square in search of Jeremy.

"Devon, I have bad news..."

Chapter Forty-Four

DEVON ARRIVED, BREATHLESS, outside a stone building with the jagged stubs of spires standing like broken teeth from the roof. A massive pointed archway opened in the front of the structure, granting a view of a dimly lit interior with shafts of light falling through holes in the ceiling. Inside, a square-cut pair of steps looked as if they ascended to a platform.

The sensation of power was a hiss at the base of her skull, impossible to ignore now that she'd discovered it.

As she stepped beneath the arch, a message from Chen flashed. Devon wanted to ignore it—emerging from the shadows as her eyes adjusted, the throne was a massive presence—but she remembered the tasks she'd set the teenager on. He wouldn't message unless it were important, so either he'd found out something about the player raid on Chasm View, or better, he'd picked out an exploitable demon weakness from the combat logs of players who had fought them.

She opened the message, and a dagger of ice plunged through her ribs. Jeremy had betrayed her? She couldn't quite believe it, but she knew Chen wouldn't make that kind of accusation without solid evidence. She thought back to all the responsibilities she'd offloaded on the bard. He was supposed to be helping Jarleck construct the best defenses for a base battle, building an overall strategy for the conflict, and disrupting the ziggurat construction. Had he even *tried* to make the attack on the glass supply effective? If he'd deliberately sabotaged the effort, would any of the players on the mission have realized it? She would have assumed so, but maybe she'd underestimated his skill in deception.

Ultimately, was the completion of the ziggurat her fault for delegating to the wrong person? If this throne didn't work a miracle for her side, would she always know that she'd made the critical error that led to Ishildar's downfall?

Devon suspected that yes, she would bear the guilt. No amount of rationalizing would make it go away.

Chen claimed that he was going to raise a posse to drag answers out of Jeremy. After, he would bring the traitor to her for punishment.

Devon inhaled deeply through her nose. All right. Done was done. She couldn't let the man harm her efforts any further by distracting her here. She composed a quick message asking Chen to keep her updated and suggesting that they seek out Jarleck and review any defense decisions that had been made with Jeremy's contributions. If there were known weaknesses in their fortifications—other than, of course, the status as a barely qualifying Fortified Camp—they could be certain the player raid knew about it. Just changing up the plan might help a little.

Then she brushed aside the messenger interface and stared up at the throne.

Carved from what appeared to be a single, massive block of gold-veined white marble, the chair towered over the room. Just the seat itself was waist-high on her, and the back rose to about twice her height. The legs ended in carvings of dragon's feet, and a row of sculpted sea birds perched on the rim of the chair back, staring down with eyes that were somehow bright despite being carved of nearly featureless white stone. Marble vines climbed the legs of the throne and twined around the arms and back, occasionally sprouting roses with petals nearly as delicate as those of their living counterparts. Between the foliage, faces peered, animal and human, draconian and felsen.

The sizzle in the back of Devon's skull rose to a boil, and she fought the urge to fall to her knees before the throne. Somehow she knew that, long ago, vassal races and travelers and residents of Ishildar came to this place to pay fealty and ask for boons from the Keeper. It didn't seem right that she should climb onto that lofty seat, even if the hall she presided over were currently empty with dust motes swirling in the shafts of light.

She didn't feel worthy, but Veia had chosen her and tested her, and in the end, she'd come forth from the Vault of the Magi with the *Raiment of the Keeper*, proving that she indeed deserved the honor.

As she climbed the short flight of steps leading to the throne's platform, an inspection window popped up in her vision.

Artifact: Throne of the Ancients
Carved by a master sculptor of the Age of Philosophy and imbued with power by a cabal of Ishildar's greatest magi, the Throne of the Ancients is the locus for Ishildar's light. For centuries, the city's Keepers have sat upon it as both a symbol of their reign and a focus item for working their greatest magic.
Requires: Keeper of Ishildar title
Requires: Level 50

Wait, what? Devon reread the description.

"Requires level 50?" she said aloud.

This didn't make any sense. She was only level 27. Why have a quest chain ending at this throne, the only hope for saving the mortal realm, when she was weeks or months away from achieving the requisite level to use it?

She sank slowly to her knees, then dropped onto her butt. When she planted a hand on the polished floor tiles, her palm slipped across the stone due to the stupid nut oil that greased her body. After recovering, she stared up at the throne.

Was she missing something?

Was the game just broken?

"Help me out here," she said to the air. "What am I supposed to do?"

If Veia had a response, the AI didn't seem interested in sharing it. No message popped up in Devon's vision, and the only answer to her question was a rustling of pigeons in the vaults of the ceiling.

Devon reached out her fingers and brushed the marble-carved claws of the nearest dragon's foot. It couldn't just end here like this, could it?

Chapter Forty-Five

"HEY! WAIT. WHAT'S going on?" Jeremy struggled in Torald's grip, trying to yank his upper arms free of the paladin's chainmail gauntlets, but his *Strength* wasn't nearly what he needed for a successful *Grapple* against the tank. He quickly gave up and instead looked at the group of gathered players as if in appeal. "If you guys haven't forgotten, there's a war on. For all the good it might do at this point, I'd still like to get to the bulwark."

Chen felt his cheeks twitch with contained rage. Part of him still couldn't believe it was true, not after everything their small group had been through together, but the data didn't lie. He hardened his jaw while he settled his emotions and then took a step closer to the bard. Jeremy's hat had been knocked askew. It now sagged over his right ear, and the ostrich plume was bobbing in Torald's face. The paladin ignored the distraction, his face locked in a grim expression.

Jeremy winced in pain, making Chen think Torald had just increased the pressure in his grip.

"Ordinarily, I'd take my time questioning you in hopes that you might redeem yourself with a confession," Chen said. "Five years as our group's healer ought to have earned you that much. But there is no time. It's too late already, really. Where will the griefer attack come from? Tell us, and even though it's impossible for us to part as friends at this point, there's a chance we'll just let you walk away if we somehow survive today."

Jeremy blinked and shook his head as if confused, but then he stiffened and looked at Chen with a mixture of shock and regret. "Aww, shit. Dude, it's not what you think."

"Oh really? So you didn't contact this Nil person to tell him that Devon was vulnerable? You didn't bring the Blood-soaked Blades over the Skargill Mountains where they massacred the Skevalli royals? You haven't been in contact with the raid, conveying information about our defenses?"'

Jeremy grimaced. "Well, yeah. But it's still not what you think."

He looked as if he would have slumped his shoulders if Torald hadn't been squeezing his arms so hard that his neck had kind of disappeared between his collarbones. Instead, he dropped his gaze to the ground between him and Torald. "I know I should have told Devon, but sometimes she's so conservative when it comes to risks, you know?"

"You should have told her what? That you betrayed her?" Chen pounded a fist into his palm. "You know what? I'm not listening to this. Either you tell us where you instructed the players to attack, or we kill and spawn camp you and start tracing your IP to a physical location."

"Dude, wait. I'm not a traitor, okay? Yeah, I brought those guys here. But it was because Devon needed more fighters than we were going to be able to recruit, and whether we like it or not they are probably the highest-level guild on the server."

Chen could see Torald's frustration building, and as much as he wanted to give permission for the paladin to let loose on the traitorous bard, something didn't seem right. Jeremy had always been a bit slippery, but now that Chen had him dead to rights, he was smart enough to realize it would be impossible to talk his way out of trouble.

"You have two minutes to finish explaining," Chen said. "But don't assume I believe you."

Jeremy swallowed, then glanced around Temple Square. "I need a good vantage point, and I need to borrow Jarleck's spyglass. If you can give me that, I'll do more than talk my way out of this. I'll show you my plan."

Chapter Forty-Six

AFTER MOPING FOR a good thirty seconds, Devon forced herself to climb back onto her feet and think things through. As she stepped around the side of the throne, intent on at least examining it from all sides, a blue-white glow sprang to life near the ceiling, and Bob drifted down to hang in front of her face.

The wisp booped her nose. Devon smiled faintly as she laid a hand on the arm of the throne. The stone was cool under her skin. "Hey, Bob."

"So don't take this the wrong way, but I thought chainmail bikinis had gone out of style."

Devon glanced down at her undergarments, a reinforced leather bra and a pair of boy shorts cut from something soft, lambskin maybe. When she'd first logged in, her undergarments had been made from roughspun cloth, and as she'd leveled and obtained better gear, her undies had upgraded to match. She guessed it was one of the perks of power or something.

But still, it certainly wasn't chainmail. Bob was just being a jerk as usual.

"Or maybe this is your Princess-Leia-in-Jabba's-lair outfit."

She sighed. "I needed the speed buff."

"Whatever excuse you want to make, Princess."

"You know, I'm really not in the mood."

"Right. You're supposed to be sitting on the throne and saving the world. Which begs the question..."

She shook her head in frustration. "I don't understand. It says it requires level 50."

"I see. And you, ever the literal-minded, have decided to give the throne a once over and go find something else to do while the city burns."

"Actually, I figured there must be some piece I was missing. I thought a closer examination might yield some answers."

Bob shimmered, the wisp's best approximation of a sigh. "Well, as they say, you do you. *Or* you could just try sitting on it anyway. Think about it. If a sword required 40 skill points in *Two-handed Slashing* and there was a rabid lemur trying to disembowel you, would you just lie there and let the beast dig in with its little claws, or would you pick up the sword and try to hit the lemur with it anyway?"

Devon drew her eyebrows together. "I'd probably just try to punch it or something."

"Okay, so what if your hands were tied and you couldn't punch it?"

"Then clearly I wouldn't be able to pick up the sword either."

Bob gave a frustrated wiggle. "Okay. You don't need to be so pedantic. I'm pretty sure you know what I meant. Better to have loved and lost than never to have loved at all."

She wrinkled her nose. "Dude, your analogies are crap."

"I'm just saying, is there something physically preventing you from sitting on the throne?"

"I dunno."

"Right. You don't know because you haven't even tried."

Devon thought back to her early days in the game. Back then, the unidentified ivory fang that had eventually been fashioned into her dagger, *Night's Fang*, had been a crude weapon requiring 60-something points in *One-Handed Piercing* to wield effectively. When she'd tried to use one to hit a tree, she'd fumbled the attempt and nearly stabbed herself in the process. But Greel, who had also lacked the requisite skill, but who had more piercing practice than Devon, had managed to inflict a necrotic wound with the fang.

She blinked, thinking. Rather than the hard skill or level cap used by many games to control access to items and gear, it seemed like Relic Online had soft caps, a system that simply reduced item effectiveness for unqualified characters. At level 27, she was definitely closer to the "suggested" level of the throne than she'd been when trying to use her handful of skill points to wield a 60-skill-requiring dagger.

She dashed around to the front of the throne. Maybe there was hope after all.

As she grabbed hold of the massive chair's arm and pulled herself up, a popup appeared.

You lack the level requirement to effectively use the Throne of the Ancients.
Warning: The power of the ancients has often been likened to Wild Magic. The means by which the artifact achieves the user's desires are often unpredictable. Fumbles and critical failures may amplify this characteristic.

Still, it's pretty much your only hope. So, yeah, good luck.

She glanced at Bob as she finished climbing onto the seat. The wisp shimmered with anticipation.

Devon's choices were either to sit all the way back and have her legs straight like a toddler in an adult chair or to sit on the edge with her elbows on the chair arms at shoulder height. At least that posture was a little more commanding than the kid at the grown-up table thing.

"You know, you're pretty annoying sometimes," she said as she settled onto the front edge of the seat. "But you sometimes have good advice."

Bob shone brighter. "Thanks, Champion."

Chapter Forty-Seven

WELL, AS DEFENSES went, the state of fortifications around the refugee camp was...interesting. Emerson hadn't seen Stonehaven grow up from its early days but he now appreciated the security that the settlement's double stone walls had offered.

The bulwark was a glorified rubble heap. Stone blocks from ruined buildings were piled to a height of about twelve feet. Those blocks that had retained enough of their original squaring off had been stacked, creating something a bit more sheer and formidable, but much of the barrier seemed to have been tumbled together. The outer facing was steeper, boasting the bulk of the proper stacking work, and where there'd been enough supply of wood, sharpened stakes protruded from the wall.

On top, earth had been packed into the spaces between blocks to provide a makeshift wall-walk, allowing defenders free movement to different areas that might need extra bodies.

Emerson stood on that earthen path now, gazing toward the south where streets emptied into the savanna. Beyond the edge of the city, just a few feet of empty grassland stood between Ishildar and the demon horde. Except to call it a horde no longer seemed accurate. It was a proper army now, divided into companies and platoons and sorted by utility. Flying imps maintained wedge-shaped attack formations that hovered maybe fifty feet above the ground forces. The infantry, spear-wielding demon thralls and ravagers with adamantine claws, formed blocks of dark flesh at the head of the major streets. Just visible at the flanks of the army, massive demon elites rode upon hellhounds the size of army tanks.

Compared to the demon force, Ishildar's defenders could scarcely be called an army. Near the edge of the city, Devon's Stone Guardians stood ready. They, at least, would make the demons fight for ground anywhere within reach of their massive stone arms. As for the rest of the defenders, those who weren't twenty feet tall with fists of rock, well...

He looked down at his notched *Practice Short Sword*.

Maybe he'd take down a few of the beasts before the bulwark was overrun.

Lined atop the wall beside him, Stonehaven's NPCs looked on with grim acceptance. They knew they would die here, but, like Emerson, they wouldn't go without a fight. The defenders held their silence; there wasn't anything to say. The only thing left to do was act.

Out on the savanna, a horn sounded. Thousands of thralls stomped in response, raising their spears to hip level. The wicked iron points were raised slightly above horizontal, and their tips caught the light of the sun. Ravagers bent their knees, crouching like runners in the starting blocks. Hellhounds howled.

When a second blast from the horn sounded, the imps shrieked and flew higher, hovering in preparation for a dive. The ravagers burst from their crouches, and the earth shook as they charged for the city. The thralls followed, marching in strict cadence.

To Emerson's horror, the hellhounds exploded into motion and approached at a dead run, snarling and slobbering. The closest hound leapt over a low building at the edge of the city, claws squealing and throwing sparks as they gouged stone when the beast landed.

The bulwark wasn't looking like it would offer much defense against *that.*

He glanced in Stonehaven's direction, the settlement hidden behind rows of Ishildar's ruined buildings. The hours he'd spent inside its walls strolling along footpaths that cut through waving green grasses seemed a distant memory now. The settlement was lost, and the city would soon follow.

The nearest ravager squad charged down the street toward his position. Emerson could see the yellow fangs poking from behind the monsters' snarling lips. Low, bestial whines rose from their throats. The wave of demon flesh broke against the bulwark, the initial ranks smashed by those that came behind. Demons started crawling over their fallen brethren, snarling and howling.

Breath caught in his throat, Emerson stabbed his sword down, skewering a ravager through the mouth and plunging the point into the soft flesh at the back of the beast's throat. The demon gagged as ichor spurted from the wound. It fell backward, flesh pulling off Emerson's blade as around 15% of its hitpoints disappeared. The falling body knocked another of the beasts off the bulwark as it fell. Both demons hit the stone flagstones with soft-sounding thumps. Ravagers around them screamed in annoyance. Soon enough, both fallen monsters were rushing forward again.

Emerson swiped the sweat from his eyes. As he raised his blade at a demon that had just crested the wall, a howling hellhound charged through the ranks of infantry, scattering a few as it cleared space to bunch its haunches in preparation to leap.

As the hound sprang, Emerson took an unwitting step back. Fearful shouts peppered the air all around him. The hellhound's shadow passed over him, and silhouetted by the sun, he spied arrows streaking from the archer platforms. The ammunition struck the hound's armor and bounced off without shaving off a single hitpoint.

He shook his head, despairing.

As the hellhound landed behind the bulwark, a humming rose from the stones and buildings all around. It sounded almost celestial.

Emerson whirled, searching for the source, and realized that the buildings were beginning to glow. He fell back as a ray of searing light lanced across the scene and blasted a hole through the hellhound.

"Holy crap!" someone shouted. "When did the golems get eye lasers?"

Chapter Forty-Eight

ASHLEY STOOD WITH one shoulder braced against the cliff face which was, apparently, the outer face of the outcrop that defended Stonehaven's back. Finally, they were out of the sauna-like savanna sun. The low-hanging boughs of an acacia tree brushed the top of her head, little twigs poking her scalp, but it was still glorious to stand to her full height. She rolled her other shoulder, working out the stiffness, and bent each of her knees in turn. If she never combat-crawled another inch in her life, she'd be okay with that. The method of advancement might have gotten them into position without being detected, but it sure as hell hadn't been fun.

As she rotated to lean her opposite shoulder against the cliff, a ranger-class player ducked under the tree and spoke to Nil in a low voice. "The opening is about fifty yards to the left. Just like Jeremy said."

Nil nodded as if the report had been a foregone conclusion. "Are the sappers getting to work?"

"Three entered the tunnel," the ranger replied. "The others are prepping more charges. We should have a confirmation that everything is set in the next five minutes."

Nil turned to Ashley and a pair of rogues standing near her. "Jeremy claimed that talented climbers would be able to ascend the cliff directly and take out any resistance up top. Does that seem right?"

Ashley didn't even need to look up to confirm. Her *Climbing* skill was tier 4, 38 points to be exact, and as long as the cliff wasn't either glass or overhanging farther than it ascended, she wouldn't have a problem. "Yeah. As soon as we're ready. And as long as the demolition doesn't collapse the whole damn cliff."

Nil smirked. "If those numb nuts in the tunnel screw up that bad, I think we're all hosed."

Ashley shrugged. "Then yeah. I'm good to climb."

Another of the rogues, a guy who had taken the spymaster specialization, took a few steps out from the cliff face, shaded his eyes, and peered up. "I figure I can manage. Question, though. Seeing as we are basically on top of Stonehaven and Devon's peeps still have no clue they're about to be smashed, why didn't we attack this way before?"

"Because, genius, this whole region was half-covered in jungle at the time. If you thought the combat crawl was bad, imagine hacking through the miles of vines and thorn bushes. Oh, and, the narrow tunnel we are about to blast wide open was recently started by Devon's dwarf miners. Jeremy said they're trying to create a postern gate to allow access for some kind of residential annex or something. So even if we *had* hacked our way through all that jungle, we would've arrived back here with no way to get inside."

The spymaster rolled his eyes when Nil looked away. "If you'd told us all that, or for that matter, if you'd told us much of anything about this mission, I wouldn't have to ask this kind of stuff."

"And since you shouldn't be asking questions anyway, I'm fine leaving you ignorant. Your job is to do what you're told so I don't have to waste my time chatting."

The spymaster's jaw hardened. Ashley tensed, just waiting for a fight to break out and ruin their entire element of surprise. Fortunately, the rogue got himself under control. "Anyway, yeah I can climb that. I imagine anyone over 20 skill points can."

"Then consider yourself deputized to round up anyone who qualifies. Be ready to climb as soon as we receive word that the demolition efforts are good to go."

As the spymaster slumped off, Ashley almost felt sorry for him. But he should have known better than to antagonize Nil. Anyway, the more people who were upset at the leader, the easier it would be to form her splinter guild.

As Nil stalked off, no doubt to browbeat some of the other guild members, Ashley leaned back against the cliff. She looked up through the screen of acacia leaves into the sky above. Sure, player-versus-environment, or PvE, game content wasn't her thing. But if she *were* into just plodding along and mowing through game content to gain levels and items, not to mention learning about the boring stuff—game-world lore and NPC back stories—Stonehaven would be a nice base camp for her play sessions. Maybe even a place worth fighting for.

So she *got* it, honestly, and she even felt kinda guilty for coming along on this raid, if only because Nil was so adamant that they make the defenders' lives miserable while taking out their settlement. But it wasn't like she could switch sides now, so when the hissed words rippled through the group, calling the climbers to prepare to scale the cliffs and for everyone else to gather at the mouth of the tunnel, she laid her hands on the rough granite and searched out incut ledges that provided decent grip.

"Now," Nil's god-voice boomed across the landscape.

Ashley jumped and actually looked up in panic even though she knew the signal had come through external voice chat. After taking a deep breath to still her nerves, she started climbing.

The cliff was maybe 150 feet tall, a fatal drop even for someone with her skill level in *Tumbling*. Even so, she reached the top in less than a minute or two, gaining the rim before the wall shook as the charges exploded. Throwing a leg over, she quickly jumped to her feet and looked side to side for Stonehaven's guards.

Ashley yelped in surprise when, not ten feet away, she saw the mottled black-and-pink flesh of what appeared to be a...demon? The creature had dropped to a crouch, planting a clawed forefoot on the top of the cliff, and small wings flapped as it tried to keep its balance. As it looked over the edge, no doubt spotting the raid group filing into the newly blasted tunnel, it snarled.

Ashley raced forward, grabbed the demon by one of its stubby horns, and dragged her dagger across its throat before it could raise an alarm. Dashing forward in search of cover, she scanned the rest of the clifftop for further sentries.

She shook her head in confusion when she spotted two more demons. One had cupped claw-tipped fingers around its mouth and was calling down into the settlement.

She slowed when she realized something was seriously wrong here. Ashley's thoughts whirled as she tried to figure out what was going on. Had Devon formed an alliance with demons? That hardly seemed like something she would do. Dropping to a crouch and using her *Meld with Shadows* ability—for all the good it might do in such an exposed position—Ashley leaned over the far edge of the cliff and peered down into Stonehaven.

Okay, so something strange was definitely going on. Not only were Stonehaven's front gates standing wide open, but also the settlement seemed to be nearly deserted.

And those few NPCs that were inside the walls weren't human; they too were demons.

Before she could try to get some kind of warning down to the others, the rest of the guild burst from a dust-filled tunnel at the foot of the cliff. With a roar, raiders streamed into the settlement and started running for what Ashley assumed were assigned positions.

A popup appeared in her vision.

Stonehaven's ownership is now: Contested (2%)
Tailoring Workshop: Contested (10%)
Shrine to Veia: Contested (15%)
Simple Cabin: Contested (25%)
Simple Cabin: Contested (32%)
Inner Keep: Contested (2%)

The list went on and on, scrolling through what seemed to be most of the buildings in the settlement. Next to that window was a second informational popup.

To claim this settlement, you must move all structures from a contested to a captured state. Once the settlement has been fully captured, you must hold it without contest for forty-eight hours. Once those requirements have been met, Stonehaven will belong to the Blood-soaked Blades, Leader: Nil.

Chapter Forty-Nine

SITTING ON THE throne was like riding a rocket into space. Devon felt like her bones were being shaken apart, like her teeth were rattling out of her jaw. At the same time, she wasn't even moving. Power gushed through her in an uncontrollable torrent, like lightning roaring through her from her toes to the crown of her head.

It was all she could do to hang on and not be blasted into bits. Yet somehow, she was managing to dip her mind into that raging river and deflect just a fraction of the stream onto a side pathway that split and surged down the connection between her Stone Guardians and the throne.

Through her bond with the golems, she felt the energy lance from their eye sockets, turning demons to charred husks wherever the beams struck. Still, the power offered more. One by one, the guardians began to collect the streams of energy, forming them into great shields, scintillating domes that arched over the giants' heads. Within the hemispheres, power gathered and condensed until Devon felt as if the pressure might crush the golems. And then, abruptly, shields gave way one after another. The blast waves raced out from each of her giants, rolling over the city and savanna. The surges left buildings and players and NPCs untouched, but where the concussion passed through demonic ranks, Ishildar's enemies disintegrated, exploding in clouds of dust.

Still, the geyser of power flowed through her, and the bulk of the magical energy swirled up to form a massive funnel cloud overhead. It was a tornado of light, an immense construct that spanned the heavens.

Gritting her teeth and clinging tight to the arms of the throne, Devon shouted with the effort of just keeping the golems working toward her goal. She didn't and couldn't instruct them in how to use the streaming energy for Ishildar's defense. But they were made for this purpose, constructed in ancient times to stand against dark forces. Slowly but surely, they advanced toward the edge of the city, lasering clouds of imps from the sky as they formed more blast waves.

The demon army faltered, and some of the squads began to make tentative retreats.

Faintly, Devon could hear the battle cries of her human, mistwalker, dwarven, and felsen forces as they first hesitated, then climbed down from the bulwark and pushed the advance, mopping up small pockets of wounded demons that had somehow survived the Guardians' attacks.

As the horde drew back, a discordant shriek rose from the rear ranks of the demon army. Through the eyes of her golems, Devon saw Archdemon Gaviroth rise from the palanquin in which he'd been borne by around a score of demon thralls. He stood to a height that seemed impossible given the being she'd seen before, and a cloud of red-tinged smoke began to pour from the monster, billowing around the archdemon and over his head. Lightning flashed within the rapidly growing storm, and all around, demons began to take heart. Once again, they began a forward march.

Tendrils of smoke and flickering bolts of lightning swirled and lanced from the billowing cloud, striking groups of demons. They seemed to grant a buff, because now, when impaled by the rays of light from Devon's Guardians, the demons took much longer to die. And still, the archdemon summoned his storm.

In the middle of the savanna where hellfire had melted the player camp, and farther south where the Ziggurat of the Damned stood in the Grukluk Swamp, Devon could sense angry red pools of demonic power, and dimly, she felt them feeding the archdemon. Through the deeper perception offered by the magic raging through her, she intuitively knew that the ziggurat matched—perhaps even surpassed—the Veian Temple in strength, and that only the power in the Throne of the Ancients had a chance of overcoming it.

And distantly, she perceived lines of darkness shooting from the ziggurat, cutting through the mortal realm and connecting the base to other loci where the demon forces, commanded by other archdemon generals, had gained footholds on the continent.

She attempted to get a count, but when she focused on each ray of darkness, it was as if it darted away from her perception.

There were more armies, but as to the number and strength, she had no idea.

And it might not matter because, with a massive roar, Archdemon Gaviroth unleashed the power he'd been condensing.

Darkness rushed out from the roiling storm. As it rolled over the horde, each demon became surrounded by an angry red nimbus. And when the infernal magic washed over her Stone Guardians, their light was abruptly snuffed, all power stolen from within them, and their connections to the throne were severed. Devon's bond with the golems dimmed but didn't quite fade. She could still perceive the scene, but the stone giants had no energy to obey her commands.

With angry shrieks, the demons' march became frenzied, and Devon's small force shouted in panic as they raced back for the bulwark.

Still, the torrent gushed through Devon, threatening to tear her to bits.

The power was there, but it was all she could do to simply be the conduit, the channel that allowed it into the world. As for controlling it, might as well stand in a canyon beneath a failing dam and hope she could hold back the water.

But what choice did she have? She tried releasing one arm of the throne, grabbing for the *Greenscale Pendant* in hopes she could activate *Ishildar's Call* and resurrect the connection between golems and throne.

She nearly lost her mind as the power pounded her psyche, and it took everything she could muster to get her hand back on the solid marble arm.

The demons once again crossed the border into Ishildar, now screeching and howling and easily toppling walls with blows from their newly strengthened limbs.

Devon could feel the tendons in her neck standing out like cables as she fought to wrap her awareness around the throne's power. It might be too much for her, but she was the city's only chance.

With a shriek, she let go of the mental barrier she'd maintained, the shield between power and mind that held her together. The torrent caught Devon up and threw her along in the current, rocketing her awareness up into the unfathomable storm of power cycling above the city.

She tried to get some sort of grip, tried to orient, and finally gave up and allowed her mind to fragment, spreading wide through the cyclone of magic. For just an instant, she understood its shape, could fathom what it might be to command that much energy.

She grabbed for the power, and it was like trying to keep hold of a massive, thrashing eel from a Greek myth, a muscular, slippery beast that she could scarcely grip, much less guide. It was like grabbing the end of a writhing firehose and hoping not to be thrown into the nearby blaze.

Devon held for as long as she could, and in that moment she conveyed her desire to Ishildar's ancient power.

She wanted the demons defeated. The enemies of Ishildar and Stonehaven dead. Just...gone.

Time lurched, and reality shuddered. Devon, fragmented and tattered, existed in strobing flashes. And then suddenly, she felt her awareness condense, sucked back together as her body was violently ejected from the throne.

Chapter Fifty

SIDES HEAVING, DEVON stopped at a street corner and dug into her *Sparklebomb Backpack.* Her inventory screen opened, and she focused, grimacing, on the *Jungle Energy Potion* she'd considered giving to Greel during their swamp trek. The little pot dropped into her hand, the gritty, earthenware ceramic rough against her palm.

When she pulled the cork loose, the smell nearly made her gag. Her tongue seemed to swell up in preemptive protest. But her *Fatigue* bar was flashing—92%. She plugged her nose and poured the potion contents into her mouth, and before she could second-guess herself, swallowed the tonic in a single gulp. Her eyes went wide as her stomach clenched, sending the concoction halfway back up her esophagus.

She swallowed, hard, then gagged and coughed and desperately fished for her *Everfull Waterskin.* After a handful of deep swallows, the taste of compost-laced motor oil wasn't entirely gone from her palate, but she didn't think she was going to barf.

Her *Fatigue* bar flashed one last time, then steadily emptied until it was only 45% full. Good enough.

"You know," Bob said. "As a largely abstract being, I'm glad I don't need to ingest substances to alter my statistics. For all the attention you mortals seem to pay to this eating and drinking hobby, I can't say that the experience as a whole seems all that pleasant."

"You haven't tried chocolate."

Of course, just thinking about eating right now—even a delicious bon-bon—brought a fresh wave of rebellion from her stomach, so Devon hurriedly slung her backpack into place between her shoulder blades and started jogging again.

During her flashes of perception while melded with the storm, she'd *felt* the eradication of the demon horde, ranks and ranks of monsters disintegrating as the enormous funnel cloud touched down and raged over the plain, cutting larger and larger swaths from the army. Her bones remembered the rattling and shaking of the earth as the storm tore at it, the crust fracturing under the force of the suction. Though she'd been both more and less than human at the time, a disembodied, fragmented awareness melded to an uncontrollable magical force, parts of her mind remembered seeing massive blocks of earth lifted from the surface to hover above the landscape in those last moments. She recalled a final, infinite split-second when time seemed to have stopped, the world frozen in surreal, suspended animation. Crumbs of earth and stone had halted where they'd been dribbling from the underside of the lifted sections of the savanna. Demons had looked up at the cycling storm, masks of terror on their faces.

And then, the surge, the final, ear-shattering thunderclap. Power fell on the earth like a thousand hammer strikes, utterly extinguishing the demon presence in the region.

She knew it was over, the battle for Ishildar won. But at the same time, she couldn't shake the feeling that something was amiss. In the last moments of her connection with the storm, she'd felt something slip sideways. A lurch of uncontrolled energy. Devon knew the theory of wild magic. With the good came the bad, or at least the unexpected. And she worried that it wouldn't all be good news when she arrived back at Temple Square.

And she couldn't forget there was still the player raid to contend with. Her mind rebelled, hating to think of Jeremy's betrayal, but she hadn't heard anything from Chen since he'd told her he planned to raise a posse.

She ran with her mini-map up to avoid wrong turns, and as her little map blip drew near to the location pin for the square, she kept her ear cocked for sounds of battle or celebration or...anything really.

The Temple District was oddly silent.

Devon forced more energy into her legs, her boots pounding the stone pavement.

Along the northern border of the area Jarleck had fortified, the bulwark was lower than in other exposures, between six and eight feet high. She scanned the top of the rubble heap for defenders but saw no one. The wall here would have been sparsely guarded given the demons' approach from the south, but the absence of fighters gave Devon hope. Maybe the worries of a player raid had turned out to be unfounded. Maybe, after such a tremendous battle against an overwhelming force, her followers and allies were taking some well-earned rest.

She spotted a point where the bulwark's outer wall wasn't too steep, and she quickly climbed to the top.

Halting on the earthen path that had been packed into the top of the wall, she looked down into the square and surrounding streets. Devon froze as she took stock of the situation.

Scattered about the square, players sat on crates and stone blocks and in some cases, cross-legged on the ground. They rested elbows on their knees, kept their heads bowed as if in complete exhaustion. In the quadrant where the Skevalli refugees had congregated, there was a little more movement as the non-combatants slowly went about their chores. A few of the diminutive felsen were crouched on their heels, their voices a somber burble as they spoke in their native tongue. Devon caught small snatches of the conversation, but she only had a few skill points in *Felsen Language*, and she couldn't piece any meaning together.

The scene struck her as far too subdued. She'd expected to find a victory celebration or fresh preparations to fend off a player attack, but not this.

All at once, the realization slapped her like a wet towel to the face. Where was everyone else? Altogether, there were maybe one hundred players and around sixty or seventy NPCs in the square. Before the attack, the entire refugee population of Stonehaven had been crammed into the area as well.

Explanations flashed through her mind, one after another. The demons had targeted Stonehaven's NPCs specifically, wiping out every one of her followers. Or maybe, with the demons gone, the citizens had rushed to reclaim their homes. That wouldn't be so bad. It would be good, really, even if she'd imagined she'd be the one to lead them back.

But the first explanation didn't really hold up. To entirely wipe out Stonehaven's population, the tradespeople especially, the demons would have needed to breach the bulwark. She saw no signs of that, and she doubted the Skevalli and felsen would have come through unscathed in that case.

As for the latter idea, as hopeful as it was, the mood in the square didn't fit. And she seriously doubted the players would have let innocent NPCs leave the fortified area unaccompanied.

As she started down the inner slope of the bulwark, she accidentally kicked free a small stone that tumbled down to the square. The clatter brought players' heads up, and some jumped to their feet.

Shadows emerged from behind the row of pillars at the edge of the Veian Temple, and familiar figures stepped down the stairs. Hailey walked beside Emerson, followed by Chen, Torald, and Jeremy. Owen was a somewhat-shadowy presence at the back of the group.

Devon's gaze shot to Jeremy, then darted to Chen.

"The raid?"

Chen pressed his lips together. "Long story. But we don't need to worry about them."

"Wait, what?"

"I screwed up," Jeremy said. "Should have told you my plan."

"Which was?"

"At first it was just a contingency. I thought I could figure out how to use them based on the conditions when they arrived. I planned to tell you once I had them near enough to matter. But then they attacked your Skevalli friends, and stuff just got out of control. I figured I'd better redeem myself by turning the plan into a success *before* I admitted the massacre was basically my fault." He shrugged. "Anyway. I know 'sorry' isn't good enough."

She blinked a few times, trying to wrap her head around what he was saying. "But they're still nearby, right? So still a problem. And where is everyone else?"

As her friends shuffled and glanced at each other as if trying to figure out who would speak, Devon's chest started to tighten. Once again, she remembered wanting her enemies gone, feeling the demons wiped away, and then there'd been that sideways lurch of the throne's power.

"I'll speak," Owen said, stepping forward. "We don't know what happened to the raid. They don't seem to be here anymore, and none are answering Jeremy's messages—they probably realized they'd been betrayed when they found Stonehaven full of demons. They're probably back at their spawn points—we think the tornado wiped them out when it disintegrated the demon horde."

"So it was a tornado? I had this vision of a funnel cloud."

Chen smirked. "Oh yeah, you could call it that. Though in the end, it was more like one of those mega-twisters from the disaster movies."

"Okay..." Devon said. "Maybe we should just get to the bad news then."

Owen nodded, looking grim. "It happened in the final flash. I can still see your NPCs in the pattern—they weren't eradicated from the mortal plane like the demons were. It's just, I don't know where they've gone."

Devon shook her head, confused. "They vanished?"

Emerson stepped forward and took her hand. "That's not all. It might be easiest if we showed you."

Chapter Fifty-One

THE CLOSING CREDITS started scrolling up the massive screen as music flowed from the surround-sound speakers. Outtakes from the movie's filming were playing in small picture-in-picture windows in the corners of the screen, but Devon couldn't focus on them. Already, she could scarcely remember what the film had been about, just that there'd been a couple of misfit city dwellers, a fashion designer and a freelance cartoonist, and they'd fallen in love at a coffee stand in a farmer's market. Or they'd met there, anyway, and then fumbled around trying to sort out their respective neuroses before finally learning to just be themselves or something.

It wasn't the sort of movie she usually went for, but then just going to an old-fashioned flat-screen movie was something she'd done probably less than five times in her life. Why watch a film projected thirty feet away when you could dive into a full-sensory VR experience?

Now she knew. Because sometimes it was nice to live in your own body, experience something happening outside the confines of your own skull. Especially when you had someone to enjoy it with.

She squeezed Emerson's hand and glanced sideways at him and once again tried to push away the memory of what he'd shown her a day before in the game. After climbing a mostly stable spiral staircase up into the bell tower of one of Ishildar's ancient buildings, they'd gazed across the savanna together.

Devon remembered Ishildar's magic pulling blocks of earth from the ground, millions of tons of topsoil and bedrock tearing free from the surrounding crust. She remembered the final destructive flash and the sideways lurch and, vaguely, she recalled being tossed from the throne's seat. She'd come to awareness, reconnecting with her body, maybe a minute or two later. Still, she hadn't comprehended the actual effects of that final blast, not until she looked out over them.

Where before, the savanna had been a gently rolling landscape, pocketed with groves of acacia trees and punctured, occasionally, by stone outcrops, earthen mounds, and the ruins of the Khevshir civilization, now the landscape was a jumbled maze. Some blocks of earth had landed on edge. Others had fallen back in their natural orientation but had landed outside the socket from which they'd been torn. They now stood like square-cut mountains, the sides nearly vertical and formed of compressed earth that looked as if it would crumble if climbed.

Massive holes gaped in the terrain, some with sides already collapsing. In other places, deep, char-coated rifts carved through the landscape, creating zig-zagging and criss-crossing canyons through what had been grassland. The path of the twister, Emerson had explained.

Before she'd brought the storm down on the savanna, the journey to Stonehaven had taken between half an hour and two hours on foot, depending on how fast someone could move. Now, over the jumbled and unstable terrain, it looked as if it might take more than a day of travel.

That was, if there were a reason to travel to the site.

Both the corvid scouts and Prince Kenjan, surveying the area from Proudheart's back, confirmed what Devon's eyes tried to tell her. Along with the glass bowl where the player camp had stood and the Ziggurat of the Damned, Stonehaven had vanished. One of the corvids, a crow named Snicket, had witnessed the disappearance, the sites flashing white in the final, destructive storm wave. They'd vanished in an instant, winking out of existence and leaving only the scars where foundations had pocked the earth.

Stonehaven's NPCs had disappeared at the same instant, apparently still tied to the settlement because Devon had been too shortsighted—or maybe too stubborn—to officially migrate the population to Ishildar.

As her friends and allies had helped her piece together the story, Devon had fought a panic attack—she thought she'd killed them all. Even with Owen getting in her face and reiterating, over and over, that they were still part of the pattern, she couldn't help remembering how she'd wished her enemies *gone.* For a few long minutes, no reassurances had been able to convince her that the extermination of the demons hadn't spilled over, due to wild magic, onto Stonehaven's innocent citizens.

Finally, Emerson had nudged Owen out of the way and wrapped his avatar's arms around her character. Taking deep breaths but not saying anything, he'd gradually brought her back to a rational state. Together with her friends, she'd sorted out an explanation.

Yes, she'd wanted her enemies gone. And apparently, Jeremy's numbskull plan had brought the player raid into Stonehaven at just the wrong time. The throne's magic, especially prone to unintended consequences since she didn't meet the level requirements, had indeed swept all her enemies away. The demons had been shipped to the void, or maybe back to the hell plane—it was hard to know for sure. And the players, along with the settlement they'd just put into a contested state and the NPCs belonging to it, had been sent somewhere *else*.

She believed Owen when he said they were still out there. What choice did she have, really? It was the only way to keep hope alive that she might find and rescue her NPC friends. And she wouldn't stop until she managed it.

Emerson was looking at her. She sighed when their eyes met, and he leaned over and kissed her cheek as he squeezed her hand. "I know it's not easy to stay positive, but you're doing a good job. I'm here, okay?"

She nodded, a faint smile curling her lips. "I know. And I know we'll find them."

"Damn straight. I kinda like your idea of trying to use the throne to locate them."

She smirked. "That's just me being selfish and trying to justify grinding out enough levels to use it safely."

"You'll probably need those levels to deal with the other archdemons, right? So no problem."

Devon laughed. "Yeah, maybe. But you're not supposed to encourage me when I want to abandon my responsibilities to go crawl through some dungeons."

"You? Abandon responsibilities? As if."

The final credits were rolling off the screen, and the lights in the theater were beginning to slowly turn on, pulling details from the largely empty rows of seating. Emerson dropped her hand and reached his arm over her shoulders instead, pulling her into a half-hug.

"Anyway, before I can leave Ishildar, I need to get the Skevalli set up with places to sleep and some sort of food supply. Without demons breathing down our necks, that should be pretty easy."

Emerson smiled crookedly. "See, always thinking of the people that depend on you. I'm pretty sure you are incapable of just playing like a normal person. I bet the only person who has logged more in-game time than you lately is Hailey. And it's not like she has a choice." He paused for a second, his face lighting up as he seemed to remember something. "Oh, been meaning to tell you that I was able to deal with her bank account thing. Her assets weren't much to speak of, so with a little creative data engineering, just some tweaks to the recorded estate plan, I was able to convince her bank to reopen the account. Deposits will come through as usual, which is all E-Squared cares about. They won't bother to check the account owner."

"Which is?"

"A charitable trust configured to make regular donations to research institutes searching for cures for autoimmune diseases like Hailey suffered from. Qualifying institutes need to prove they've chosen candidates for trial therapy who can't afford to buy the institution's favor. Hailey's salary isn't enough to drastically impact research, but for the candidates chosen for therapy, it may make a difference."

"Does she know?" Devon asked.

"I'll tell her when I get a chance. For the time being, I'd rather focus on you. So, dinner? I'm thinking we should go out."

"You mean you don't want me to cook for you?"

Emerson's eyes widened in faint alarm until he seemed to realize she was joking. "It's not so much your cooking. More that you use your laundry for curtains. Figure we could use a night on the town."

She laughed. "Let's go."

Chapter Fifty-Two

WORST WEEK EVER.

Ashley sighed as she shaded her eyes against the glare coming off the salt pan. She wasn't sure what was worse, the fact that it was always a billion degrees in whatever godforsaken desert they'd been teleported to, or the added fact that everyone else in the guild seemed to think it was awesome. Why? They were trapped in the middle of nowhere, inhabiting a settlement they'd only attacked because they wanted to be annoying, and the only combat to be had within a day's walk was against a bunch of scarabs and scorpions and some variety of dust elementals.

But the moment Nil had realized he could command any of the NPCs that had been teleported in, forcing them to give massages and cook meals and basically wait on the guild like a bunch of slaves, he'd set the guild up like sultans in the inner keep. No one seemed to give a shit about advancement at the moment. They were too busy eating gourmet meals—how the cook, Tom, managed to create something tasty from beetle meat was beyond her—being fanned by dwarves stripped down to their short pants, and putting back mug after mug of dwarven ale.

But they'd get tired of it eventually, and when that happened, Ashley hated to think what Nil would come up with as entertainment. Stonehaven's citizens might be just NPCs, but cruelty, even to simulated beings, just wasn't cool.

So before the novelty of playing Egyptian Pharaoh wore off, Ashley needed to figure out where the hell they were and how to provide a distraction. Whether that was a raid on a nearby town or—ideally—player settlement, or whether she'd manage it by luring a bunch of sandworms to attack Stonehaven, she wasn't sure.

As for her splinter guild...yeah, no. Not a good time. Even if she could still put together a coalition, it wasn't like she could just break off while they were trapped here with Nil's sycophants.

So with a sigh, she took a swig of her waterskin—at least the settlement had appeared on top of an oasis...she shuddered to think what would have happened to them otherwise—and started marching into the salt flats.

"You're fricking nuts you know, trying to level while you could be living it up."

Her shoulders hunched as she heard Nil's voice coming from atop the wall behind her. But Ashley didn't look back. She kept walking into the desert.

Dear Reader,

Thank you so much for reading *Throne of the Ancients* I really hope you enjoyed it! As a working writer, I utterly depend on readers to spread the word on my books.

Please consider leaving a review on Amazon for this book and for other authors you enjoy. I promise that I read every review (yes, even the critical ones). Sometimes, they help me shape the story to come, and often, they are the reason I get out of bed and in front of my computer long before the sun rises. Thank you!!

If you would like to grab free books and participate in my reader community, head over to www.CarrieSummers.com and join my reader group. We have a lot of fun writing collaborative stories over email, talking about books, and other great stuff. Plus, the group is how I let readers know when new books are out.

So, what's coming? The next book in the Stonehaven League series will be out Fall 2019, so keep an eye out. In the meantime, you can check out my other fantasy series, *Chronicles of a Cutpurse*, *The Shattering of the Nocturnai* and *The Broken Lands*.

Once again, thank you for reading!

All best,
—Carrie
carrie@carriesummers.com

BOOKS BY CARRIE SUMMERS

Shattering of the Nocturnai
Nightforged
Shadowbound
Duskwoven
Darkborn

The Broken Lands
Heart of the Empire
Rise of the Storm
Fate of the Drowned

Chronicles of a Cutpurse
Mistress of Thieves
Rulers of Scoundrels
Queen of Tricksters
Empress of Rogues

Stonehaven League
Temple of Sorrow
Fortress of Shadows
Cavern of Spirits
Citadel of Smoke
Vault of the Magi
Throne of the Ancients

Made in the USA
Monee, IL
05 October 2024

67254157R00204